AWAKENING

BLOODLINE BOOK ONE

TIERA RICE

Eula Rae Printing & Publishing, Rockland County, NY

Awakening is a work of fiction. Names, characters, places, and incidents either are the product of the author's imagination or are used fictitiously. Any resemblance to actual persons, living or dead, events, or locales is entirely coincidental.

AWAKENING

Copyright © 2016 by Tiera Rice

Published in the United States by Eula Rae Printing and Publishing, an imprint of Depending on the Day LLC, Rockland County, New York.

ISBN 978-0-9976748-0-4
eBook ISBN 978-0-9976748-1-1

Cover design: www.damonza.com
Formatting: www.thebookdesigner.com
Editor: Caitlin McKenna of Scoria Press

Printed in the United States of America

www.eularae.com

To my brother, Rudy. You said the magick words which pushed me to follow my dreams—to put pen to paper and write.

To my parents and youngest brother, Sean. Your unwavering love and encouragement is more appreciated than anything I could describe.

To my daughter, Raevyn. You are my strength and when I look at you, I am reminded of why I continue to write.

SAN FRANCISCO, CALIFORNIA 1996

Rays of sunlight beamed down on the woman as she took a sip of her iced tea. She leaned back into her chair, her brown eyes focused on a young mother walking down the street with a toddler in tow. The woman closed her eyes and smiled, lifting her head towards the sky. A gentle breeze flitted by, causing strands of her dark hair to fly into her face and tickle her nose. As she began to wrap her hair into a ponytail, she felt a familiar presence approaching.

"I've been expecting you, Păzitor," she said to the Keeper as he pulled up a chair to sit next to her. She noted the shabby state of his clothing and the grave look he was giving her.

"You understand why I am here, Vrajitoare," he said.

"I do." Gently holding her swollen belly, the woman shifted in her seat to regard the Keeper. "We have avoided the affairs of the Strigoi for many centuries, but I have foreseen what destruction awaits us should we fail in this task." The woman gazed at her belly sadly and let out a deep sigh before returning her gaze to the Păzitor. "We must do everything necessary to prevent that from happening—the Order of the Dragon must not gain control or all will be lost." The Keeper merely nodded in agreement. "Where is the fiintă?" she asked.

Reaching inside the collar of his jacket, the Keeper pulled out a small corked potion bottle affixed to his necklace. Inside the bottle was a swirling mass of brilliant white light.

"She's beautiful," the woman whispered in awe, eyes reflecting the glow of the light. She held out her hand and he handed her the bottle.

"Indeed," he said in return.

The light continued to dance in the bottle. At the touch of the woman's hand, it changed from white to green. The Keeper's eyes widened as he watched the light continue to change to red and, finally, to gold.

"I have never seen the Essence take that color before." He beamed at her—for the first time, he was hopeful. Still mesmerized by the light, the woman uncorked the bottle and put the rim to her lips. She closed her eyes, tilted her head back and drank the contents in a single draught.

As she swallowed, her whole body seemed to glow until the essence was all ingested. Her skin became flawless and clear, shaving years off of her features. As her skin returned to its normal fair color, she could feel the Essence searching within her before nestling in the pit of her womb, becoming one with her unborn daughter. She inhaled deeply and opened her eyes, now bright and flecked with gold.

"It is done."

CHAPTER ONE

BRĂILA, WALLACHIA 1480

My head swung from left to right, golden-amber eyes searching for anyone who could be lurking in the trees. Aside from the ruffling of leaves in the gentle wind, there was no other movement and all was quiet. I slowly rose from the murky water, weighed down by my bow and quiver, and rushed to hide behind a large bush.

It was a crisp cool evening and I shivered underneath my damp clothing before crouching as low as I could comfortably go. As I was reaching for my bow, I suffered a blow to the head and bit my tongue as my head snapped towards my sternum. I was propelled forward and landed on an upturned piece of bark jutting from a nearby tree. The bark jammed into my stomach, knocking the wind out of me, and I staggered as I pushed myself to my feet.

Warm wetness trickled down my neck, and I winced as my fingers pressed against the deep gash in my head. My fingers were covered in the stickiness of blood. I scowled at Fabian.

"Was that really necessary?"

"You have to be on guard at all times," he said. "There was no reason why you shouldn't have sensed me coming."

I rolled my eyes and sighed in annoyance. "I *was* on guard—I knew you were coming," I fibbed.

He narrowed his eyes at me. "I could see you from a distance—you were complacent."

I groaned. "Ugh—it is the eve of my Vârstă de Maturitate, surely this allows me time to rest?"

His eyes softened only just. "Antanasia, I don't mean to be harsh, but rest is awarded when deserved, regardless of the day."

I frowned, "I know..."

"As a member of the Brotherhood, you have an obligation to make sure you are prepared at all times. The Order's Vampyres are powerful, and merely hiding behind a bush is not enough to stop them. Think of the risk your mother took to make sure you were safe, and all those who weren't able to be saved."

I nodded and stood up straighter—he was right. When the Vampyre king had gone mad, he used the Order to satisfy his new obsession: destroying the human race, whether by slaughtering or placing it in chains. The Brotherhood had seen a victory three years ago when they killed the mad king, but his death only added fuel to the fire—his son was even more motivated to see the plan carried out; I couldn't let him succeed.

Fabian smiled. "Just a little while longer—you're nearly there."

I returned his smile and nodded. Just then, the hairs on the back of my neck stood up. I quickly nocked an arrow and pulled my arm back in a draw as I turned towards the male figure that was flying at me. I aimed and released the arrow, then immediately started running in the opposite direction, unsure of who was after me but knowing that an arrow wasn't enough to stop him.

My feet carried me away from the water and deeper into the woods. The wetness of my clothes slowed my movements and my feet squished inside my boots. I cursed the extra weight and the sounds that my shoes were making. Quickly undoing the ties of my overcoat, I threw it while dodging around a tree. The chill bit through the fabric of my clothing and my skin broke out in bumps.

I made a sharp left, past a large rock face. My attacker stumbled behind me and the sounds of pursuit seemed to fade—my movement was enough to increase the distance between us. I scaled the nearest tree and rested on a sturdy branch about fifteen feet up. I looked left and right, searching for Fabian—he had to be out there, along with my attacker, and I didn't want him to catch me off guard again. Shortly after, I heard footsteps and my attacker stopped several feet away from my tree. I narrowed my eyes as I recognized who it was: Nic.

"I know you're close—I can sense it," he said, slowly circling the area. As quietly as I could, I reached over my shoulder for another arrow. He froze. As I drew, he looked up at me. "Well, there you are."

I released the arrow just as he pulled a dagger from his belt and threw it at me. Trying to dodge it, I lost my footing and fell to the ground. Nic used this to his advantage and made haste to pin me.

"You almost hit me," he grunted.

We tumbled around on the ground before he was able to successfully hold me down. I kicked out, determined to unbalance him, struggling to release his hold on me. I lay there with my knees bent and arms pinned to my sides. My hand grazed my boot and I gazed into Nic's eyes, overcome with emotions. I pushed them aside; there was no time for distractions. He leaned in close to my face, leaving only inches of space between us.

"I never tire of seeing you underneath me."

"Is that so? Well, I feel I must tell you," leaning in close, I licked his ear lobe. I gently bit his ear and whispered, "I never tire of being underneath you."

Nic was so focused on my lips that he didn't notice the dagger I took from my boot. I plunged it into his side, then shoved him off me and took off running as fast as I could. I heard him curse and the squelching of flesh as he pulled out the dagger. It was made out of steel, so I knew it wouldn't cause him much harm. I was close to the border and crossed the county lines, losing Nic, and ran for miles until I was in Chilia. I was slightly out of breath and chastised myself for not going to the stables to retrieve Fyuree before heading to Chilia.

Fyuree was my white horse—a gift from Mother when she was but a foal, "to bless my travels and reveal my enemies". She had the deepest blue eyes that seemed to hold the Universe in them. I shook my head, already dreading the run back home. Not only would it be tiresome, but Fabian would not be pleased that I ran off during training.

Oh, well.

I needed to visit Cristian—the blood always tasted best when gathered directly from the source. He was my Black Swan, one who was friendly with Vampyres and familiar with our culture. I tried not to drink from him often. Even though it didn't take long for the humans to replace lost blood, it still left him weak.

I first met Cristian two years prior on one of my hunts:

I left Fyuree tied to a nearby tree, along with my bow; I didn't need it for this hunt. Cristian was riding back to his home from a neighboring village on a beautiful brown mare. He was lean with light-colored hair to his shoulders and somewhat pleasing to the eye. I hid in the trees and watched him, waiting for the perfect opportunity to make my move. Just as I was about to leap forward, I heard more voices walking towards my intended target. I nestled back against the tree and saw three men in a jovial mood stumbling along the path. There was a brute of a man, with a beastly face and smelling of manure. He was accompanied by two average-looking men, one tall and one short. I caught a whiff of something just as strong as the ma-

nure. Ale, I thought, if the smell was anything to go by.

It was the brutish one who noticed Cristian first.

"Well, what do we have here?" Cristian stiffened and turned around. The brute stopped walking and smirked. His companions followed his lead.

"Looks like a pansy," said the short one.

"He does, doesn't he," the brute responded, looking at Cristian. "Are you a pansy?" He asked, walking closer to him.

"What do you want?"

"What do you have?" asked the tall one as he snatched a bag off the saddle of the horse and started rummaging through it; he pulled out a red corked bottle. Cristian's eyes widened.

"Give that back!" He reached for the bottle but the short one pushed him. I could feel and smell the increase of his fear.

The tall one held up the bag. "I think I'll keep this."

"No! Prithee," Cristian pleaded, "Anything but that!" The brute punched him in the face and Cristian fell to the ground.

"Shut that hole in your face," commanded the brute. Cristian stood up and tried again.

"Prithee, my sister is very sick—that is the only thing that can cure her." I started to sympathize, as I never even got to know my kin. I pushed the feeling aside; I couldn't allow myself to become attached—it was cause for distraction.

"He said to shut that hole in your face." The tall one went to strike him, but Cristian quickly dodged the hit and snatched the bottle from his hand. He was fast. This made the tall one angry. He snarled. "Why you little..." He pulled out a dagger and moved to attack Cristian. Still hidden in the tree, I spoke up.

"Three against one isn't very fair—cowardly, if you ask me. Drop your weapon and let him go. No one has to get hurt." All four men looked around to try and pin-point my position.

The brute stepped forward and said to Cristian, "A woman speaks for you." Then he addressed me. "Cowardly you say. Is it not cowardly to hide in the bushes? Come out. Let me see that pretty face." His companions sniggered at the comment.

"Of course," I bowed my head even though he couldn't see it, then jumped fifteen feet from the tree to the ground, landing as smoothly as a cat only a few feet away from the brute. The smirks instantly disappeared from his companions' faces.

"How did she do that?" I heard the short one whisper. The brute ignored him and walked closer to me.

"My, my, my, aren't you a sight for sore eyes." He reached out and stroked my cheek with the backs of his fingers. "I think I'll leave the pansy's stuff and take you instead." He faced his comrades. "What say you, men? It'd be the perfect ending to the perfect night." He stepped up to me, inches from my face. When he spoke his next words, I could see his teeth caked in an unknown black substance. "We'll take turns with you, fucking you until you squeal."

I turned my head away from his hand and replied, "I think not."

He dropped his hand. "Oh?"

I looked deeply into his eyes, slowly smiling. "You have little knowledge of how to use that nub in between your legs." His comrades laughed heartily while Cristian backed away towards his horse.

"Shut up," the brute spat as he narrowed his eyes at me. "You got a mouth on you. I like that." He roughly grabbed my jaw. "I would have lots of fun with that mouth of yours."

I slapped his hand away and spat in his face. "Don't touch me."

He snarled and bared his teeth. "You little cunt!" He slapped me and my head snapped to the side. I licked the blood from my split lip. My vision blurred for an instant. I knew, on the outside, my eyes would be turning black and I growled. He hesitated and I could smell the sour stench of his fear. For the first time during this encounter, he seemed uncertain.

"I wouldn't do that again if I were you," I warned.

"And what are you going to do about it? You think you can

beat me?" He chuckled. "We'll see about that."

He raised his hand to strike me again. I threw my left arm up, blocking his attack, and rammed my right palm into his nose with lightning speed. The brute yelped and sunk to the ground, holding his broken nose. Blood dripped through his fingers and down his front. The tall one stepped forward.

"If she wants to fight like a man, she can die like one," he said through clenched teeth, brandishing his dagger. Following his lead, the short one flipped out his dagger.

I threw my head back and laughed. "I have danced with children manlier than you lot."

Both the tall and short one wore expressions of pure disdain. While they were distracted, Cristian used this opportunity to secure the rest of his belongings on the horse. He hadn't noticed that the medicine bottle had fallen from the bag and rolled away. The brute was still squirming around on the ground, trying not to choke on his own blood, while both of his men came at me with weapons in their hands. I don't have time for this— I must feed soon.

I closed the gap between myself and the tall one, moving in the blink of an eye. I grabbed the dagger from his hand and stabbed him in the neck. Crimson covered me as his blood spurted onto my clothes, and he slumped to the ground, gurgling. I then focused my attention on the short one. His jaw dropped and his eyes were wide. I could smell his fear, and saw that he was standing in a puddle of his own making.

The dagger fell from his hand and he took off running. He didn't get far. I chased after him, tackling him to the ground. My Hunger was too great at this point, and I sunk my fangs into his skin. The ale in his blood made me dizzy, and I stopped drinking from him. I took his head in my hands and twisted until his neck snapped—leave no witnesses. I wasn't far from Cristian, and noticed that he had been watching the scene in shock. No longer feeling threatened, my eyes faded back to red.

I walked towards Cristian and bent down to pick up the

medicine bottle. Holding it out to him, I said, "I think you need this." He slowly took it from me and didn't say anything at first, just stared. I rose my eyebrow and smirked at him. He cleared his throat and bowed his head.

"My apologies. Thank you m'lady." He glanced back at me, and I was impressed that he hadn't run away screaming. "Your eyes...I always knew your kind existed," he said softly.

I smiled. "Yes, there are a number of us, though we are still the minority."

"I never thought I'd meet one..." he trailed off, looking at me in awe.

"Your sister is sick, you say? May I ask what ails her?"

He shook his head, clearing himself of his reverie. He looked crestfallen. "White plague, m'lady. She is so fragile, and is coughing up blood. For now, the rest of us have been spared. I travelled a long ways to a special healer and spent all my savings on this medicine. It is our last hope—I can't let my little sister perish."

"I'm sorry to have to tell you this, but there is no cure—that medicine will not help your sister." Waves of pain flowed from him and broke over me. I flinched slightly and stood there thinking for a moment. "But I can help her."

The light shone back in his eyes. "You can? But how?"

"She shall drink from me, but we must act soon—she is well within the sickness."

He took my hand in his and kissed it. "Bless you m'lady. Thank you, thank you."

I smiled. "I need you to do something for me first."

"Anything."

"A meal would be much appreciated."

He bowed his head. "Of course, m'lady."

After he let me feed from him, we travelled to his home. I followed Cristian into a shop and up the stairs, and saw a little girl who had just entered the hallway. She was pretty but looked *sickly, with shallow cheeks and sunken eyes. She ran to Cristian and hugged him, smiling brightly. This sight filled me with warmth and I admired her strength, given the position she was in.*

She released him and her brown eyes gazed in my direction before returning to Cristian. "Who is she?"

Before Cristian could answer, I walked towards her and bent down to her level. "I am Antanasia. What do I call you?"

"Adelina," she responded shyly and went into a coughing fit. I frowned at the blood sprinkled on her bottom lip and placed my hand on her shoulder.

"Precious Adelina, I am here to help you." Her eyes flicked to Cristian and he nodded, smiling encouragingly.

We went to his room, where I explained what I was. Adelina's eyes widened and I heard her heart beat faster. She gripped Cristian's hand tightly but said nothing. I explained that she was to drink a substantial amount from me, and that my blood would be able to fight off the disease that was in her. I sat next to her and bit into my wrist. She wrinkled her nose at me when I told her to drink.

"It is the only way," Cristian said.

Adelina gulped and weakly took my wrist, bringing it to her lips. She took several deep swallows and then fell back into Cristian's pillow, convulsing.

Cristian jumped up. "What is happening to her?"

"It is normal," I replied calmly. "The Vampyre blood is strong. It is killing the plague and will take a toll on her, but I assure you that she will be okay." Shortly after, Adelina stopped shaking and slowly sat up. Her cheeks had more color and her eyes twinkled. Cristian flew to his sister's side and took her hand, holding it tightly.

"Are you okay?" He asked.

"I...I think so. What happened?"

"It was the effect of having much of my blood." I explained.

"She looks much better!" Cristian turned to me. "I thank

you."

"Do not thank me yet. Though she is better, there is a little of the sickness within her. She must take a little more."

I let his sister drink for a short period of time and soon, the white plague was no longer upon her. Adelina also had some of my abilities, like speed and swift healing, but those wore off as time went on. Since that day, Cristian became my dearest friend. I would visit with him when I wasn't training and he would let me feed from him. His parents gave many thanks and blessings for healing their daughter, and the whole family vowed to keep my identity a secret.

My clothes were dry by the time I reached Chilia. I found Cristian in his father's shop chiseling a piece of wood; they were carpenters.

"Good evening," I greeted him. Cristian jumped at the sound of my voice and regarded me.

"Your Highness." He bowed his head and smirked. I rolled my eyes.

"Stop," I said, walking closer to him. "You know I hate that." I kissed him on the cheek as he responded.

"I do. That's why I do it." He returned my kiss and I chuckled. He loved to joke at my informal nobility. Had it been another, I would be upset; I disliked the reminder of who my father was. But, Cristian being my dearest friend, I allowed it. He was soft spoken and easy to confide in—he was like the sister I never had.

He put down his chisel and wiped his hands on a rag. "Is Fyuree outside?" He asked, "I have an apple for her."

"She is not—I ran here."

He gazed at me wide-eyed, and then shook his head, smiling. "Your kind never ceases to amaze me."

I shrugged. "They continue to amaze me," I said, thinking about my training and the war that was currently going on. "How does your family?"

"They are in good health, thank you." I nodded. "And yours?"

I sighed. "You need not ask. Mother and Fabian are insisting on longer training hours, and the Seer is insisting on more magickal sessions; it is very tiring."

"Can you blame them? We all know what the Order is capable of." I flared my nostrils. *Aye, I know what they are willing to do.* I'd seen firsthand just how far the Order would go. Just last week, they'd captured a few of our knights. Every day we received a package containing a part of them—we'd received one of their heads earlier today. "Enough about that. Tell me, how goes the cute one?" Cristian asked with a smirk.

I laughed, absent-mindedly twirling the ring Nic had given me two years prior. "Nic is like his father—train, train, train. If I'm not battling, I'm working magick. "

"Had you made no claims to him, Nic would be mine." Cristian winked. I blushed, thinking about my betrothed. I knew the Gods had created him for me the moment I laid eyes on him. "I have something for you!" Cristian announced, pulling me from my thoughts. He took my hand and led me up the staircase that was hidden in the back of the shop. His family lived in the apartment on the second floor.

"I just finished it." He walked to his desk and picked up a five-pointed star necklace. Its precious stones shimmered in the candlelight—there was a different stone at each point of the star: ruby, opal, emerald, sapphire, and aventurine. I'd broken the clasp while training, and Cristian had offered to fix it for me. I grinned from ear to ear, taking the necklace from him. It was a gift from the Seer, given to me at a very young age.

When the king had gone mad, the current Seer and other Witches broke free from his reign and created the Brotherhood. They believed that by teaching me their magick I would be strong enough to defeat the Order. This necklace had the magick of all the Seers before her and was very powerful. Though made from silver, it had a special coating so as to not burn my skin.

"Many thanks to you!" I threw my arms around Cristian in a tight hug. I had grown so accustomed to wearing my necklace that the last few days without it had been uncomfortable.

"No thanks needed, m'lady." He helped me fasten it around my neck and immediately I felt complete. "I hope it comes in handy tonight."

I thought about that night and what was to happen. On the eve of my Vârstă de Maturitate my Gift would be revealed to me. It is customary for every Vampyre who reaches their eighteenth year. The Gift appears in a Vision or can just *happen*. Everyone had hoped that I would inherit Mother's natural Gift of Sight. Although not a practitioner of magick, and not a Vampyre, Mother always had her Gift—and that made her very powerful. It was believed that my having that ability, coupled with being the daughter of the mad king, would ensure my success. According to the Seer, I was the one who was meant to stop the Order and reclaim the throne. I felt Cristian's hand on my arm.

"You will win, you know," he said matter of factly. I gave him a small smile. I tried not to think about the war too much because it was distracting. Distractions can get you killed. But I was uneasy—it was a big task at hand and there was a lot of pressure on me. Shaking my head, I looked Cristian in the eyes.

"I do. But it will prove challenging on an empty stomach. May I?" I asked.

"Of course," he responded, rolling up his sleeve. Feeding from Cristian was always a pleasant experience. With his blood came a sense of calm, and it reminded me of the sweetness of a ripe nectarine. It was a refreshing feeling having the blood roll down my throat and into my belly. We shared stories and laughed—he was truly like the sister I never had. The sky was darkening as evening became night; it was time to take my leave. "Good luck, Princess." He winked.

I wrinkled my nose at his use of the word "Princess". "Many thanks," I said, bowing my head as I made my way out. "I shall let you know how it goes."

"Princess, Princess!" A pair of arms wrapped around me. I turned around and found myself facing Adelina. I couldn't help but become attached to the little girl—she warmed the still heart in my chest. It was comforting to know that she had reached her now seventh year of life because of me.

"The only true Princess here is you, little one," I commented, tapping her nose and hugging her back. She giggled.

Oh, how I long for a little sister.

"Are you leaving?" she asked me.

"I am."

"Will you return?"

"I shall try for the day after tomorrow." She gave me a cheeky grin and I returned the smile. "Until then." I gave her a kiss on the cheek and one last hug, before doing the same to Cristian.

I took my leave. It was getting cooler but that didn't bother me. Being half Vampyre gave me the ability to withstand nature's elements—where humans might be freezing or suffer from frostbite, I merely felt a tickle on my skin. I took a deep breath and started the journey home. In no time at all, I could smell the signs that I had reached my village: the manure from the farm; freshly chopped wood; metal from the iron worker. All these scents were comforting to me. They reminded me that even though I was a Vampyre forced to fight this war, I still had a home to come to.

I felt a pang of sadness for the humanity I missed out on.

It was still a mystery how I was even born, as my mother was human. We are a small breed, only a few hundred of us in existence, and it was uncommon for humans to give birth to Vampyres—the mothers would die from carrying the baby or while giving birth to it. Vampyres are too powerful for the human body to hold. In addition to giving birth to a Vampyre even though she is human, Mother also miraculously survived the jump from the tower, which should have been fatal. Not completely unscathed, though; she had lost vision in her right eye. Those in the Brotherhood, myself included, wondered how she was even alive, with the jump and being married to the mad king. Mother used to tell me it was her humanity he fell in love with. I didn't think he was capable of such compassion.

I couldn't fathom the idea of living with a man as insane as my father. I admired Mother's courage—to jump out of the tower and risk everything must not have been an easy feat. To survive such a jump, become partially blind, and then join the Brotherhood all while mothering a child, showed a strength that could not be measured.

"I was wondering when you would be back," said a voice from behind me. My breath caught and I turned around to see Nic walking towards me. I ran and threw my arms around him.

"My love!"

He draped his arms around me and kissed my forehead, then picked a leaf from my hair. "You treat your love so harshly?" he asked, rubbing his side.

I looked in his eyes and smirked. "It was only a scratch! Mayhap you should tell your father, the Keeper, to not have you attack me. Besides, you should be proud that I was not distracted, unlike you."

He nodded. "This is true." He pulled me closer to him. "But I don't mind being your distraction." He brought his lips to mine, and all else was forgotten except the feel of his love for me, the brightening glow of his spirit warming my own soul. Reluctantly, I pulled back. Nic gave me a questioning glance.

"Mother is watching," I said.

"Ah," he responded. "I don't want to upset her."

"She adores you," I commented, "but I must prepare for the Ritual."

"I remember my Vârstă de Maturitate; I was nearly a prune before my Gift was revealed to me."

"Aye, you gave your mother a fright appearing right next to her when you were supposed to be in your bath." I laughed.

"But I *was* still in my bath." He winked.

I giggled. "Although that is true, most Vampyres don't consider projection a Gift—you are of magick too, mayhap?"

"Mayhap I am and they know nothing." We shared a good laugh and stood quietly in each other's arms.

"Have you had any word from her lately?" I asked suddenly, referring to his mother. He gave a small smile.

"Nay," was all he said. She'd left on a mission for the Order, and the punishment for communicating with the Brotherhood was death. And still, she risked it. For him—her only son. Neither of them spoke of the organizations they chose to serve, but you could see it in their eyes—they couldn't bear the thought of meeting each other on opposite sides of the battlefield.

"Well," I said, trying to bring him to the present, "I must go."

"Of course, my love," he responded, bowing slightly. "Until tomorrow."

"Until tomorrow."

I walked to my front door and tried to brush off some of the twigs that had gotten caught on my britches. We had one of the bigger stone houses in the village, and Mother liked it nicely kept. I could already smell the lilies and it brought a smile to my face. Mother always smelled of lily of the valley.

"Where have you been?" she asked when I opened the door, her eyes searching me. One was clouded with blindness—it was a permanent reminder of her escape from the castle. It was all I ever knew, but her blindness shocked others who were unfamiliar with her.. "You know to bring a companion with you should you leave the village."

I groaned. "Mother, I went to feed, and I don't need a companion—I can take care of myself."

She walked to me and gave me a sympathetic look. "I know you can," she responded, caressing my cheek. "I know I'm hard on you—I just don't want anything to happen to you." I inhaled her scent and took her hand in mine.

"Nothing will happen. We will succeed." She gave me a weak smile.

"Of course, you are right." She shook her head. "Now go—you must get ready. I will draw a bath for you."

I took a candle from the dining table and made haste to my room. After lighting the lamps, I undressed and picked the rest of the debris from my hair. As I was brushing it, I started singing.

I rise again for the night is mine. I walk the streets claiming time. The moon is dark but my mind is bright. I gain my strength from the night.

It was a song that had appeared in a past dream that resonated with me—I chose it to be my personal song of empowerment. There came a soft knock on my door.

"Come in." Mother walked in and looked at me.

"Beautiful—just like your mother." She smiled and I laughed.

"Oh, come now, Mother. You would love me still if I resembled the mad king."

"Indeed I would, but it is a blessing you do not. Now go, before the water gets cold."

I nodded before making my way to the privy. I was greeted by the smell of lotuses. Mother had pots of water with floating pink and white lotuses all around the room—they were very good for opening up to one's inner self. It didn't hurt that they had a pleasing scent as well. I sank into the warm water and let out a gratifying sigh. I had been training really hard for as long as I could remember, and had been waiting for this moment for a long time. I hoped that receiving my Gift would only aid in my mission.

It isn't every day you go against Dracula's heir, I thought.

I laid back, inhaling deeply and closed my eyes. I asked the Gods to reveal my Gift to me. Almost immediately, my eyes rolled to the back of my head and I was assaulted by images, past and future—flashes appearing so fast, they almost seemed like a single image. Mother jumping out of the tower; me battling foes, humans and Vampyres alike, using magick and blades; me going limp as I was overcome with Visions; me running through the forest. Then, as suddenly as the images appeared, they just stopped and all was black. This darkness was cold and complete. It was everywhere. I heard nothing, saw nothing, smelled nothing, *was* nothing; it suffocated me.

I jumped up, splashing water all over the floor. My skin crawled and I was shaking, wholly terrified. Mother ran into the room.

"Are you alright?" She took my hand in hers. "What did you see?"

I gripped her hand tightly. "The end," I whispered. "I saw the end."

CHAPTER TWO

NEW YORK, NEW YORK 2015

*T*rees whizz by me as I sail through the air. I crash into the side of a cliff, and leave a small imprint of my body before slumping to the ground. The loud crack and sharp pain in my chest tells me that my ribs are fractured. Still on the ground, I begin to wheeze. I wince and blood spatters on my lips as I go into a coughing fit; my lung is punctured. I rest for only a moment, trying to ignore the pain of my now-healing ribs and lung as the bones shift and muscles sew back together. I am up and running before my attackers can locate me, my arms pumping by my sides. Trees blur as I run past them, careful to avoid branches and squirrels alike. My breaths are hurried and visible in the early morning air. A sense of dread washes over me, and I cry out as the silver arrow pierces my back.

I jolted awake to the sound of my screams. My heart was racing and I was breathing heavily. I could still feel the arrow tearing through muscle and sinew. I mentally counted to seven while trying to slow my breathing. It took me a minute to gather my bearings. *Home. I'm at home.* I sighed, noticing I was on my bedroom rug. *Nadia, get it together!*

Beads of sweat dripped down my forehead and onto my nose. This nightmare had been haunting me for the past few weeks, always the same. I looked up at my bed and found a pair of deep blue eyes staring at me. My cat, Nefertiti, meowed at me and I stroked her white fur.

Nervous anxiety, you are dead. Lord and Lady soothe my

head. Bring to me your calming peace. As I will, so mote it be. Immediately, I relaxed, then untangled myself from the sheets. I stretched towards the ceiling, loosening my stiff joints. My ears perked up at the sound of a bird whistling outside of my window. I looked out, smiling at the blue jay perched on the fire escape. The sun streamed brightly into the room, illuminating the clock on my side table. It read 7:32.

Geez, it's early. I scratched Nefi behind the ears and bent down to pick up the sheets. Throwing them on the bed, I promised myself that I would straighten it up later. I heard a loud growl and frowned at the sounds coming from my stomach. No longer concerned with the nightmare, I padded across the room to my bathroom. Nefi trailed behind me and took her place outside of the door, placing herself on guard duty. I washed my hands and started considering my breakfast options. Then I looked in the mirror and paused. Leaning in closer, I tilted my head to the side, furrowing my brows.

Well that's different. I blinked a few times, staring hard into my normally hazel eyes. They were now golden amber. I didn't put too much thought into it, considering hazel eyes are known to change colors often. But I frowned upon inspecting the rest of my face—my skin was extremely clear, and there were no blemishes in sight. I thought back to the night before, wondering if the banishing spell I'd cast may have had something to do with it. I shrugged. Besides that, my face was still "cute"—so I've been told—with dark brown curls clustered over my head. I nervously bit the inside of my cheek. The lines that usually adorned the side of my lip were nowhere to be found. *Very different.*

I shrugged as my stomach growled again.

"Mamă," I called out, heading towards the kitchen. Silence answered me. *She probably went to the store or something.* We had a three-bedroom, two-and-a-half-bathroom condo in SoHo. Since I was studying prelaw at NYU, I loved the convenience of being close to campus.

I opened the fridge to gather ingredients after deciding to make fried eggs with toast and cold cuts. Just add cheese and *viola*: the perfect breakfast sandwich! I concentrated on making it as quickly as possible. The first bite was like heaven. I closed my eyes, savoring the blended flavors of ham and Swiss cheese, and then washed it down with a sip of orange juice. As I ate, I thumbed through my text messages. Though it was only 8am, I had several unread text messages and Facebook notifications. I clicked the first message.

*HAPPY BDAY!!!!*glowed at me, surrounded by gift and cake emojis. I crinkled my nose and sighed. *It is my birthday.* The front door opened just as I took another bite of my sandwich. Mamă.

Abandoning the last of my sandwich, I rushed to greet her. I almost tripped over Nefi in the process—she loved walking in between my legs. Mamă's hands were filled with grocery bags, and I reached out to take some from her.

"Good morning," I said and she smiled.

"Bună dimineata," she responded. "Happy birthday!"

I smiled brightly. "Thank you."

"How do you feel?" she asked as I followed her to the kitchen.

"Ugh" I made a face. "Nineteen is so pointless. At least with seventeen, you graduate from high school, and at eighteen you're 'officially' an adult. But nineteen? Nineteen I don't get. The only good thing about this age is that it leads to a new decade. Otherwise, today is just another day." She whirled around so fast that I almost ran into her.

"No," she said forcefully. "Nineteen is *not* pointless and today is definitely not *just* another day." I stared wide-eyed, surprised by her outburst. "Always appreciate your birthdays, fiică; appreciate every day..." She frowned, looking deep in thought. I stepped closer to her and placed my hand on her arm.

"What's wrong?"

Shaking her head, she smiled again. "Nimic."

"Are you sure?"

"Yes, fiică. Thank you."

"Whatever you say."

Mamă planned on making a special dinner tonight, so there was a lot to unpack. My mind wandered back to my dream and I made a face as I pulled out carrots from a brown paper bag.

"What's wrong?" she asked, pulling me from my thoughts. I placed the carrots on the counter.

"Hmm? Nothing's wrong. I just didn't sleep well last night." She stopped right before putting the milk in the fridge, glancing at me. "I had a nightmare," I continued, "and it left me a little shaken."

Milk now forgotten, she asked, "What happened?"

"I was running through a forest and was stabbed with an arrow. Then I woke up." I kept it simple, leaving out the other details. I didn't want her to worry more than she already would. Clearly, it didn't work, judging by the look on her face. Mamă narrowed her eyes at me. I should have known—it's hard to fool a Witch. Vrajitoares take dreams and nightmares very seriously, finding meaning in each one. Surprisingly, she didn't push the issue. "I've been trying to figure out what it means. I've had the same one for a few weeks now," I admitted. Mamă's eyes widened.

"Atentie—be careful," was all she said. I snorted. *Overreacting as usual.*

"Oh, relax—I'm sure it's nothing. Besides, I always carry my knife with me." I found it at an auction I went to with Mamă last year—I loved the phoenix that was carved into the hilt.

"That still concerns me." I rolled my eyes, reaching over

Mamă to put a can of vegetables in the cabinet. She grabbed my shoulders and turned me towards her. She studied me and stiffened.

"Geez, Mamă, what is it?" She released me, taking a couple of steps back.

"Ochii tăi..." She answered softly.

"Oh!" I started unpacking another bag. "It's cool right? I didn't know hazel eyes could turn that color."

"That's because they don't," she muttered.

"Huh?"

Mamă shook her head and I shrugged. We finished putting the groceries away in silence, each lost in our own thoughts. I started folding up a paper bag when I noticed that something was still inside. It was a small velvet box, and it seemed to pulse when I picked it up.

"What is this?" I asked. She looked up, perkier than before.

"Open it," she instructed. Opening the lid revealed a beautiful silver pentacle necklace, which sat atop plush velvet fabric. It had different stones at each point of the star, and looked oddly familiar, though I didn't recall ever seeing it before.

"It's beautiful," I said in awe, brushing my fingers gently across the stones. My hand grew warm where it made contact. "What stones are these?"

"All these stones represent the five elements: earth, air, fire, water, and spirit. Emerald is earth, aventurine is air, ruby is fire, sapphire is water, and opal is spirit," she explained.

"I love it! Thank you." I looked at Mamă and found her studying me. I pulled the necklace from the box. "Can you help me put it on?" Nodding, she took the necklace from my hand and stepped behind me to fasten it around my neck. I wrapped my fingers around the pentacle and could feel the pulse more strongly now; it was magick. It was still warm, and I wondered if it had been cast upon recently. "Did you bless it? It feels warm..."

Mamă furrowed her brows, looking subdued. She sighed, shaking her head. "Nu fiică..."

Something isn't right. I could sense her uneasiness, and I searched her eyes. "What's wrong?" I asked for the second time this morning. She didn't answer at first. She closed her eyes, inhaling deeply. When she exhaled and opened her eyes, her expression was weary.

"Nimic," she finally responded. "It suits you. I wish I'd given it to you earlier." She smiled, but it didn't reach her eyes. *What isn't she telling me?* I looked deeply into her eyes, searching for the answer, but she looked away. "That necklace has been in our family for centuries," she said, "it has the power of all the Vrajitoares before you. If you feel hopeless or scared, let it guide you; it will always protect you."

I admired the necklace again, enjoying the glimmering stones. Tucking the necklace into my shirt, I surprised Mamă by throwing my arms around her and embracing her tightly.

"Thank you," I repeated sincerely. Mamă hugged me back and lightly kissed the top of my head.

"Te iubesc."

"I love you, too." We stood holding each other until I felt a familiar presence walking down the hallway. "Vi's here!" I exclaimed, hurrying towards the front door. Excitement coursed through me. I hadn't seen my best friend from high school, Viviana Lupei, since her graduation two months prior when she earned her Bachelor's from the University of California San Francisco. While I'd be starting my junior year in the coming fall, Vi would be looking for an apartment in the city. Mamă laughed at my reaction.

"Such a strong Witch—your senses are getting sharper, fiică. She wanted to surprise you for your birthday, you know." I was almost at the door.

"What? Surprise me?" I shook my head. "She knows that's not possible." Mamă laughed. I never told Vi of my family's culture—I was sworn to secrecy. But once in a while it would slip; sometimes I would just know things. Just as my hand grasped the handle, a knock sounded on the door. Although I knew she was here, I was genuinely thrilled to see her. I opened the door, grinning from ear to ear.

"Happy birthday!" Vi embraced me tightly. I hugged her back, noticing she had a lovely perfumed scent about her. Vi was tall, standing at five-eight, and had a figure that most girls would starve themselves for. Even this early in the morning, Vi was still gorgeous, with her grey eyes and perfectly tousled waves of hair.

"Hey Vi," I greeted her. I found it fitting that her name means "energetic", because she was definitely a lively character. I tapped her on the shoulder. "Okay, can't breathe," and she relaxed her hold on me.

"Oops, sorry." I stepped aside, giving her room to enter.

"Bună dimineata, Viviana," Mamă called from somewhere inside the condo.

"Morning, Mamă Anica," Vi yelled back. Turning towards me she asked suspiciously, "You knew I was here, didn't you?"

I smiled sheepishly and nodded. She threw her hands up, feigning disappointment.

"Whatever! One of these days, I'll surprise you. In the meantime, let's celebrate—you're finally nineteen!!" She was practically beaming. "Hey, what happened to your eyes? Are you wearing contacts?"

"Yes! I figured new age, new look, right?" It pained me not being honest with Vi, but no matter how guilty I felt, I had to maintain our secret.

"They're awesome." Vi commented, making her way to

the living room. I followed behind her, listening to all the birthday plans she had made. She was going a hundred miles per hour, and Mamă smiled as we walked past. Vi was in the middle of telling me about a new club that she wanted to take me to; it had recently opened in the Lower East Side, and so far seemed to be quite popular. I shook my head, grinning.

"Vivi, Vivi. It's not that big a deal. I honestly forgot it was my birthday until I looked at my phone."

She dismissed my comment. "Nonsense, it's just as important as any other year."

"That's what I said." Mamă walked into the living room. I rolled my eyes.

"Why does everyone keep telling me that?" They both laughed at me. Mamă and Vi shared small talk, updating each other on the past couple of months. I sat next to Mamă, listening. Vi was just telling us that her aunt had let Vi borrow her apartment on the Upper West Side since she was in France for the summer.

"That's awesome! I'm definitely sleeping over," I promised.

"Duh," Vi agreed. I stood up, looking at the clock on the wall.

"Ugh. I have to start getting ready." I was a paralegal intern at Dalca and Dalca, LLP. Glancing at Vi, I asked, "Will you be around for dinner tonight?"

"Yes, birthday girl. In fact, I'm going to drive you to work—which by the way, I can't believe you're working today—then I'm coming back to help Mamă Anica." I smiled and shook my head. *It must be nice to have such a fun disposition towards everything.*

"Oh, Vi, you don't have to do that."

"Hush. I want to. Besides, I enjoy nightlife in the city more than day life. I'll have fun around here helping to set up for your birthday." I laughed. Vi shooed me away to get ready. "Mamă Anica and I have some things to discuss."

"Okay, okay," I said, defeated. I headed upstairs to my room wondering what they were up to.

∞

An hour later, I was sitting in the passenger seat, riding next to Vi up Third Avenue towards the office with the windows rolled down. The radio was playing in the background and Vi was telling me about this guy she was seeing: Adrian Serban.

"He's so fascinating and mysterious," she was saying. "Just out of reach."

"Sounds...interesting." I giggled. Traffic slowed to a trickle. A gentle breeze flowed through the open window, ruffling my hair. The scent I noticed earlier reached my nose and I glanced at Vi, finally able to place it.

"You smell nice. Japanese Cherry Blossom?"

"Yeah," she responded. "How did you know? I only put a little bit on."

I shrugged. "It's strong I guess."

She gazed at me. "I barely smell it and I'm the one wearing it. You have a really powerful nose." I gave a small smile; I wasn't really sure why the scent seemed to come off so strongly to me.

Again, I shrugged. "I admit it—I'm a freak of nature." She laughed. "So, tell me more about Adrian." Her eyes twinkled as she began naming all the hobbies and such that they had in common.

Damn this traffic. I can't be late for this meeting! The gruff voice came out of nowhere and I sat up, stiffening.

"Did you hear that?" I asked, completely cutting Vi off.

"Huh," she said, looking somewhat annoyed. "Hear what?" I listened again for the same voice, but the traffic had picked up, and all I could hear were other drivers leaning on their horns and people talking on the streets.

"Nothing, sorry." I settled back in my seat, slightly embarrassed. *What was that?*

Vi's gaze lingered on me for a moment longer before she faced the road again. We were around the corner from the office and all my thoughts were focused on what I had just heard. It made my head tingle. *It was probably just the radio,* I surmised. Vi pulled in front of the office and put on her hazards, giving me a warm smile.

"Have a good day, birthday girl—don't work too hard."

I smirked. "I'll try not to."

I stepped out into the warm sun, trying not to think of all the other ways I could be enjoying this gorgeous eighty-two-degree day. Vi honked before she peeled off. I didn't have to open the office for another fifteen minutes, but I liked being a little early—it gave me time to make coffee. Welcomed cold air blasted on my face as I walked through the door. The central air was set to seventy degrees and compared to outside, it offered much relief from the heat.

I worked in a charming little office with two desks in the front space, a conference room with a kitchen area off to the side, and Mr. Dalca's office in the back. My friend and coworker, Darius, didn't have to be in the office for another thirty minutes. I'd met him during my first year at NYU. He was only working at Mr. Dalca's office as an assistant, and would be taking a semester to study at the Shanghai campus this coming fall.

I shrugged off my blazer, placing it on the back of my chair. There was a small silver-plated box on my desk with images of flowers and symbols I didn't recognize etched into the sides. Beside it was a note in Romanian which read: Am crezut că ar dori să aibă această înapoi. "I thought you would like to have this back".

I eyed the box and note skeptically. There are only a handful of people who knew that I spoke some Romanian, and even so, they would have given me a gift in person, or so I thought. I looked around the room, searching for who-ever had left it. Suddenly, I felt silly—I knew I was alone in the office. I hesitated before picking up the box and opening it. Inside was a beautiful yellow gold ring set with an opal in the center surrounded by rubies on both sides. There was an inscription on the inside, which was worn and unreadable, though I could tell it was in Romanian. *How old is this thing?*

I focused on the ring and could sense mild energy com-ing from it. It was smooth and had a white aura, which helped to ease my mind. I took the ring from the box and placed it on my right ring finger, somehow knowing it would fit perfectly. Once on, a sense of loving calm came over me, and I was overwhelmed by a Vision.

I stare at the breathtaking man before me. He looks back at me with riveting, hazel eyes, and he's smiling brightly. He has short, raggedy brown hair and beautiful olive skin. I watch as he places the ring on my finger and I am enveloped in his love for me. We are standing in a field of jasmine with the sun shining upon us.

"You are my essence," he says to me.

Someone was shaking me and I smelled honey.

"Nadia! Nadia!" Coming back to the present, I found my-self on the floor. I looked up into brown eyes. Darius was leaning over me, giving me another small shake. "Nadia, are you okay?" I shook my head, clearing it of the residual imag-es left behind from the Vision.

"Yeah, yeah," I replied as he helped me up. "Thank you."

"What happened?"

"I guess I fainted or something. I didn't eat too much this morning and the heat probably got to me," I added, thinking quickly. He looked hesitant and I smiled. "Seriously," I reas-sured him, "I'm fine."

"Well...okay. If you say so." Darius walked towards his desk. "Way to start your birthday." He winked. "Did you get my text this morning?"

"I did—thank you, love," I responded, smiling.

"You're more than welcome."

"Hey, are you coming over later?"

"Oh, honey. I wish I could but I need to pack for this weekend." He made a face. "I hate packing."

"Don't we all." We laughed.

"We'll get together soon, though. If you need anything, let me know."

"Yes, sir."

"And by the way, I'm loving those contacts!"

I let out a nervous giggle. "Oh, thank you." I glanced at the clock on the wall and noticed that I had been in the Vision for three minutes.

Though a short scene, it was extremely vivid. I'd only ever had one other Vision like this, many years ago. It was of a woman, wearing a silk dress with sleeves that draped to the floor. She rubbed her pregnant belly and whispered, "I won't let him have you," before jumping out of her open window. I shook my head, still not understanding it to this day.

I took off the ring and gently placed it back in the box. Closing the lid, I hid the box with the note in my blazer pocket. The Vision had left me weak and hungry. I walked to the kitchen, question after question running through my mind. *Who was the ring from? Why did the note say I'd like to have it back? Most importantly, who was the man from my Vision?* Even now, his features were starting to slip away from my consciousness.

I grabbed a French vanilla cup and placed it in the Keurig. Freshly ground coffee is much better, but beggars couldn't be choosers right now. I closed my eyes, and rubbed my temples, my head tingly again.

I hope she's okay. I wonder if I should call 911...

I looked up, wide-eyed. "Darius," I called out.

"Yeah?"

"Did you say something just now?"

"Um," I could see his confusion in my mind's eye. "Nope."

"Ok, never mind. I must be hearing things." I let out a small giggle.

He laughed. "It happens to the best of us."

Crap! What is going on with me? I was always intuitive, but hearing thoughts was very new to me. My thoughts swirled as I slowly sipped my coffee, gripping the mug tightly to stop my hands from shaking. I took my time finishing my coffee, trying to figure everything out. The honey scent was growing stronger, and I stiffened when Darius walked into the room.

"How are you feeling?"

"My stomach is starting to bother me," I answered honestly. "I don't think I ate enough his morning; I'm going to grab something to eat. Do you want anything?"

He shook his head. "Oh, no thank you. You just take care of yourself right now." I loved working with Darius, but his scent was too much for me right now. It took everything in my power not to run out of the office. Once outside, I took a few deep breaths, instantly feeling better. The breeze made the outside smells of car exhaust and burnt nuts much more manageable.

The great thing about working in Manhattan was the overabundance of restaurants at my disposal; I never had to travel far to find something to eat. I walked across the street to *Midtown Pizza*, following the appetizing aroma of pepperoni. Unsure of what I would be hearing, I focused on blocking out all thoughts before I went inside. But I was lucky; I had arrived before the lunch rush, and thanked my Higher Power for the lack of people in the restaurant. The smell of garlic, sausages, cheese, and fresh dough surrounded me. My stomach growled loudly and I decided on two slices of pizza with onions, green peppers, sausages, bacon, mushrooms, and black olives. *Yum!*

I sat down while I waited, mind wandering back to the ring. I considered mentioning it to Mamă—maybe she'd know where it came from. I threw my head back and sighed deeply. Suddenly, my skin broke out in goose bumps as a chill ran through me—I was being watched. I surveyed the restaurant, my head on a swivel, but I didn't see anything out of the ordinary. As lunch breaks started, more and more people were entering the restaurant.

"Nadia—two everything slices!" I quickly made my way to the counter, grabbed my pizza and headed for the door. I still felt eyes on me as I walked out, but there were too many people for me to pinpoint where the gaze came from. I relaxed once I got back to the office. Thanks to my mental blocks, Darius' honey scent didn't seem to bother me as much.

"That smells like heaven," he said from behind his computer. "What did you get?"

"Two everything slices," I replied with a smile, walking to my desk.

"I may have to get a couple of slices."

"You should," I agreed, turning on my computer. "Any messages?"

"No, just a few things to do. Mr. Dalca wanted you to see him when you got back." He pointed to the stack of papers on my desk. "He also left those for you to copy and file and asked that you call Mrs. Rizzo about the case." I nodded, putting my untouched pizza on my desk.

"Thanks. I hope this doesn't take long—I'm hungry." Darius sniggered while I headed towards my boss's office. I knocked gently. "Mr. Dalca?" I called out softly. "You wanted to see me?"

"Yes, Ms. Gabor, please come in."

I opened the door and took two steps into the office. It wasn't decorated how you would expect a lawyer's office to look. Instead of leather chairs, his were upholstered with brown chiffon fabric. The walls were a light blue color, creating a more welcoming environment. His degrees hung on the walls, and next to them were shelves filled with law books, but also some on European history. "Would you like me to close the door, sir?"

"No, no. This will only take a second. Come in, come in." He motioned me forward. I took a few more steps inside. "First, I would like to wish you a happy birthday."

I smiled brightly, impressed that he remembered. "Thank you!" The corners of his mouth turned up ever so slightly.

"You're welcome." He continued, "I also wanted to check on you. Darius mentioned that you had a fainting spell? Are you feeling okay?"

"Oh," I replied, embarrassed. "It wasn't a big deal. I think it was just because I didn't eat enough this morning and the heat made me dizzy. I'm okay now though; thank you."

He gazed at me intently, as if he knew that I wasn't being truthful. I looked away. It felt like minutes ticked by before he spoke again.

He nodded. "Please make those copies and call the client, and then you are free to go." I stared at him, surprised.

"Thank you, Mr. Dalca!"

He waved it away. "I want you to enjoy your birthday and take the rest of the day to relax; I don't want any more fainting spells." He eyed me knowingly.

"Of course. Thank you again, sir. I really appreciate it." *The rest of the day off is practically unheard of in this business.* I started to dance-walk back to my desk but then thought better of it; I didn't want Mr. Dalca to reconsider his letting me go home early. *I hope my pizza is still warm.*

"Everything okay?" Darius asked.

"Yes. He wished me a happy birthday and asked me how I was feeling. He, um," I hesitated, but he would know soon anyway. "He also said I could leave after I finished those two tasks."

Darius' eyes widened, dumbstruck. He quickly recovered and said, "Wow! That's awesome! Well, hurry up so you can leave!"*Lucky.* I pretended like I didn't hear his thought.

"I'll get right to it—after I devour this deliciousness in front of me. Want a bite?" I offered, holding out a cheesy slice.

"Don't tempt me." He shook his head. "You eat—I'll get my own in a little bit. Thank you, though." I nodded and began to eat, letting the taste and aroma consume me. All too soon I was finished with my lunch, and settled into my chair to call our client. I wasn't looking forward to speaking with her; Mrs. Rizzo had proven to be a pain to work with. Picking up the phone, I swiveled my chair to face Darius.

"Wish me luck?"

He chuckled. "Good luck."

The next twenty-five minutes were filled with the difficult task of trying to gather information from Mrs. Rizzo, and explaining why her case would take longer than usual. I was as patient as I could be, but she was starting to give me a headache. Finally, we clicked off and I let out a heavy sigh.

"That went as well as I expected," I said to Darius. He looked at his watch.

"Only twenty-five minutes—that's a record."

"Man, that woman is a piece of work."

He shrugged and shook his head, smirking. "They all are."

Darius headed to lunch while I put all of Mrs. Rizzo's information into the system. I sent a quick email to Mr. Dalca, letting him know the information had been inputted. Afterwards, I picked up my phone and sent Vi a text letting her know that I was almost done, if she wouldn't mind heading over. Grabbing the stack of papers off my desk, I went to the copier.

I was grateful to have a shorter shift and was looking forward to having dinner with Mamă and Vi. I felt a pang of sadness. *I wish Tată were around.* My father passed in a car accident when I was a baby. It hurt that I never got to know him, and Mamă rarely spoke of him. I couldn't believe that another year had gone by without him in my life. I pushed the feelings aside—this was going to be a good birthday celebration. *Stop depressing yourself.*

I had about two-hundred hundred pages to copy into three files. It didn't take too much time but it was a tedious process; I also felt bad about all the trees I had killed to complete the task. I rushed to put the files away and headed to my desk, checking my phone to see if Vi was here. She'd messaged me: *Will be another 30 min or so—had to make a stop. Sorry!*

I replied with *No problem, see you soon!* But I groaned. *Oh, well.*

I dashed to Mr. Dalca's office. The door opened just as I lifted my hand to knock. "Oh!" I lowered my hand, taking a step back. "I just wanted to let you know that I was done making the copies, but my ride isn't here yet. Is there anything else that you would like me to do?" I added.

He thought about it. "No," he said finally. "Thank you, Ms. Gabor. Perhaps you can walk around and enjoy the weather?"

I nodded. "That sounds like a plan."

"Great! Well, enjoy your weekend, and I'll see you on Monday."

"Thanks, Mr. Dalca, you too." As I was walking back towards my desk, an idea occurred to me. I turned to Darius, who had just come back from his lunch break. "So, Vi won't be here for a little bit. Is there anything I can help you with?"

"Girl, you are too sweet. Get out of here. Go sit outside somewhere and wait before Mr. Dalca finds something for you to do," he said, putting his bag down. "But thank you for offering."

"Okay, okay—I'm leaving." Turning to get my blazer, I doubled checked that the box and note were still in my pocket and gave Darius a hug.

"I'll text you later, but have a great weekend, girl. Take care of yourself," he added.

"I'll try, and thank you again."

"No problem."

"See you Monday!"

I decided to go to the café on the next block over for an iced coffee. Once I had my coffee, I sat outside people-watching. They bustled past, every single person looking as if he or she were on a mission. I looked up at the cloudless sky, the image interrupted by skyscrapers and high-rise buildings. *It really is a nice day...I wonder what Vi and Mamă have up their sleeves.* My phone pinged—it was Vi, letting me know she was a few minutes away. I stood up to start walking back towards the office. It was more humid than before, and beads of sweat instantly formed on my brow. I could see Vi parked right in front. I waved to her, quickening my pace. She had the air conditioner on full blast, freezing the sweat as soon as I entered the car.

"Sorry I was late!"

"Not a problem. Thank you for offering to drive me in the first place."

"Anytime. So, how was work?"

"It went by fast." I didn't mention the ring. "I had some papers to copy and a phone call to make. I was lucky Mr. Dalca let me leave early."

"Yeah—how does that even happen?"

I shrugged, shaking my head. "I have no clue, but he told

me to enjoy my birthday."

"You have a sweet boss." She nodded appreciatively, then put on her blinker and pulled into traffic. "I can't wait to see your face once we get home!"

My eyes widened. "Uh-oh! What did you guys do?" I lowered my head, covering my eyes with my hand. "I told you guys it wasn't a big deal."

She gave a mischievous smile. "You'll see." She navigated through traffic with ease, beating most of rush hour. We sang along to Bruno Mars and reached my condo in thirty minutes. Once in the hallway, I looked around unsure of what I'd find. *I hope they didn't plan a party or something crazy like that.* I walked slowly towards the front door, still reviewing possibilities in my head.

"Go on," Vi said slyly, "there's nothing to be scared of." I gave her a suspicious look and opened the door. Enigma was playing in the background; it's Mamă's favorite band. *Nothing seems out of place...*A delicious scent of cabbage rolls and grilled sausages wafted towards me. As I headed closer to the kitchen, I could also smell bean soup and baked potatoes. My stomach growled. I walked into the kitchen to find Mamă pulling the potatoes out of the oven.

"Oh my..." I stopped, eyes wandering around the kitchen. "What did you guys *do*?!" The kitchen was decorated with *Happy Birthday!* signs, and the counters were filled with enough food to feed an army. Nefi meowed in greeting. I bent down to pet her as Vi walked in behind me.

I shook my head, laughing. "I love you guys. Who else is coming, though? This can't be just for us."

Just then a knock sounded behind me and I turned around to see my old friend, Gabriela, step into the kitchen. I squealed in delight.

"Told you I'd surprise you," Vi said triumphantly. Mamă smirked and Vi gave her a high-five.

"Gabby!" I rushed to her, giving her a hug. Gabriela was my closest friend when we lived in California and I hadn't seen her in years. Gabby looked the same as I remembered, standing about five-four with mocha-colored skin and gray eyes. Her thick curls were set in a ponytail, allowing her face and bright smile to stand out. We always kept in touch, but recently it had been challenging planning a visit because of our conflicting schedules.

"Happy birthday," she said, embracing me tightly.

I took a step back. "Zeită! I've missed you so much! I'm so glad you're here!" I could barely contain my excitement, and I found myself hugging her again. She laughed. I released her and addressed Vi. "Is this why you were late?"

Vi nodded. "Yup! I had to pick her up from the airport." She stumbled slightly when I threw my arms around her.

"Thank you, thank you!"

"You're welcome."

"Gabriela, it's so nice to see you again." Mamă gave her a hug, too.

"Thanks for having me. It worked out perfectly." Gabriela explained that she was in town for her job, and had contacted Mamă to arrange her visit for my birthday dinner. I squealed.

"I'm so glad you're here," I repeated.

"Me too." She turned to Vi and asked, "Is there anything I can do to help?"

"No," both Mamă and Vi responded simultaneously.

"Both of you go sit down in the dining room—dinner will be ready shortly," Mamă instructed. I dropped my blazer on a chair in the kitchen, having no choice but to head to the dining room. With my arm looped through Gabby's, I led her there. The dining room was decorated in a similar fashion as the kitchen, with birthday signs taped to the walls. There was a floral piece in the center of the table.

"Wow—they decorated nicely," Gabby commented as we

sat down.

"Yeah. I knew they were up to something, but this is more than I was expecting. They really managed to surprise me this year. So, how long will you be in town?"

"Until the middle of September."

"Great! I can bother you until then."

Gabby laughed. "Well, I haven't started working yet, but until I do, you can bother me anytime." I smiled. "So, anything new with you since we last spoke?" she asked.

I thought about it for a second. "Not really. Just working and saving—I'd like to take a trip in the near future." I smiled. "What about you? Besides your job, what's new in your life?"

"Not too much, honestly, but it's funny you mention a trip; I've been doing a lot of traveling as well, trying to see it all, even though it's mostly for work."

"Doesn't matter—at least you're getting out there." I made a face. "I'm a little jealous," I said, smirking.

Just then, Mamă and Vi came out with platters of food and a big bowl of soup. My stomach grumbled as the food was set out on the table.

"Smells good," Gabby commented.

"Thank you, dragă."

I hope Nadia likes it.

My heart beat faster as Mamă's thought flittered across my mind. *Not again!* I tried to ignore it and instead echoed Gabby's appreciation of the aroma. "It smells amazing, Mamă. I can't wait to taste it!" She gave me a curious glance before sitting down.

"Yes, I hope you like it," she said, voicing her thought.

"I'm sure I will." She seemed sad. *What's wrong, Mamă?* She glanced sharply at me. My eyes widened and I looked away. *Had she heard me?*

Vi sat on the other side of me and rubbed her hands together. "Okay! Let's eat!"

"Yes, let's," I agreed. I decided to start with the bean soup and poured some of it into my bowl. I took a spoonful and swirled the soup around in my mouth, enjoying the flavors of onion and celery mixing with the sweetness of paprika. I gave an appreciative sigh. No one could cook like Mamǎ.

Mamǎ Anica can cook her ass off! I smirked—apparently Vi shared the same sentiments. It didn't take long for me to finish my soup and soon I was piling grilled sausages, cabbage rolls, and potatoes on my plate. We made small talk, raising our voices over the clanking of forks and knives.

"What happened to Darius?" Mamǎ asked.

"Oh, he said he had to pack for this weekend, so he couldn't make it."

"That's too bad—I like him. You two would make such a cute couple."

Vi snorted and I laughed heartily. "He's gay, Mamǎ."

"I know he is, but still."

Gabby smirked and put her fork down. She pulled an envelope from her bag where it hung on the back of her chair. "Here, let me give this to you before I forget. It's from me and Vi."

I took the envelope from her and tore it open, exposing a beautiful navy blue birthday card with gold lettering and designs. Two concert tickets for Lenny Kravitz slipped out and I snatched them up, brimming with excitement. The card fell on the table, unread. I glanced from Vi to Gabby, grinning sheepishly. Jumping from my chair, I gave them both tight hugs.

"Thank you, thank you, thank you!" I jumped up and down. Lenny Kravitz was one of my favorite artists and I couldn't wait to see him perform live.

Vi giggled. "You're welcome."

"I'm glad you're happy with them," Gabby said. Mamǎ

watched the whole exchange with a smile on her face. It was the first time all day that she looked relaxed.

"Oh, no! Which one of you is going with me?"

"Don't be foolish," Gabby replied.

Vi shook her head. "Yeah, we got those for you to enjoy. Maybe you'll meet someone tomorrow at the club." She wiggled her eyes brows suggestively.

I snorted, sitting back in my chair. "Yeah, right. Who says I'll meet anyone? One of you may be my date after all." They laughed. Mamă stood up and started clearing away the plates. "What are you doing, Mamă? I'll clean up." I reached for the plate that was in her hand.

She lightly slapped my hand. "Nu. It's your birthday; you sit and relax." *I can't wait to see her face when I bring out the papanaşi cu brânză de vacişi affine.*

I squealed. "You made papanash!" I was so excited about dessert that it took me a minute to realize Mamă, Vi, and Gabby were staring at me. "What?"

"How did you know that I made papanash?" Mamă asked.

Now aware that I had responded to her thought, I came up with an answer quickly. "I smelled it," I replied, biting my lip. No one said anything for a moment.

Gabby was the first to break the silence. "What's papanash?"

"It's a cheese donut made with blueberries," Vi explained.

"And is my absolute favorite," I added.

Vi looked at me. "That nose of yours never ceases to amaze me."

"Yup, that nose of mine." I gave a nervous giggle, then stood up. "I'll go get them!" I rushed out of the dining room. *Zeită! What's happening to me? This mind-reading thing is getting worse.* I was picking up the tray of papanash when I heard footsteps behind me: Gabby.

"Are you okay?" she whispered.

I turned to face her. "I've been feeling a little...different today," I admitted. "First, it was my eyes...." I began pacing the kitchen, talking to myself.

"Yeah, I was going to ask you about your contacts."

"...now I'm hearing things." I looked at her.

"They're nice, though."

"I think I'm going crazy, Gabby."

She threw her head back and gave a vigorous laugh. *Is she really laughing at me right now?* I looked at her, dumbfounded. "You're silly." Gabby fixed her eyes on me. "Did you ever think that maybe you have a gift?"

I stopped pacing and stared at her. Just like Vi, I had never told Gabby of my family's culture. *Does she know? But how?*

"What?" she asked, shrugging. "I read a lot."

"It's nothing. But what you say makes sense; you know we're all special in my family," I winked. In actuality, it was possible—all the Vrajitoares in my family had special gifts and talents.

I didn't mention my other senses being heightened, like the fact that I could see the speck of dust floating near her head.

"Hey! Are you guys bringing dessert, or what?" came Vi's voice from the dining room.

"Coming!" Gabby followed me to join the others. I placed the tray on the table and sat down.

"What took you so long? Were you trying to eat them all?"

I snapped my fingers. "Damn, you caught us!"

We each took a pastry and the chatter resumed. Gabby was reaching for another pastry when her phone pinged. Her fingers flew across the screen as she responded to the text. Finished, she looked at me and Vi sadly.

"I have to meet up with my coworker to begin our project."

"Do you need a ride back to your hotel?" Vi asked.

"Oh, no thank you—I can take a cab."

Vi waved her hand dismissively. "It's not a problem; I was going to leave soon, anyway."

"Are you sure?"

"Of course!"

"Well, thank you very much." Gabby turned to Mamă. "Thank you for letting me join for dinner."

"You are welcome here anytime."

"Thank you both for coming and for the tickets!" We shared a group hug.

"I'm sorry I won't be able to help clean up," Vi said to Mamă.

"It's no problem at all, dragă. Thank you for helping me prepare dinner." She gave Vi a hug. "It's always lovely to see you."

"I'll be back tomorrow to kidnap your daughter for the day." Vi smiled.

"Tomorrow?" I asked. "What's going on tomorrow?"

"You'll see." She winked.

"Oh no," I groaned. Vi laughed, grabbing a couple of papanash before making her way to the door.

When they were gone, Mamă and I sat at the table, letting our food digest. "Thank you so much for this and for dinner."

She smiled sadly. "You're more than welcome, fiică."

I sat up straight, "Mamă, what's going on? You seem so sad today."

"Nimic. I'm just tired. Blame it on old age." She gave a small laugh. I felt that there was more to it, but I accepted her answer and kissed her on the cheek.

"You go relax, Mamă, I'll clean up. This was amazing and

so much more than I expected."

"I'm glad you enjoyed it." She stood up and stretched. "And you're right—I think I will go rest." She seemed deep in thought as she made her way to her bedroom.

Oh, Mamă, I wish you would tell me what's going on. As soon as I thought it, I realized how hypocritical I was being. It felt like I had more and more secrets as the day went on. I tried to put the pieces together as I cleaned, but I was more confused than ever. *Zeită, give me answers.*

CHAPTER THREE

BRĂILA, WALLACHIA 1480

Mother had a task trying to calm me after my Ritual bath and even still, I had a fitful night's sleep. I tossed and turned, haunted by the images of my Vision in the form of a dream. This time, the story the images created seemed more complete, and as I was running through the forest, I could hear footfalls behind me and the creak of a bowstring being drawn back. All too soon, the arrow pierced my back. I woke up screaming. Mother threw my door open and rushed to my side.

"What's wrong?"

"The Vision," I replied breathlessly. "I was shot with an arrow." I reached over my shoulder and rubbed the area of my back that the arrow had pierced, remembering the burn from my dream. *It had to be silver...*I stared straight ahead, still seeing the woods around me. *Is that the cause of the darkness?* I was fearful of being in the darkness again.

"Shh." Mother held me, stroking my hair while my head rested on her shoulder. "Do not fret, my child, all will be well. Remember the words of the Seer: 'these are but visions—their true meaning yet to be known.'"

She was right, of course, but I couldn't rid myself of the feeling that there was no underlying meaning and the Vision was as final as it felt. I lifted my head and glanced at her.

"You are right, I mustn't forget. I think I shall go hunt to clear my head." I stood up and stretched.

"I think that is a wise idea," she agreed. "But bring some-one with you."

I rolled my eyes, ignoring her statement. "Do you need anything while I am out?"

Mother thought about it for a second. "Aye, stop by the market and fetch some things for supper. I will have Una make a stew." Although she was our servant, Una was more like family to us. She had been mother's personal attendant when they lived in the castle. When Una found out Mother was still alive, she snuck out of the castle to join her. I admired her loyalty and courage.

I nodded. "Of course."

She excused herself while I dressed in a light gown and my overcoat. My being a Vampyre was common knowledge to those in my community, but I tried not to feed on them if I could avoid it—I would need to travel some distance to a nearby town. Plus, feeding on someone I had no connection to added to the appeal of the hunt. I was looking forward to enjoying the day since I didn't have to train. After tying my long dark hair into a bun to get it out of my face, I left the house, walking out into the bright sun. I strolled towards the stables to visit my beautiful Fyuree. She neighed excitedly when I entered. *Such a majestic creature.* I pet her muzzle before reaching to the nearby shelf to retrieve an apple. She ate it in one bite. I refilled her manger with oats and corn and gave her fresh water.

My skin tingled, and I smiled as strong arms gently wrapped around my waist. I rested my head back against Nic's chest, inhaling his scent.

"Good day, my love," he breathed over my head.

"Mmm. Good day." I turned to face him and his lips locked with mine in a long, passionate kiss. The kiss grew deeper and I gripped his hair tightly. He growled and bit my lip, his fangs drawing blood. I pulled away and looked at him while slowly sucking the blood from my lip. Then my eyes darkened and I sent him a message: *Run.*

He raced through the stable doors and I counted to twenty before I gave chase, following his scent in the air. I sped through the village, passing old women pushing carts of fruit and men shoveling cow dung. Once I was in the forest and on a familiar path, I slowed down. Finding his scent again, my arms pumped by my sides as I continued to pursue him. A light coat of sweat began to form on my forehead.

I love the chase. He wasn't always the prey, but today I was feeling a little dominant. I caught the scent of fresh water, and could hear it flowing smoothly just below the small cliff ahead. Jumping over it, I landed in a stream. I took off running again and slowed to a jog when I entered the clearing. *Our clearing.* This place would always be dear to me; it was in this field of jasmine that Nic had vowed to always be by my side.

My skin tingled and I could sense that he was close by; I looked around. There. He walked forward from the other side of the clearing and I charged at him. As I neared him, Nic made no move. In two steps, I was upon him...and then through him. I faltered, landing on the ground. In that same instant, I felt the heat of a body pressing me down. He flipped me over and I stared into his eyes. All fight left me then.

So much for being dominant.

His eyes burned with desire and I felt a stirring from deep within my lower belly. I wrapped my legs around his waist, my underskirt rising inch by inch as I ground my hips, teasing him. I felt him harden through his trousers and a shiver ran through me. As I reached to wrap my arms around his neck, he swiftly pinned them to the ground. I flexed my fingers to test his grip, but that only made him tighten his hold on me.

"You distracted me once, but I shall not be fooled twice."

Then he kissed my neck and bit me. A moan escaped me as I threw my head back. As his fangs pierced my skin, a current went through us. Our minds became one: his thoughts were my thoughts; my memories were his. *Conexiune de Spirit.* This connection was a level of consciousness that only those who were truly meant to be could achieve. It was the reason why we could communicate without words.

Nic retracted his fangs and left a small trail of kisses across my collarbone. He sat up once he reached the ties of my overcoat, tearing it open. In one swift movement, he ripped the remaining garment from my body. Although my hands were now free, I remained still, watching him with lust stirring within me. He slowly lowered his head to my chest, kissing me softly. My skin erupted in goose bumps where his lips touched. His head shifted to the right and his lips were upon my breast. I let out a contented sigh and closed my eyes.

I felt Nic's breath on my nipple and it hardened in between his lips. My fingers found their way into his hair and I gripped tightly when he flicked his tongue across my nipple. He suckled on it, causing a wetness in between my thighs that only he knew. A small moan escaped me, and he moved to attend to the other side. His fangs gently grazed my nipple before he bit me. I growled at him, and he quickly removed my hands from his head and held my wrists tightly in one hand.

Ignoring my attempts to break free of his grasp, Nic continued to nibble down my abdomen, stopping at the rim of my skirt. He tugged at the lace and started untying it. I ceased struggling when he pulled my skirt down, revealing my forbidden fruit. He sat up, eyes traveling down my body as I lay there in my most natural state. I could smell his arousal and I bit my lip in response. He let go of my hands and gently wrapped his fingers around my thighs.

Starting from my knee, Nic kissed up the inside of my

thigh. My breath caught when he reached my center and used his tongue to part my lips. He licked and kissed with such intensity that I dug my hands into the grass, ripping up clods of dirt. I arched my hips, pushing his tongue deeper into my center, and started shivering in sweet delight. Just before I reached the height of my pleasure, he stopped. My eyes snapped open and I groaned in frustration. I was about to question him when he entered me and I gasped as we became one.

He held himself up with his hands on either side of my head, and I seized his arms. His movements were slow at first, a steady tempo that made me ache with impatience. Then he quickened his pace, inching deeper into me. I dug my nails into his skin and screamed out in ecstasy. I could sense his pleasure in my mind, and that made our dance all the more intense.

Staying inside me all the while, Nic flipped me over so that I was on all fours. I turned my head to the side and rested my cheek on the ground as he again found his rhythm. I felt his lips on my back, and then fangs breaking skin. I moaned loudly, startling the squirrel on the nearby tree. Our connection was so deep that I could feel him in my soul. I bit my lip to quiet myself and tasted blood, which only added to my arousal.

I felt strong fingers wind their way through my hair. Nic tugged and I snarled as he pulled my head back. I reached back with my right hand to grab his hip. With each thrust, I pulled him into me, forcing him deeper. My nails dug into his backside and, again, I found myself at the edge of my desire, desperately clinging to this moment. Nic started breathing more heavily and I heard him grunt. That was all the confirmation I needed to let go as we both rode the passionate waves of our lovemaking.

We laid there with our eyes closed, snuggled together. I

felt a gentle breeze on my skin and listened to the birds chirp. For a moment, all was forgotten. I was not a princess training to defend her people and take the throne. Instead, I was simply a woman lying in a field of jasmine, connecting with her lover. *If only we could stay like this forever.* Suddenly, my stomach grumbled and Nic shook with laughter.

"Fancy a bite?"

I hunched onto my elbow and rested my head in my hand. "You know me too well." I smirked, then stood, feeling refreshed. "Let's hunt."

He followed suit, standing to stretch. Then he held out his hand. "After you," he offered.

I took off heading west, weaving my way through places where the sun had yet to shine its light. The air tickled my bare skin. Twigs and branches dug into my heels as I ran, but they bothered me not. I could hear Nic breathing heavily behind me. I threw a quick glance at him and then stopped running. I'd heard something. It sounded like a whispered conversation.

"Do you hear that?" I asked Nic.

He put a finger to his lips and I nodded. I followed quietly behind him as he started tracking the sounds' location. We moved silently through the trees, stopping every so often to listen. Nic halted suddenly and again I heard the distant voices of two men. I pointed in the direction the voices were coming from. He motioned at me to flank them and ran to position himself opposite me, surrounding the men. Our plan was simple: attack from both sides, leaving our prey with nowhere to hide.

I climbed the nearest tree, my nails digging into the bark, and stopped on a sturdy branch. Now able to see more of the woods, I looked around until I spotted two men relieving themselves on a tree. Judging by their armor and the cross and dragon that were embroidered on their flag, they were knights of the Order. I suddenly grew suspicious and my vision blurred; I could tell that my eyes had blackened. *What brings them here?* I could hear their rhythmic heart beats in my head and smiled. *Easy prey.* Though I couldn't see Nic, I could sense him in a tree across the way. The knights laced up their trousers and started walking back from whence they came.

Nic's voice fluttered across my mind. *Now.*

I leaped from the tree, landing smoothly, and then raced towards the closest knight. I was too fast for him to sense, and he grunted when I tackled him.

"What the..." his companion started, but the rest of his statement was cut off when Nic tackled him to the ground. Together, we ripped off their helmets and sunk our fangs into their flesh. The knights writhed about, swords clanking against their armor as we fed. Soon, I let go my knight—I needed information. He raised his head, and with a steady gaze, raked his eyes up and down my naked body. I grabbed him by the throat and lifted him into the air until we were at eye level.

"What business do you have here, Swan?" I growled. He clawed at my hand, struggling to breathe. I released him and Nic was behind him in an instant, having drained the other knight unconscious. He rubbed at this throat with an iron-clad hand, and I watched him intently, waiting for an answer.

"Fuck you," he coughed out.

Nic punched him in the back of the head. "I believe the lady asked you a question."

The knight glared at him defiantly. "I'd rather die than betray the Order."

"Then so you shall." Those were the last words he heard before Nic grasped his jaw and pulled his head from his neck. Blood spurted on us and I licked some off my arm.

"And what of this one?" Nic asked me, glancing at the

unconscious knight.

"Leave him."

"You are growing soft."

"Nay. He is unconscious—he will make a lovely meal for the Gods' beasts." I smirked at him. Nic had opened his mouth to respond when we heard a woman's shriek, followed by several voices shouting. I didn't think we were that close to a village, but I quickly pulled the armor off the knight and began undressing him. Nic mimicked me, and we rushed to put on their clothing to cover our naked bodies. The screaming grew louder and more frantic.

I ran towards the sound with Nic at my heels. The forest was suddenly full of the squawks of birds, and the trees were sparse enough for me to see them flying away from a cloud of smoke. We didn't have to travel far before we encountered deer, squirrels, and many other beasts running in our direction—and I could see why; there were several people running towards us, covered in flames.

From where I stood, I could see a blazing village. Men, women, and children scattered in all directions. Moving among them were more knights of the Order, slaughtering those they could reach. A knight grabbed a boy no older than a tot and shoved his sword into the boy's abdomen.

"Take heed Mihnea's orders—no one is to be left alive that does not comply!" He called out to the other members, clearly in charge.

"Raz, what of this one?" asked a knight holding up a trembling middle-aged man. "He asked that he and his family be spared."

The leader thought for a moment before responding. "Kill him."

"Nay, sir—" The man's screams were silenced when a sword was thrust into his gut.

Raz grunted and dropped the boy into the dirt as though he were nothing more than a sack of potatoes. He walked away.

Before I knew what was happening, my feet carried me to the boy's little body.

"Antanasia!" Nic implored, but I barely heard him. Chaos was erupting all around me, but all I could focus on was saving the little boy. I found his entry wound and roughly bit into my wrist. My blood started flowing freely from the gash, and I held it over his injury. His skin began stitching itself together and I breathed out a sigh of relief. But it was short lived, for the boy did not move once it was completely healed.

"I beseech you, wake!" I shook him gently and still he did not move. I tried again more vigorously, with no luck—he was gone. I felt a burning deep within me. *How dare they murder children!* I yelled out wordlessly in frustration. I was sworn to protect these people—those who rebelled against the Order and refused to be in chains—and I'd failed. There came a clanking sound behind me, and I turned just in time to see a knight falter and sag to the ground. Nic stood behind him holding a blood-soaked dagger. He looked at the lifeless boy and his expression saddened.

"Scoundrels," he said, spitting on the dead knight.

Fueled by the loss of an innocent babe, I sprang into action. I ran into the closest building, ignoring the flames that were licking at my skin—it would heal soon enough. Past the blazing table and chairs, I saw an older child hiding in the corner with her hands over her head. She was surrounded by flames, and I was sure the roof would cave in shortly. I ran and kneeled before her, holding out my hand.

"We must leave." She screamed and shook her head, shrinking away from me. The shriek of splintering wood sounded and the wall began to cave. "Come, now!"

Needing no more convincing, the little girl took my hand and I picked her up, racing to the door. No sooner was I outside than the roof collapsed and all that remained was burning rubble. I held the girl tightly and looked around, searching for a safe place. I spotted a hollow at the base of a large tree at the edge of the village. Moving with lightning speed, I reached the tree and gently placed her on the ground.

"Stay here. Go as far back into the hollow as possible," I instructed her, and started walking away to find foliage to conceal the hollow with. I felt a sharp pull on my arm, and turned to see her peering at me with terror in her eyes.

"Don't leave me!" she yelled frantically. There was a river of tears flowing from her almond-shaped eyes.

I squatted down and took her head in my hands. "What do they call you?"

"Jeniviva," she answered in a shaky voice.

"That's a beautiful name. I am Antanasia. Jeniviva, I will never leave you, I promise." She smiled weakly and threw her hands around me in a tight hug. A warm feeling swam inside me and I hugged her back. I kissed the top of her black hair and pulled away, looking into her eyes. "But, I must stop those who did this and save as many of the others as I can. Do you understand?" She nodded. "Stay here. I will come back for you as soon as I can."

I found a piece of bark and several twigs, which I placed in front of the hollow. With that, and Jeniviva at the back of the tree, no one would know she was there. I dashed towards what was left of the village. Most of the screaming had stopped. All of the houses and vendor stands were now nothing more than flaming wood and melted cob. There were a few stragglers running about, but most of what still moved was fire. I didn't see Nic anywhere and my chest tightened with worry.

Then I heard him in my head. *I'm well.*

That was all the confirmation I needed. I sped through the village, searching for more survivors. Anger and sadness filled me at the amount of bodies littered about, more villagers than knights. I didn't find anyone else alive, and prayed to the Gods that Nic had gotten them to safety.

I ran to the other side of the village and there Nic stood, piercing a knight with his own sword. He looked up as I approached.

"That's the last of them."

"There were but a handful of knights..." I stood there, in the middle of the burned-down village full of corpses. "Look at what they've done."

"Aye. They must have begun the attack around dawn, surprising the villagers. There were Vampyres among the Swans. But," He took my arm and turned me towards him, "none of them still breathe." That offered me a little solace and I gave a weak smile.

"Although that is good news, I am still full of grief. They raided the village looking for me—I have failed them, Nic," I said, motioning towards the dead bodies sprawled on the dirt.

"But there are even more that were saved using the knights' horses—be mindful of them as well." Just then, I remembered Jeniviva and sprinted to the tree. Thanks to a Vampyre's impeccable memory, it was no challenge to find it. I pulled away the bark and twigs, growing worried. "What are you looking for?" Nic asked behind me.

"The girl—Jeniviva. She should be in the tree!" I stood up, frantically looking around. "There is no time to explain; we have to find her!"

"There!" He pointed suddenly, and I saw movement in the bushes, several yards away. I sped through the foliage, stopping abruptly at the scene before me: the knight I'd spared gripped Jeniviva by her hair and held a blade to her throat. She squirmed about, struggling to break free of his grasp.

"Let the girl go." I took a step towards him.

"Come closer and she dies," he warned, and Jeniviva stopped struggling, eyes filled with terror. I froze in my tracks. "I was just telling her that you wouldn't return—she's nothing more than food to you. You will drink her dry once you're bored. All of your kind do."

"What is he talking about? You're not a monster, are you?" Jeniviva asked, eyes searching mine.

"Nay, I'm no monster," I replied, and then regarded the knight. "*He* works for a monster. If you have such strong feelings, why follow Mihnea?"

"Mihnea is more powerful than you'll ever be; I'd rather be on the winning side." I took a step forward, and Jeniviva yelped as the knight pricked her hard enough to draw blood. I hissed, fangs bared.

"Stay back, I say!" The knight warned me.

A surge of anger went through me and my necklace heated against my chest. "I could have killed you before, but I was merciful; this time you won't be so lucky."

The knight didn't notice Nic approaching him from behind. In a swift movement, Nic pulled the knight's windpipe from his body. The knight opened his mouth and began spluttering blood. He released Jeniviva and sank to the ground. Nic stood there, covered in blood with the windpipe dangling from his hand. He looked down at the knight's body, wearing an expression of loathing. I went to Jeniviva, but she skirted away from me as I approached.

"You are hurt—let me help."

"Stay away from me!"

I frowned. "But I can heal you."

"You *are* a monster, just like the man who killed Mama and Papa."

I felt a pang of sadness. "Aye, I am a Vampyre like the knight who took your parents, but I am no monster—you've seen who the true monsters are."

"Do you eat people like he did?"

"I feed, but do not slay, unless threatened. I don't believe in doing that." I stepped closer. "There are others who believe as I do, and together we fight villains like the one who took your Mama and Papa." She said nothing as I took yet another step towards her. "You have no reason to fear me; I will never harm you." I held out my hand. "Let me heal you."

She searched my eyes and, finding only truth to my words, took my hand. I pulled her towards me and embraced her in a tight hug. In our short encounter, I had grown to care deeply for her. I kissed her forehead and inspected her neck. Blessedly, the wound was only surface deep. I bit my thumb and smeared blood across her lesion; instantly, the broken skin closed up and smoothed over.

"All better," I said, smiling at her. "I want you to meet someone." I held her hand and turned to Nic. "This is Nic—he trains with me to fight the villains. Nic, this is Jeniviva."

Nic slowly took her other hand in his and kissed the back. "Pleasure to meet you, my lady."

She blushed a deep shade of crimson and mumbled, "You too." I giggled as Jeniviva tightened her grip on my hand and shuffled her feet to hide behind me. She tugged on my pant leg and I knelt beside her. "We have to find Luca," she whispered in my ear.

I grew alarmed. "Luca?"

"Aye, my baby brother. We have to go back for him—I am all he has left." I glanced at Nic and he frowned.

What else are we to do? Nic's voice sounded in my head.

I looked back at Jeniviva's sweet face, staring deep into her eyes, and said, "I'm sorry, Jeniviva, but *I* am all you have left."

The image of the lifeless babe was clear in my head and I shared it with her, praying to the Gods that I was wrong, but knowing I was not. The twinkle in her eyes dimmed and they filled with tears as she began sobbing heavily. I picked her up and held her tightly, enveloped in her sorrow. Slowly, her sobs quieted and she hiccupped, still resting on my shoulder. A thought occurred to me.

"Have you ridden on horseback before?" I asked her. She shook her head, sniffling. "Would you like to?" This time she lifted her head and looked at me. She nodded and I smiled. "I have a beautiful white horse called Fyuree, and you can ride her anytime you'd like. How does that sound?"

"Good," she hiccupped again.

"Excellent! We shall go to my village and you can meet her. Would you like that?"

"I would," she responded, a little more brightly.

You are good with her.

I faced Nic, still smiling. *She's precious.*

I put her down and took her hand in mine. "Come." We started walking back to Bräila. A few steps in, she surprised us by taking Nic's hand, too. He said nothing, but smiled at her.

"I miss Mama and Papa and Luca." She sniffled as more tears threatened to spill.

I squeezed her hand. "I know, but they are with the Gods now, watching over you."

"Why did those men do that to our village? We've never harmed them."

"Because they are heartless and cruel," Nic answered for me.

Jeniviva was silent for a second and then said, "Can you teach me how to fight? I want them to pay for this." She spoke with such conviction that I was certain she was much older than she appeared. I glanced at Nic and then stopped walking, kneeling before her.

"Aye—we can teach you basic sparring, but you have no reason to worry—I will always protect you. Remember my promise?" She nodded. "Good girl."

We continued walking towards home, listening to Jeniviva talk. She spoke of her family and how they'd come to be at the village where we found her. She asked lots of questions about my family and what life was like at my home. I kept some of my responses short and simple, unable to explain that my father had created the organization that killed her entire family. Those were things to be discussed at a later date. She spoke of the things she liked to do and asked if there were other children at the village that she could play with. Her young and bubbly energy was infectious, and I couldn't help but smile the whole time. It was amazing how resilient the youngling was—how, for now, she was able to bounce back from losing her whole family.

The sun was lowering from its apex when Jeniviva's chatter and movement slowed and she yawned. It was after midday and we still had a ways to go. Long distances were nothing to us, but she was only a child.

We would get there much quicker if we ran, Nic thought. I nodded in agreement and he regarded Jeniviva. "My lady, do I have your permission to carry you? We would reach the village much faster by running."

She rubbed her tired eyes and bobbed her head. Nic picked her up with ease and she laid her head on his shoulder. One hand supported her back while his other hand rested on the back of her head. His eyes met mine and he nodded. I raced in front of him, leading the way as he trailed behind me. The sun's rays beamed down on us, and I began perspiring early into our journey. I used the back of my hand to wipe off bugs that were sticking to my forehead.

In no time, I smelt the familiar scents of lilies and fresh-baked bread, and heard the recognizable sounds of children laughing and men smithing iron. I slowed to a walking pace, inhaling deeply. Nic stopped behind me, still holding

Jeniviva, who was now deep in slumber. I gently shook her and she opened her eyes.

"We are here." She sluggishly lifted her head, peering around her. She jumped from Nic's hold and took my hand.

"I'm hungry," she told me. That reminded me of Mother's request to get supplies from the market.

"Right. I must run to the market for vegetables and beef. Do you want to accompany me, or would you rather visit Fyuree with Nic?"

"Can I come with you and then we can see Fyuree?"

"Of course!"

"I will get Fyuree's saddle ready," Nic said.

"That would be wonderful."

We walked the short distance to the market and Jeniviva looked around while I gathered an onion, carrots, potatoes, beef, and celery for Una to make stew. The vendors welcomed Jeniviva and she even got a free papanash. *She will fit in nicely here.* She ate her pastry as we strolled towards my home.

"Your village is very pretty," she commented.

"You mean *our* village is pretty—this is your home now." She didn't say anything, but she beamed at me. "Here we are." She looked up at my house and her eyes widened in awe. Her expression made me laugh. I opened the door and she followed me to the smoke kitchen. After putting the food in the larder, we searched for Mother.

I found her in her chambers, writing. Mother's room was fairly plain, with only sconces on the grey stone walls. Her bed covers matched her surroundings—she didn't like to become too attached to an area, and should someone come searching for us, there were no clues of her true identity.

"I've returned," I announced. She looked up at me, expression unreadable.

"And who is this child?" she asked, gazing at Jeniviva. As I opened my mouth to respond, Jeniviva stepped forward.

"I am called Jeniviva, madam." Jeniviva bowed her head, keeping her gaze downward so as not to stare at Mother's clouded eye.

"Pleasure. I am Ecaterina." Mother smiled, bowing back. "Such a proper one," she commented.

"Aye, she is."

"May I ask a question?" Jeniviva asked Mother. She nodded for her to continue. "If you are like me, then how is it that Antanasia is a Vampyre?"

Mother looked at me. "And bold too." She smirked.

"Aye. I believe her to be older than she appears."

"That answer is still unknown to us, child," Mother answered her.

"Jeniviva is anxious to meet Fyuree." I grinned and placed a hand on her head.

"She is a beauty. Take her to the stables and return to me."

I nodded and turned on my heel, with Jeniviva following close behind me to the stables. "Your mama is beautiful."

"She is," I agreed.

"What happened to her eye?"

"A reminder of her journey from the tower." Jeniviva frowned and I sighed. "Long ago, Mother was married to the mad king—"

Jeniviva gasped. "Is he your Papa?"

"Aye, he is," I nodded. "Mother felt trapped, as she told me, and did not want to be involved with Father's insane ideas. When she learned that she was pregnant with me, she thought of ways to leave, to protect us. In the light of the moon, she decided that jumping from the castle tower was the only way to escape him."

"She is brave."

"That she is." We reached the stables and found Nic with Fyuree saddled and ready to go. "Do you mind if Nic gives you your first lesson? I must speak with Mother."

Jeniviva shook her head and hugged me tightly. "Don't go."

I put my hand on the back of her head. "Jeniviva, I will return shortly. I am only going to speak with Mother. Remember my promise—I will always be here for you." Jeniviva didn't respond at first, seeming to consider my words. "Nic will be with you the whole time I'm gone," I added. She released me and smiled before hurrying to my horse, in awe. "I will return shortly," I repeated.

I walked across the courtyard back home, and braced myself for the conversation I was about to have with Mother. She was outside waiting for me. Before she spoke, I gave her the details of how Nic and I found Jeniviva.

"As precious as she is, she must not stay here."

I let out an exasperated sigh. "She has no one but us. Where is she to go? Who is to look after her?"

"Children are a distraction. This is not the time for distractions."

"She can learn and play with the other children. When she is able, she can—"

Mother cut me off. "We are at *war*, Antanasia. Be wise!"

I didn't respond right away, struggling with my emotions. *I understand what Mother is telling me. But then again, I have grown fond of the child and I need to protect her.* To Mother, I said, "I made her a promise. I intend to keep it." I turned my back on her.

"Antanasia..."

"If you wish her gone, then you tell that little girl who lost her *whole* family that she is not welcome," I said.

Mother did not answer and I knew the battle was won. I went to the stables, but they were empty. At the back of the stables, I found Nic and Jeniviva near the outskirts of the village. Jeniviva was atop Fyuree, riding slowly while Nic held onto to the saddle. I watched them before approaching—the sight of them filled me with warmth. It was then I realized how much love I felt for them. It broke me inside that I couldn't save Luca. Right then, I vowed to the Gods that I would never fail Jeniviva.

CHAPTER FOUR

NEW YORK, NEW YORK 2015

I am running, breathing fast. I stumble over a branch but don't slow my pace. It is still not enough: the hunters catch up with me and the arrow finds my back and goes through me with ease.

I sat up, drenched in sweat. I took deep breaths to calm myself. *This nightmare has got to stop! I need to have a decent night of sleep!* Sighing heavily, I ran a hand through my hair, completely frustrated. I got out of bed, going through my usual morning routine with Nefi meowing behind me.

I started getting dressed, and was looking for a hair tie when my eyes came across the silver-plated box from yesterday. I'd put it on the desk next to my knife before going to bed last night. The note came to mind: *I thought you would like to have this back.* Opening it, I stared at the beautiful ring, thinking back to yesterday. I took a deep breath before placing it on my finger, wondering if anything would happen again. No Visions appeared to me, and I admired how good it looked on my hand.

I shrugged, deciding that I was going to wear it today. *Maybe I have a secret admirer. But who could that be? Who would give me a magickal ring?* I couldn't think of anyone off the top of my head. Perhaps it was a surprise from Mamă after all. It looked so familiar—maybe Tată had given it to her and she wanted me to have it. I shook my head, not completely sold on this theory. I made my way downstairs and found Mamă in the kitchen pouring two mugs of coffee.

"Mmm. That smells great," I commented, taking a mug from her. I listened for a second, until I was satisfied I wasn't picking up her thoughts. *Maybe yesterday was a one-time thing.*

"How did you sleep?" she asked.

I shrugged. "I had the nightmare again."

Mamă put her mug down. "Is there anything else that you can remember—something that stands out?" I considered my options: tell Mamă and maybe get some answers or suffer in silence, trying to figure it out myself. Mamă raised her left eye-brow and gave me a knowing half smile. "Fiică, if there's anything I can do to help, I will, but you need to talk to me." I sighed. "You know I'm here for you," she reassured me.

"I know. It's just—I don't want you overreacting or anything." Walking to the fridge, I pulled out the leftovers. I seemed to be the only one of all my friends who didn't think it was weird to have dinner for breakfast. Nefi meowed hopefully, weaving her way in between my legs. I smiled at her, momentarily distracted.

"I won't overreact. Iți promit. Just tell me what's on your mind."

I was standing at the microwave waiting for my food to finish heating, and I turned to face her. "I don't see the faces of the men chasing me," I began, "but when they catch up to me, they always kill me with a silver-tipped arrow." Mamă gasped. "It feels so real," I continued, "I wish I knew what it meant." Mamă wore a worried expression. "What? Why have you been looking so sad lately?" There were lines on her face that I had never noticed before, and she seemed less energetic than usual; I was beginning to worry about her health.

Mamă pinched the bridge in between her eyes and let out a deep breath. Then she looked up at the ceiling as if thinking of where to start. "There's so much I want to tell you." Food forgotten, I dragged Mamă to the table and sat next to her. Finally, she looked me in the eyes, and then frowned. She took my head in her hands and shook her head, furrowing her brows.

I took her hands off my face and held them in mine. "Mamă, what is it? What do you want to tell me?" She looked down, finally noticing the ring. Her eyes grew.

"Where did you get that?"

She brought my hand closer to her face so that she could better examine the ring. Her expression was one of pure shock, and I knew that something wasn't right.

"Stop being silly, Mamă. I know that it came from you. Tată gave it to you." I looked down at it. "Thank you so much for giving it to me. I love it." I glanced at her. "I didn't understand the note though; why would I like to have it back? I don't remember ever having it before."

"So that's the ring. It's more beautiful than in the pictures," she whispered to herself. Then she looked me in the eyes. "Oh, my baby. My poor, sweet baby," she said. "That's not from me."

I was confused. "If it's not from you, then who is it from?"

"A very special man; one who loved you very much." I immediately thought of Tată and my Vision, thinking that it was my parents whom I saw. Mamă looked distressed. "I don't think it's a good idea for you to wear it."

"Why not?"

"Because you don't know where it came from. How do you know it's not dangerous?"

I was suddenly offended. "Because I saw its aura and it *felt* fine. It was given to me. It's beautiful and fits perfectly."

"Of course it does; it was made for you," she replied in a low voice.

"What are you talking about, Mamă?" She wasn't looking

at me anymore and I was starting to get irritated.

"There's so much you don't know."

"Well, then fill me in," I said firmly.

"Where do I even start?" She seemed agitated.

"Mamă, start from the beginning," I encouraged her.

She looked away, lost in thought, and then smiled sweetly. "Your Tată was such a charming man," she began. My heart swelled and I suppressed my irritation. Mamă rarely, if ever, spoke about my father, and I was excited to hear more. "Frumos," she continued. "When we first met, it was like love at first sight." She gave a nervous giggle. I smiled. It was cute seeing Mamă act like a little school girl with her first crush. "He was a mysterious character, always seemed to be involved in this...group."

I gave her a questioning look. "What do you mean 'group'?"

Mamă closed her eyes, looking weary again. I wondered if Tată was into something illegal. "Your father was involved with an organization whose mission was to protect all that we hold sacred."

"So, he was in the military," I said matter-of-factly.

"Yes and no." She hesitated, choosing her next words carefully. "A long, long time ago, an organization was formed to defend Christianity." I raised my eyebrow and cocked my head to the side. I wasn't sure where she was going with this, as we are a family of Witches. "It was called the Order of the Dragon." The name sounded familiar to me, but I couldn't figure out how I knew it. "The members were specially selected, but there was one family whose patriarchs always made the cut, and—" Mamă stopped mid-sentence and stood up. It took me a moment before I was able to feel Vi's presence. "We will finish this at a later time," she said, walking out of the room.

I was disappointed; this was the most I had learned about

Tată. I knew there was so much that she didn't say, but I still couldn't understand what had her so worried. Not to mention, I still hadn't learned anything about the ring. I sighed and plastered a smile on my face before opening the door to let Vi in. At that point, I had built up quite an appetite, and I remembered my plate in the microwave. I offered Vi a plate, which she declined, saying she would just pick off mine.

I pulled my plate from the microwave and walked into the dining room. Vi followed behind me. "So what are we doing today?" I asked.

"My dear," she said, "I am taking you to lunch, and the rest of the day is up to you." She sat down next to me and Nefi jumped into her lap.

"Yummy," I exclaimed. "Where to?"

"How about Soyo," she suggested, absentmindedly petting Nefi. I smiled brightly. Soyokaze was a quaint Japanese restaurant in the Village and one of my favorites.

"You'll hear no objections from me." Then I called out, "Mamă, want to come to Soyokaze?"

She answered from the laundry room. "Nu, mulțumesc."

"Are you sure?"

"Da, I'm sure. You two have fun—I'm going to bring some food over to Mrs. Agnes."

Mrs. Agnes was our next-door neighbor: a kindly old lady with a few grandbabies whom I loved to play with. I shrugged and turned back to my food, making a mental note to bring Mamă some leftover sushi. Vi and I talked about what else we could do after lunch, trying to choose between shopping for that night or the movies.

"We could always do both," Vi suggested with a smirk.

I rolled my eyes. "One thing at a time."

"Whatever! It is my mission to make sure you enjoy yourself today."

I got up and took the plate to the sink to wash it. "Vi, I always have a good time with you."

"Aww, thanks." She giggled.

We made our way to my room for a quick touch up. According to my weather app, it was going to be warmer than I'd originally predicted, so I decided to change clothes. I was flipping through the hangers with Vi and Nefi by my side.

"Hey, nice ring," Vi commented, taking my hand and examining it. "Where did you get this?"

"It was on my desk at work yesterday. I think I have a secret admirer," I replied, wiggling my fingers.

Vi chuckled, "I wish I had an admirer like that; this ring is beautiful. It looks really old." She studied it for a second longer, then turned her attention back to my clothing rack. "You really don't have any idea who it's from?"

I shook my head. "Not a clue."

"Well, did the person leave a note or something?"

"Yeah, but it was weird. It said, 'I thought you would like to have this back,' but I don't remember having it in the first place."

"Um, isn't that a little creepy?" Vi asked.

"Well, I don't get any bad vibes from it, so I'm sure it's fine." I didn't want Vi getting worried about the ring, too; Mamă's concern was more than enough.

Vi was unconvinced. "Whatever you say."

I didn't say anything more about the ring. It was true that I didn't have the foggiest idea of where it came from, but my intuition told me the ring was safe. Whoever had left it knew where I worked, but for some reason, that didn't concern me. It probably should have, considering someone had been watching me at lunch yesterday. I made a face, looking at the ring again. I decided that I would meditate for answers later, but for now, I was comfortable wearing it.

An hour and a half later, Vi and I walked arm and arm down Fifteenth Street. I was wearing a maroon sundress with silver Greek sandals, while Vi wore a loose teal shirt and grey shorts. Nothing strange had happened so far, and it left me in a good mood. I gazed at the cloudless blue sky through sunglass-covered eyes. We were discussing places I should go for the study abroad program at my school.

"I think you should go to Italy," Vi said.

"Italy would be great, but that's so typical. I want to go somewhere different, like Turkey, Albania, or Romania."

Vi rolled her eyes. "You *would* want to go to Romania."

I shrugged. "What? I mean, it's where my family's from—why not go visit?"

"Because," she said matter of factly, "Italy has vino, gelato, and sophisticated Italian men."

I burst out laughing. "Vi, you're ridiculous."

She smirked. "You know it's true."

My stomach growled loudly. Vi raised her left brow. "Hungry? I think the whole city heard that," she quipped. I laughed.

"Yeah, I bet. Guess I didn't eat enough for breakfast, again." I thought back to yesterday. *That's odd; I definitely made sure to eat more this time.* I picked up the pace; my stomach was starting to hurt, and I couldn't get to the restaurant fast enough.

"Hey, slow down," Vi called to me, running to catch up. "There will still be some food left when we get there." I smiled but didn't respond.

Uh-oh. She's acting strange again.

No! I didn't want to be hearing Vi's thoughts. Today was supposed to be *normal*. My hunger pains were becoming increasingly uncomfortable, making it difficult for me to put up any mental blocks. Smells were starting to overload my senses and I was getting dizzy. I could smell the sushi just a block away, the Japanese Cherry Blossom Vi was wearing, the piss on the fire hydrant and the cigarette smoke from the man across the street. I tried to take a deep breath but all I could do was gag.

When we finally arrived at Soyokaze, I quickly ran inside. It was somewhat better than outside; at least the scents were nicer. However, I could hear a mish-mash of thoughts from the other patrons. My stomach grumbled loudly at the smell of tempura, teriyaki, and noodles. I tried to ignore it as I took in the décor.

I hadn't been here since last year, but it was just like I remembered. The light was dimmed, giving relief from the brightness outside. The back wall had been painted a deep red with silver Japanese characters written on it. The left wall was all shoji paper sliding doors, making me feel as if I had stepped out of NYC and straight into Japan. Looking at the other side brought me back into the city: it was a floor-to-ceiling window, giving a view of the busy street.

"Hello, welcome to Soyokaze! How many?" The hostess greeted us with a thick Japanese accent. I clenched my jaw and placed my hands over my abdomen as my hunger got worse.

Vi glanced at me. "Just us. Can we sit at the sushi bar, please?" she added. The hostess nodded, grabbed two menus, and motioned for us to follow. I appreciated how well Vi knew me—I loved watching them prepare the rolls. Luckily, it wasn't crowded near the bar, as most of the patrons were seated at booths. The sounds decreased to a more manageable level. I took a deep breath to clear away some of my dizziness. We thanked the hostess before she moved back to her post. Slumping in the chair, I placed my sunglasses on the bar. I regarded Vi, who was staring at me. I had to swallow a few times to moisten my throat before I could speak.

"What?"

"Are you feeling okay?"

"Yes; I'm just hungry." I didn't mention any of my other symptoms; I was still trying to figure that out for myself. She continued to study me, and I sighed. "Talk to me. What are you thinking about?"

"Nothing. You just seem different lately." I made a face. "It's not bad, I swear. Your eyes—" she paused. "That new color is intense."

"Yeah, I decided to try something new." I shrugged, growing uncomfortable with being examined. I leaned away from her scrutinizing gaze. "Anyway, it's more than that," she continued. "They seem sharper and your skin is crazy clear. You look good." I scowled at her. "Not that you don't look good any other time," she added quickly. "Maturing works well for you." She winked and I laughed, though I could still feel her lingering gaze.

"Thanks, I guess." The scent of lavender floated towards me, and I looked up to see an exotic woman with long dark hair walking in our direction. She was elegant, with almond-shaped eyes, and seemed completely out of place in this restaurant.

"Hello, my name is Jeni, and I'll be your server today. Can I start you off with something to drink?" She smiled sweetly. Jeni had a slight accent, though I couldn't place where it was from. I secretly wanted *sake*, but law prohibited it, so I was forced to order a Sprite instead. Vi requested a glass of merlot.

Gross. I made a face. "Red wine is nasty—how can you drink that?"

"You're just not used to it, is all," she responded as Jeni walked away to grab the drinks after checking Vi's ID. I shook my head.

"No way!" I stuck my tongue out. "You can have that." I watched Jeni—there was something about the way she moved; almost like she was gliding. My stomach growled again and I turned my attention to the menu. "What are you thinking of getting?" I asked Vi.

Jeni had returned with our drinks. I was about to thank her when I caught her looking at me. Her expression was unreadable as her eyes bored into mine. I felt a hint of recognition, but it was gone so quickly I must have imagined it. She smiled, and said she would give us more time to figure out what we wanted.

"Hmm," Vi said, considering her options. "The New Yorker roll sounds good. Or maybe I'll get the beef teriyaki." I flipped through the menu for the third time; everything seemed like a good option to me. I began salivating over the smells of tempura and miso soup wafting from the kitchen. I squeezed my eyes shut and ground my teeth together through another hunger cramp. *Shit.*

"Are you okay?" Vi asked again. The pain was getting worse; it felt like I hadn't eaten in a week. Moments passed before I could respond.

"I'm alright, Vi, just really hungry." I let out a deep breath and gave her a weak smile. "I'm getting the sashimi platter." It wasn't my usual dish, but I figured since it was mostly raw, it should take less time to prepare, right?

"I know you love food, but geez, are you even going to be able to eat all that?" I shrugged.

"I'm really, *really* hungry. Besides, I can take home my leftovers for Mamă."

The platter was made for two, so it should be more than enough for my increasing appetite. I took a sip of my Sprite, hoping the carbonation would mask some of my hunger—it didn't. I suppressed a growl and focused on trying to figure out how I knew Jeni. As if sensing I was thinking of her, she returned to take our orders. Vi had decided to get both the roll and the teriyaki; I stuck with my sashimi. Jeni walked off to put in our orders and my stomach growled. Again. *This is really beginning to annoy me.*

Trying to distract myself from the pain, I took another sip of Sprite while Vi began to tell me the ideas she had for the rest of my birthday weekend. Her eyes twinkled as she became more and more excited about her plans. I rolled my eyes and shook my head. Oh, man.

She took a sip of wine. "We'll start out at Relik."

"Relik is that new Goth club you were talking about yesterday?" I asked. She nodded. I'd heard of Relik; it was the newest, hottest gothic club in the neighborhood. I'd been on a Goth kick lately, so I was definitely open to trying the club out.

"Then there's an after party I was thinking we could go to," she continued.

"We don't have to go crazy, Vi."

She wasn't listening. "Oh! And you can meet Adrian." She sighed lovingly. I snorted, making bubbles in my soda. She looked at me darkly.

"Sorry—had to sneeze." I ignored another hunger pain, and asked through clenched teeth, "So where did you guys meet?"

"We met at the club," Vi replied. "He looked so good dancing; I *had* to talk to him before someone else snagged him."

"So, what happened? Did you walk up to him, drooling?" I joked.

She squinted her eyes and flared her nostrils at me. "No," she said, sarcastically. "Believe it or not, he beat me to it and approached me first."

"I can believe it." *Where the hell is my food?!*

Right on cue, Jeni appeared carrying a tray of assorted fish for me, as well as a roll and beef teriyaki for Vi. After she placed our food on the table, Jeni and I locked eyes again. That nagging feeling came back that I knew her from somewhere. Before I could say anything, she made to leave, telling us to call if we needed anything. My mouth watered and I took a big gulp to stop myself from drooling. I grabbed my chopsticks, considering which fish I wanted to start with.

"So, let me guess. *He* walked up to you drooling?" I asked.

She nodded, taking a bite of her beef teriyaki. "Basically." She laughed. "Once we locked eyes, that was it. We've hung out almost every day ever since."

"But what happens when you go back to Cali?" I asked, picking up a piece of tuna. I closed my eyes, savoring its flavor. "I mean, it's not like you're moving here right away." After that I took a bite of salmon, then started on the yellowtail.

"We've discussed it. He said he'll come visit every so often."

I was skeptical. "Are you sure that's a good idea? I mean you haven't known him that long..."

She huffed. "Coming from the girl who wears a ring from a stalker?" She raised her eyebrow at me. "Way to be a Debbie downer. We've learned a lot about each other these past few weeks. I have no problem with him coming to visit and us seeing where it goes."

"I guess." I was still unsure, but I didn't want to be pessimistic about her possible relationship. "You're right. I'm sure it will work out." I gave her a smile.

"Yeah," she smiled. Vi tilted her head to the side. "Um," she began, "are you even chewing?"

"Huh?" I looked down at my plate and grimaced. I had only six pieces remaining, even though we had received our order only a few minutes ago. "Oh, wow! I guess I was hungrier than I thought." *What the hell is going on?* I felt awkward; I never eat that fast, and there had been so much food!

"I'll say," Vi agreed. "Want to try a piece of the roll? This is more than I can eat, anyway." My stomach growled loudly in response. "Guess that's a yes." She laughed, putting two rolls on my plate. I gave her a small smile; I was getting concerned about my increasing appetite. A low, thumping rhythm began sounding in my head.

"Thank you," I said quietly. I took another sip of Sprite. Immediately, I wanted to spit it out. It tasted syrupy and felt foreign on my palate. Jeni reappeared, took one look at my platter, and gave me a knowing smile.

"You're hungry," she stated matter of factly. No sooner did I finish the second roll Vi gave me than my stomach growled once more. I wrapped my arms around my midsection and made a face; my cramps were getting worse.

Vi put her hand on my arm. As soon as our flesh made contact, thoughts assaulted my mind. *Is she okay? Is she going to be sick?* I stood up quickly and she frowned. "What's wrong?"

"Going to the bathroom—excuse me." I raced past Jeni, whose expression I couldn't read. I felt their eyes on me until I was in the hallway and no longer in their field of view. I leaned against the wall and looked at the bathroom door. The thumping sounded louder, and a strong smell of strawberries drifted towards me. I heard the lock click and a woman walked out, looking down in her purse. My nostrils flared as I took a deep breath, inhaling more of the strawberry scent.

"Oh!" she looked up, startled. My stomach growled and I winced as I was overcome by the strongest cramp yet. "Are you okay?" The woman started walking towards me but I glared at her. She gasped and backed away down the hall. The thumping increased in frequency, but I didn't have time to question it or the woman's reaction. Another cramp had started. I hurried to the door, fumbling to get it open. Inside, I fell to the ground hugging my stomach as tears welled up in my eyes. *Zeită! Goddess, help me!*

I rocked back and forth on the floor until the feeling passed. Taking deep breaths, I stood and made my way to the sink. I closed my eyes and rubbed my temples; the thumping sound was starting to give me a headache. I splashed my face with cold water, then grabbed some paper towels to pat it dry. I looked in the mirror and gasped—my irises were blood red, and my face was so pale I looked sickly. I felt another stirring of pain in my abdomen. *What's happening to me?* I rushed from the bathroom, barreling into another patron.

"Hey!" she yelled at me.

I mumbled a quick apology and kept making my way towards the sushi bar. The thumping was louder in the main dining area, and my headache worsened. Jeni was gone when I returned to my seat, but I could feel her eyes on me, along with someone else's. Whoever this other person was, their gaze was intense and their energy was projected onto me—I could tell it was a man.

I wonder...

More thoughts appeared in my mind, but I couldn't focus on the source. The pain in my head and stomach were making it impossible to concentrate. I snatched my glasses off the bar and quickly put them on my face, hiding my eyes from Vi. She stood up, looking worried.

"What is going on?! Are you okay?"

"My stomach is killing me." I gritted my teeth through the pain as another cramp wracked me. "And the light is giving me a headache," I added, to explain the glasses. I thought she was going to question the glasses since it was dim in the restaurant, but she said nothing.

More rhythmic thumping. More random thoughts. Thoughts in different voices, in different languages from the various patrons in the restaurant. I slumped down in my chair and rested my head in my hands.

"My head feels like it's going to explode. I'm sorry, Vi, I don't think I can do the movies or shopping right now." She gave me a sympathetic look and flagged down Jeni to get the check.

"Don't be silly. I'm sorry you're not feeling well." She sighed. "This isn't how our day was supposed to turn out. Let's get you home so you can rest." Vi began rubbing my back, and I stiffened at her touch. Underneath her perfume, I could smell Vi's natural scent of lilacs; I'd never noticed that before. I inhaled deeply and my stomach growled painfully again.

"Ow."

I closed my eyes, hugging my midsection. The voices and thumping seemed to grow louder. It felt like someone was drilling into my skull. *I think I'm going crazy.* A tear rolled down my cheek as I started rocking back and forth.

"It'll be okay," Vi tried to comfort me, but it wasn't okay; none of this was okay. It hurt and Vi's scent was so divine. I felt Jeni's presence and looked up as she handed Vi the check. She gave me a curious glance as Vi wordlessly handed her a credit card. I watched as Jeni gracefully walked away.

I hope she'll be okay. She's acting so strange. I wonder what's going on with her. Vi finished her wine and peered at me, still rubbing my back.

I wanted to tell her that this had nothing to do with her, but I couldn't concentrate on forming the words. I was acutely aware of her presence: her scent and the feel of her hand on my back. The rhythmic thumping washed over me, and suddenly something clicked: they were heartbeats. My senses were on high alert. It was taking all of my willpower to not sink my teeth into her flesh to see if she tasted as good as she smelled. I tensed at the thought. *I really* am *going crazy.*

Jeni returned with the final receipt, still curiously eyeballing me. It was getting annoying and I bit back a snippy comment. As if reading my thoughts, her eyes widened slightly and then narrowed in understanding.

Odd...

I closed my eyes tightly as Vi's lilac fragrance drifted back to me, this time with a hint of the strawberry I'd smelled earlier. I followed the strawberry until my gaze landed on the woman from the bathroom. She was frightened of me, and immediately looked away when she noticed me watching her. I could hear her heart beat faster and faster. I gripped my chair tightly and broke out in a sweat as her fear projected itself onto me.

Vi finished signing the receipt and handed it back to Jeni, who thanked us for coming and wished me better health. While Vi gathered her belongings, a thought stood out to me: *Don't worry, the pain doesn't last forever.* I looked around and saw Jeni staring at me. She gave me a reassuring smile.

What is going on? I ran out of the restaurant to get some fresh air. I was hunched over, breathing deeply, when Vi ran behind me and placed her hand on my shoulder. I stood abruptly, taking a step back from her. My nostrils were flaring. Her hand hung in the air where my shoulder had just been. She frowned.

"Nadia, what's going on?"

"I just need to get home—NOW!" I growled. She jumped at the sudden ferocity of my voice and immediately became withdrawn. "Please, Vi. I'm sorry. I'm just in a lot of pain. Please, please," I begged. She dropped her hand and nodded curtly. We made our way to the subway, getting there in record time.

The ride back to my condo was uncomfortable on several levels. I was surrounded by a mixture of smells, ranging from pleasant to unpleasant. There was a whiff of someone who was in dire need of a shower, trying to cover up their funk with a flowery perfume. I was being pressed down by body heat and the hot air of peoples' breaths. Unfortunately, it was crowded on the train, and the combination of thoughts and heartbeats made me feel like my head would split in two—there were several times that I had to focus on not passing out. To make matters worse, the tension between Vi and me was so thick you could swim in it. Besides the occasional, "How are you feeling," she didn't speak to me.

I felt bad for snapping at Vi—it was so unlike me. I was usually very open with Vi, like the time I'd had concerns about a guy she was dating—we spoke about it and she accepted what I had to say. Turns out, he *really* was bad news, and so my unease about him was well founded. But this, this I knew nothing about. I was struggling to restrain myself from attacking my best friend. I tried to trick myself into imaging things that would make her scent less appealing, like her sweating it out at the gym. Another cramp started and I silently prayed for the pain to disappear. *Almost there, almost there.*

Thankfully, the ride to my condo was a short one.

After a brief walk from the train, we finally arrived at my building. She glanced at me, then wordlessly leaned over to give me a hug. I tensed when she touched me; her scent was too strong and I was starting to lose control. I held my breath and was surprised to find it was almost effortless, even as the hug stretched out longer than thirty seconds. She pulled back, giving me a sad look.

"Feel better, Nadia. Text me later. Love you!"

"I love you too, and I'm really sorry, Vi. I'll talk to you later."

I rushed into the building and let out the remaining air from my lungs. When I got to the hallway, I could tell that Mamă wasn't home. Fumbling with the keys, I ran to my door, twisting the handle so hard that it came away in my hand. I blinked a few times, staring at it in disbelief. Walking inside, I dropped the handle on the floor. My hands flew to my temples. With my enhanced senses, I could hear the conversations in the neighboring condos; I could see the particles of dust floating in the air before me; I could smell the flowers in the pots outside of the open windows. Just when I thought things couldn't get worse, my stomach twisted in another cramp.

Zeită! Please make it stop! I pleaded. Completely overwhelmed, I sagged to the floor in tears, wishing it would all end.

CHAPTER FIVE

BRĂILA, WALLACHIA 1480

In no time at all, Jeniviva had wormed her way into the hearts of everyone in our village, human and Vampyre alike—including Mother. Fabian absolutely adored her, and he agreed to train with her on certain days if her school studies were completed. Typically, education was reserved for royalty, but the Brotherhood had a select few to administer schooling to those under our protection. Jeniviva wasn't thrilled about schoolwork, as most children aren't, but it was pleasing to see her so positive after experiencing such a loss, and connecting with the other children.

It was midmorning and the sun was high in the sky. I stood in the doorway watching Fabian at his desk, scribbling in his book. He put down his quill and shut the book, eyes on me.

"You are to train with the Seer at high noon," he announced.

I crossed my arms, aggravated. "But what of the attack? We should avenge the village!"

He stood up and walked to me. "And we shall," he said patiently.

"When? We cannot let them think this act of cruelty will go unpunished!"

He held up his hand to stop me, and I scowled. "To act out of haste is not wise, and will endanger us all."

"But—"

He spoke over me. "When the time is right, we will discuss a proper plan of attack. Until then, you will continue to train." His tone indicated the conversation was over.

I left Fabian, seething with anger and disappointment. There was still time before I had to meet with the Seer; I decided to visit Cristian, as I hadn't seen him since before my Ritual. I could also feed. I made my way to the stables, taking a deep breath before entering; I didn't want to upset Fyuree.

Fyuree nickered when I entered, and the sound brought me joy.

"I'm pleased to see you too, girl." I rubbed my fingers through her mane. "Care to ride?"

I grabbed her saddle off the hook, then opened her gate. As I gently tugged on her reins, she walked out of her stall, following me into the fresh air. I secured her saddle, checking the girth and stirrups. She let out a snort as I mounted her easily. I snatched up her reins, gripping them tightly, and shifted in my seat to get Fyuree's attention.

I squeezed my lower legs against her, not needing to tap her for her to move. Guiding her onto the trail that would lead us to Chilia, I sank into the saddle and relaxed. Once clear of the village, I clucked, indicating that she should go faster. Fyuree began trotting, and we travelled like this for some distance before I felt comfortable enough for her to increase speed. I made a smooching sound, and soon we were galloping the rest of our journey.

I slowed Fyuree to a trot and then to a leisurely walk as we approached Cristian's town. It was much bigger than where I lived, with twice as many people wandering about. I waved at familiar faces as we rode through. We passed women with baskets of goods and clothing, and smiling men with children on their shoulders. Once outside of the shop, I shifted my weight, signaling her to stop. She sniffed loudly and I climbed off of her. I petted her side and secured her to a post before fetching her some water from the nearby well. I entered the shop, greeted by the smells of cedar and oak and the hammering of nails into wood.

"Good day, Your Highness," Cristian's father welcomed me.

"Good day, Dragoş." Dragoş shared the same light-colored hair as Cristian, but where Cristian was lean, Dragoş was of a bigger build.

"Cristian is out back," he said.

"Many thanks." I turned to walk outside, but stopped when he spoke again.

"Your Highness." I faced him and he strolled towards me. "I had this made for you, to aid on your quest." He handed me a peasant knife, and I noticed it was slightly warm. I flicked it open and heat radiated from the blade. "The blade is made of silver to use on your enemies, so take heed," he explained. Upon closer inspection, I saw a phoenix carved into its hilt. The detail was remarkable; I couldn't fathom how long it must have taken to carve...or the cost of such a piece.

"It's beautiful, but I cannot accept such a gift." I held it out to him, but he shook his head.

"I beseech you, take it."

"You are too kind."

"It's my pleasure," he said, bowing his head.

I took my leave and checked on Fyuree before wandering to the back of the shop. Cristian was chopping wood and I called out to him. He waved at me.

"Greetings, Princess."

I kissed him on the cheek. "Hard at work?"

He laughed. "Aye, like always. Did you run here again?"

"Nay; Fyuree is in front."

"Oh, good." We walked around to the front—Cristian adored Fyuree. She neighed happily at the sight of us and he rubbed her muzzle. "Such a beauty." We went inside and headed upstairs. "What of the ritual?" he asked once we were in his room.

I hesitated before answering. "Chilling."

He furrowed his brows. "What happened?" I described my Visions and the dream I'd had that night. He said nothing at first, and then, "Do you know the meaning of this 'darkness'?"

"I believe it is as it seems..." Though distracted by other events, the Vision had never left me, and I shivered.

"Worry not." Cristian's voice pulled me from my dark contemplations, and I nodded. "You have the strength to defeat anything."

"Bless your kind words."

Cristian sat on his bed and rolled up his sleeve. Sitting next to him, I took his arm in my hands and began feeding. I stopped, recounting the events at Jeniviva's village, and expressed my dissatisfaction of how the situation was being handled.

"I understand your frustration, but the Keeper is right—it is best to have a solid plan in place." My mouth thinned into a hard line and he laughed at me. "Vengeance will come soon, Princess."

I sighed; he was right, as usual. I finished feeding and Cristian pulled down his sleeve, while I stood up. "It's almost time for my meeting with the Seer."

Cristian's father was not downstairs, so I didn't see him on my way out to thank him again for the knife. Cristian walked me outside and hugged me before pleasing Fyuree with an apple. I untied her from the post and climbed atop. He bid me farewell, and I started on my journey home.

I was anxious about meeting with the Seer. My skin broke out in goose bumps thinking about our last meeting only days before:

I walked up the stairs to the Seer's home, located in the

middle of our village. Knocking on her door, I heard her call out to me and entered her chambers. I always enjoyed the decorations in her home—the unusual tapestries and the way her furniture was set up. I usually felt at ease when I walked in...unless our meeting invoked other emotions.

"There is something more to you, but you know not what it is," she said, not facing me. I stayed silent, unsure of what she was talking about. She turned towards me with milk-colored eyes. "My eyes have not rested upon another as powerful as you." Still I said nothing. Although she was blind, she saw more than those with sight. Her next statement reminded me of why she was considered the wisest of her family. "Tell me of this darkness."

"I...how did you know?"

"The wealth of knowledge that lies within my old body would surprise you, child. Now, tell me of this darkness," she repeated.

"I...sensed nothing—like I was nonexistent."

"What do you think it means?"

"I..don't know."

"Don't you?"

I could feel the intensity of her gaze from where I stood and I gulped nervously. I didn't respond right away, instead giving thought to her question.

"I know not who," I said finally.

She held up her finger and her blind eyes widened. "Ah. And knowing that, what do you plan to do?"

"I don't understand."

"You soon will."

I returned Fyuree to the stables and made sure she had fresh food and water prior to leaving for the Seer's home. I took a deep breath and knocked on her door. She bid me come in, and I pushed open her door to find her sitting on the floor waiting for me.

"The girl, Jeniviva, is an asset to your mission. You made

the right decision in bringing her here." I nodded, somehow knowing she could see me, but unsure as to how a child could be an asset. "Sit," she instructed. As I took my place in front of her, she asked, "How has your mind been?"

"Quiet—I have no thoughts that aren't mine. Only when Nic speaks, otherwise my mind is my own."

"Good. Your mental blocks are strong."

"Aye, they are," I agreed. "What is today's lesson?"

"We will expand on an ability that you already possess— the ability to enter the mind of another."

"Glamouring?" I rolled my eyes. "Can't we do something new?"

"Nay, child. What *you* possess far exceeds ordinary glamour."

I furrowed my brows, looking at her. "I don't understand."

"You defied the laws of nature by bypassing time and space to enter the mind of another. You've been doing it for some time now, completely unaware. Even for your kind, that is unusual."

"But is that not glamour?"

"You do not merely inject thoughts into the mind," she replied, shaking her head. "Nay, child—you *become* the person." I stared at her, wondering what she was talking about. "This is a rare thing, and we must develop it."

"How?"

"Simply close your eyes and follow the images that come to you. But it is more than that. Instead of observing as an outsider, place yourself behind the eyes of that person. Hear what they hear, smell what they smell, see what they see. Take them into you and *become* them. It sounds more challenging than it will be."

"Um..."

"Just close your eyes, child, and make sure to breathe.

You will know what to do when the time is right. Take heed—in doing this, you open yourself up to them as well."

I inhaled deeply and closed my eyes, beginning to chant. "I open myself to receive your message."

I repeated this statement over and over, eventually only reciting it in my head. I smiled when my song came to mind. I could hear myself speaking with others in a language I did not understand. I heard a combination of sounds that were different from any music I'd ever heard. I wrinkled my nose at a foul odor that reminded me of rotting food. My vision was last to work, and then slowly an image appeared to me, though I recognized nothing of it.

I was in an alley, standing against a brick building. It had the height of a castle, as did the one across from it. I was dressed in pants and an upper garment made out of a material that was new to me, though it was as tight as the overcoats I often wore. Something whizzed by in my peripheral vision, too fast for me to identify. There was a rank stench coming from a large metal bin right next to me.

My eyes fixed on the man accompanying me. The amount of darkness coming from him was unnerving, and I wondered why I was even in his presence. He said something to me, still in the language I didn't understand, but I felt a stirring of anger and my defenses rising in response to his words. He had a blade pressed against my throat. He undid both of our pants, and I wondered what the devices were that helped them to stay fastened.

His intentions were clear to me as he roughly pulled on my bottoms and spoke so maliciously that spittle flew from his mouth. Still I said nothing, but I was formulating a plan in my head. Expecting me to reply, he hesitated at my silence. He spoke again, commanding with more force, and still I didn't respond the way he would have liked. Instead, I smiled at him and pushed against the knife, causing myself to bleed—showing that I had no reason to fear him.

I pressed him against the wall with my hand around his throat. The blade fell from his hand and finally I spoke, still not recognizing the words. Then I fed from him. His blood was tainted, and I felt my head lighten. The connection broke. I opened my eyes, blinking several times before I peered at the Seer.

"Welcome back, child. Now tell me, what did you see?"

I recounted my vision and all that I had sensed. "My eyes have never seen such things. My ears have never heard such a language. What world is this?"

"One you will come to know."

"I am not sure I want to know such a world," I replied, thinking about the foul smell and even fouler man.

"We do not get to decide what the Gods have already chosen." She nodded at me. "You have done well."

I smiled at the praise and stood up, stretching. "I give thanks for your guidance."

"It is my duty. As for you, the Gods have many plans." She too stood up, and took my hand in hers. Her expression became serious and I grew wary of what was to come. "You will soon be put to the test. Remember, the biggest challenges reap the biggest rewards. Remain strong, but do not act in haste."

She released my hand and bid me farewell. "Until we meet again," I said. I stepped outside, deep in thought about the world I'd seen. *Is that what I have to look forward to? What was the meaning of my Vision? More importantly, who was I in the Vision?*

"Antanasia!" A pair of little arms wrapped around my waist and I looked down at Jeniviva.

"Good day, youngling." I hugged her back. "How go your studies?"

She scrunched her nose. "They put me to sleep. Why must I do schoolwork? I would rather train with you."

I laughed. "Aye, but you must keep your mind sharp—it makes you a better fighter." I bent down to whisper in her ear." Do not let Mother or Fabian hear of your slumber; they would not be pleased." I smiled and patted her head.

Her eyes widened. "That shall be the last time."

"Good." We started walking towards home. "You have many tasks to complete?"

"Nay. I finished them before I took leave." I nodded. "How went your meeting with the Seer?"

I didn't respond right away, choosing my words carefully. "It left me with many questions."

"Was it fun?"

I winked at her. "Better than your studies."

She giggled, and the sound warmed me inside. We were almost to the house and I saw Nic standing outside, waiting for me. He was smiling brightly, and waved at us as we approached.

"Why so cheerful?" I asked him.

"I am always cheerful to see my love." He kissed me gently and then looked at Jeniviva. "Hard at work, little one?"

She blushed crimson and said in a small voice, "Aye. I must keep my mind sharp," she added, glancing at me.

"That you must. For a youngling, you are filled with wisdom."

"She is well guided," I said, smiling. "To what do I owe this visit?"

"Your training is not yet complete for the day."

I cocked my head to the side, regarding him. "Is it not?"

"One more lesson awaits you," he answered excitedly.

At first I didn't understand. Then it came to me. "You mean..."

He nodded, "Aye."

I was beaming with anticipation. "I shall fetch Mother!"

Jeniviva glanced from me to Nic, confused. "What lesson?"

"One I have awaited my whole life—to feed off animals."

"You were not able to do so before?"

"Nay. Until the Vârstă de Maturitate, only the blood of humans can sustain us." I was beyond thrilled.

Jeniviva hugged me. "I am happy for you."

I started towards the door to get Mother, but then I remembered something. "Come," I said to Jeniviva, taking her hand. "I shall return," I said to Nic. I brought Jeniviva to my quarters, closing the door behind us. "I have a gift for you, but it is to be our secret." I pulled out the peasant knife and handed it to her. "It was made for me, with a silver blade. It will come in handy against our enemies—I want you to have it."

"I cannot—it was made for you."

"This is true, but silver is dangerous to my kind." I flicked the blade open and pressed it against my skin, wincing at the burn. She gasped as it started to eat away at my skin like acid. Jeniviva wrinkled her nose at the charcoal-like scent that my burning flesh was giving off. I closed the knife and watched as my skin healed in seconds. "Take it. Every warrior needs a weapon; it will aid you when defending yourself against my kind." I placed the knife in her hand and she looked at it adoringly. "There is another reason why I gift this to you. Look at the hilt."

She twirled the blade around, observing the hilt. "What is this bird?"

"It is a phoenix—a bird that rises anew from the ashes of its funerary pyre. A symbol of power, strength, and renewal, much like *you*. To experience such loss yet continue to thrive is inspiring. This may have been made for me, but it was never mine to have."

Jeniviva's eyes watered and she jumped into my arms, embracing me. "Many thanks," she said through her tears.

I embraced her tightly and closed my eyes. "I care very

much for you, youngling. You must use caution when handling the knife."

She wiped her nose on her sleeve and bobbed her head. She hid the knife in her pocket just as a knock sounded on the door. Mother entered, beaming.

"I got word of the good news! This brings me much joy!"

"Me as well, and I would like to share it with you," I said to her.

On a few occasions, Mother had accompanied me on hunts, though they were of short distance and little challenge. She was curious by nature and wanted to understand how we hunt. I felt that this should be another hunt added to her list, as this signified me becoming a mature Vampyre.

"I would love nothing more."

"Can I come?" Jeniviva asked excitedly.

I shook my head, focusing on her. "Nay, young phoenix. It is too dangerous, and anything can happen." She pouted and I added, "After you have much training with the Keeper, you can join, mayhap."

This satisfied her. "I shall go to him now to see what I can learn."

She ran out of my room in search of Fabian. Mother turned to me and we both chuckled.

"She is headstrong, like you," she said.

I made a face, and we went outside to join Nic. The three of us took a stroll through the forest, Nic and I staying alert for any signs of movement. We halted in our tracks and Mother, not hearing what we did, bumped into me. She started to speak, but I shushed her. In the distance, past several trees, Nic and I could see a doe drinking from a pond.

Nic ran to her while Mother and I walked. The doe could sense something coming towards her, but was not able to outrun Nic. I felt a pang of guilt when he tackled the doe, but it was the only way to stop the doe from running. She thrashed about, trying to get from underneath Nic, but Nic's hold on her was strong. Soon Mother and I were only feet away. I saw Nic glamour the doe; she instantly relaxed and laid down.

My gown hiked up as I sat at the edge of the pond. I ran my fingers through the cool water and gazed into it, staring at my reflection. My eyes widened at what I saw—my golden amber eyes looked up at me from a different face. I crinkled my eyebrows and leaned closer to the water.

"What do you see?" Mother asked me.

"Nothing," I lied, and smiled reassuringly.

This was something to bring to the Seer's attention. Mother smiled back and looked at Nic, who was stroking the doe's coat. He took my hand and rubbed his thumb across my knuckles—it was time. I had been trying to embrace this Curse that I was born with, feeding off of the life force of others so that I could survive. It would be easier now that I had passed my Vârstă de Maturitate and turned eighteen; I'd no longer need human blood.

Nic had already bitten the doe and nodded, indicating I should do the same. I peered at the animal, feeling a familiar ache in my belly. Bending over, I sunk my fangs into her neck. The blood had a tangy flavor and was very different from human blood, but it was pleasing all the same. I closed my eyes, inhaling the pine scent on the doe's hide. Nic rubbed my back, and a myriad of emotions overcame me— love, contentment, and appreciation. To be sharing this moment with two of my dearest family members was something to be treasured. Although we were silent, so much was said.

Soon, Nic placed his hand on my shoulder, signaling me to stop. I glanced at him and he urged me to move on to the next step. I gazed deeply into the doe's eyes, travelling into her subconscious. After thanking the doe for providing me with nourishment, I informed her that she was free to go.

With that, her gaze cleared, and immediately she took off for the woods. I was extremely proud of this accomplishment. The thought of not having to always feed from humans was a pleasing one.

The air shifted. Something wasn't right and both Nic and I tensed, smiles leaving our faces. Mother took pause and stopped smiling after looking at our expressions. A silver arrow appeared through the trees, and Nic and I jumped to our feet. I motioned for Mother to follow me while Nic ran towards the archer. She followed my lead, zigzagging to throw off our attackers, but she was much slower than I. I grew uneasy and turned around to find Mother sagging to the ground. As I ran to her, I saw the arrow sticking into her leg. I went to pull it out so that I could heal her.

"You must go!"

"Mother, I can at least carry you," I protested.

"Nay! I will only slow you down!"

"But..." An arrow flew past my head.

"Go now, Antanasia! RUN!"

My eyes filled with tears and I gave her one last look before running through the trees. I felt a sting as an arrow grazed the side of my arm. Growling, I picked up speed and hid behind a thick bush of star gentians with bated breath. I heard the crunching of dry leaves as a Vampyre approached carrying a crossbow, with her sword sheathed. There was a cross and dragon etched into her armor—she was a knight of the Order. Anger bubbled within me. My necklace thrummed against my chest, and I felt a power building inside me.

"Come now, let's not make this any more difficult than it already is," she said, looking around. I remained silent, my anger rising. "I can offer you a trade," she added. "You for your pathetic human mother."

Before I knew what was happening, I found myself inside her mind. The fear of losing Mother; the interruption of such an important moment; the senseless war I was forced to fight—all the emotions I was feeling I sent inside her tenfold, overwhelming her psyche. She screamed, dropping her crossbow and sinking to her knees, holding her head. She shook her head vigorously, as if that could make the pain stop.

I pushed a little more and her piercing screams startled the animals around us. Birds flew from their nests while squirrels and chipmunks scurried in the opposite direction. Blood poured from her ears, and I grinned maliciously at the sight. As blood started leaking from her eyes, she quieted and collapsed to the ground, landing on her face. I came back into myself and wiped the sweat off of my forehead.

A twig snapped behind me and I spun around, prepared to defend myself. Nic came near and I breathed a sigh of relief. Upon closer inspection, I noticed his appearance was somewhat hazy—it was his projection.

"I have your mother," he announced.

"Oh, thank the Gods!" I stood up.

"But she is very weak. It took some time for me to return to her aid. The arrows were dipped in poison and it started to corrode her system."

"Where are you?" I asked hurriedly.

"We are back at the village. I gave her some of my blood and she is resting."

I sprinted through Nic's projection, heading back towards the village. Consumed with worry, I recited every blessing I could think of to aid in Mother's recovery. Nic was waiting for me when I arrived, and I embraced him tightly. He kissed the top of my head and pulled back.

"I was unable to track the other knight."

"That is a concern for another time. Right now, I need to be with Mother."

I walked past him and made my way to Mother's room. I

could sense her sickness before I pushed open her door. Una was sitting in a chair near her bed, wiping her forehead with a damp cloth. She caught sight of me and returned the cloth to the bowl on the side table. She stood up to leave, squeezing my hand as she passed. The sight of Mother brought tears to my eyes. Her skin was tinged with blue and her breathing was labored. I moved to her side and grabbed her hand.

"I'm sorry, Mother—this is all my fault."

If I hadn't wanted to bring her with us, she would be in good health now. If she let Fabian turn her when they first met, she would be in good health now. Suddenly frustrated, I let out an exasperated sigh. I kissed her forehead.

"Rest now, Mother," I whispered and exited her room, closing the door behind me. Nic was still outside when I walked out.

"Where are you going?" he asked.

"Keep an eye on Mother. I will return shortly." I raced through the village until I found myself outside Fabian's home. I barged in without knocking, startling Jeniviva, who was sparring with him.

The Keeper turned to Jeniviva. "We will continue later."

She bobbed her head and ran through the door. I slammed it behind her and glared at Fabian. "Do you still believe we should wait?"

"You are dissatisfied. I understand. But again, to act in haste is not wise."

"They almost killed her!"

He held up his hand, his calm demeanor only adding to my frustration. "But they didn't." I scowled. "We must wait until the time is right to attack."

"Fuck waiting! We will all be dead by then!"

"Antanasia—" he began patiently.

"You are weak, Keeper." And with that I turned on my heel and stormed out the door. I plopped to the ground and covered my head with my hands, tears rolling down my cheeks. *What more damage must the Order do before we act?* I felt a little hand on my shoulder and looked up into Jeniviva's concerned gaze.

"I'm scared," I admitted to her.

"As am I. But you are strong. I believe you must do what feels right to you."

I cocked my head to the side. "How did you get to be so wise, young phoenix?" She shrugged and I kissed the back of her hand. "Thanks for that." I stood up and wiped away my tears. "I think I'll go clear my mind."

I wandered off, distracted by my anger and frustration. This time, I took a different path through the woods. *I am the Princess, why must I listen to the Keeper? I shall develop my own plan of attack. Gods give me strength!* I took my time in the woods, appreciating the beauty that surrounded me. Little beasts scattered about, peeking at me from their hiding spots. I trekked up a small mountain and settled on a boulder, observing the valley below.

I started to feel ashamed of my behavior towards the Keeper. I might not agree with him but Fabian was only doing what he believed was best. There was no reason to blame him for the attack on us. I shook my head, suddenly disappointed in myself; I needed to stop letting my emotions get the best of me. I decided I would go apologize to him; princess or not, he was my elder in both the human and Vampyre world. Fabian had been a part of this war since the beginning, and helped raise me when my own father was too busy murdering innocent people—he deserved respect, especially mine.

It began to grow dark as the day came to a close. I'd taken a long time gathering my thoughts. A gentle breeze ruffled through my hair as I got to my feet. I closed my eyes, enjoying the feel of it on my skin. I set off towards home, maintaining my balance on the downward slope of the mountain. I hadn't ventured far before I grew troubled. Ears perked, I spun around, listening for something, *anything*. It was eerily quiet, and the hairs on my arms stood on end. Another breeze tickled my skin and whispered to me secrets of blood and death. My necklace heated almost to the point of being painful as one person came to mind: *Mother!*

I bolted down the mountain, moving faster than I ever had. By the time I reached the village, my feet were bloodied and my arms were covered in scratches, but I ignored them. I skidded to a halt at the brightness illuminating the village, and terror gripped me. Smoke rose in the air, and for the second time in days I watched an inferno eating away at a village. *My* village, my *home*. This time there were no screams and no people running about. I saw charred bodies blanketing the ground, filled with arrows. I could smell burning pitch and oil, and realized what happened.

We were followed earlier; the knight that escaped had come back with reinforcements. Their archers began the attack with flaming arrows, and then the foot soldiers charged through the village to massacre those who were still alive. This time, the Order was determined to leave no witnesses. I heard nothing but the crackling of fire as it fed on everything around it.

I sped through what was left of the village, concerned about everyone's safety, especially Mother, Nic, Fabian, and Jeniviva. I stopped in front of our home, the fire hurting my eyes. There stood nothing more than a pile of stones and melted clay. I prayed that someone had gotten Mother out before the house was consumed by flames. I went in search of Nic, Fabian, Jeniviva, *anyone*. But I didn't find a single soul; I had to believe that Nic and Fabian were safe and protecting Jeniviva and Mother.

I walked to the perimeter of the village and intuition struck as I heard the wind sigh to the left of me. I turned and my eyes fixated on a tree with a naked body dangling from its limb. I walked slowly towards it, gripped with fear. As I reached the base of the tree, I looked up at the mutilated body of my mother, swaying in the wind with blowflies around her. She was covered in deep gashes—her blood dripping into puddles underneath her. Her blind eye was dangling from its socket, and some of her fingers and toes had been roughly cut off. I fell to my knees and cried out to the Gods.

I should have acted when they first attacked! They will not get away with this!

Refusing to leave her body hanging in the air to be food for more of nature's beasts, I set to work. I gathered wood, splitting it to create a pyre. Removing the rope from around her neck, I placed her gently on top of the wood. I crossed her hands over her chest and crossed her feet, closed her eyelids, and picked as much debris from her hair as I could. As I kissed her forehead, I sniffled, and a few tears landed on her face. I grabbed a flaming piece of wood from a burning hovel and used it to light the pyre. The flames hungrily lapped up the materials, and soon it was blazing.

"May the Gods watch over you now."

I turned away and my eyes darkened. There was no more waiting, no more planning—I was going to take care of Mihnea and the Order *now*.

CHAPTER SIX

NEW YORK, NEW YORK 2015

They are close by; I can feel their presence. The morning dew seeps into my skin as I continue to run through the trees. I know it is coming right before the silver arrow pierces my back.

My eyes snapped open. I was slumped on the ground, in a T-shirt and my underwear, leaning against the wall in a bathroom. *What's going on? Where are my clothes?* I furrowed my brows and looked around. Though private, this was definitely not *my* bathroom. I started to panic. The light from outside made the bathroom extremely bright—almost to the point of being painful. I squinted my eyes. *What time is it?* Light was streaming through the window, and I could hear a bird chirping as loudly as if it were right next to me. *How did I get here?*

I stood up and stretched. Physically, I felt great. Better than great, actually; I felt amazing and healthy and the complete opposite of how I'd been feeling before. I didn't spend long marveling at my sudden change—I still didn't know where I was. I took a deep breath and grabbed my pentacle necklace to calm my nerves. *Panicking is not going to help me right now.*

I fought the urge to use the bathroom; I didn't want to make any sound. Looking in the mirror, my jaw dropped at my reflection. My eyes were no longer blood red, instead sporting their new golden-amber color. Though my skin was paler, my cheeks had a rosy tint to them. I stared at my full lips and noticed a red smear running down my chin to my jaw line. I closely inspected the smear and ran my tongue over it. Immediately, my pupils dilated and my canines lengthened at the iron taste in my mouth. I gasped, stumbling away from the mirror, and slapped my hands over my mouth.

*No...*Tears formed in my eyes. *What is happening to me?* Flashes of text on Vampyre lore flew across my mind, all leading to the same conclusion, but I refused to believe it. I pinched myself to see if I was dreaming and winced at the pain. *This isn't real. This can't be real. Vampyres don't exist!* And yet here I was, experiencing an Awakening—the Change from human to Vampyre that only occurs in those born with the Curse. I thought it was a myth.

I reached panic mode again.

Question after question popped into my head, none of the answers making sense. This new discovery was a temporary distraction; I still didn't know where I was, and I felt on the edge of freaking out. Closing my eyes, I counted to seven, taking calming breaths. *Concentrate.* I needed to focus. The answers I sought would come in time, but for now, I needed to find out what had happened. *How had I ended up in someone's bathroom? And whose bathroom?*

There weren't many clues here, but I was afraid of what I would find outside the bathroom. I turned on the water to wash the blood from my face, and braced myself before slowly opening the door. In the bedroom beyond I halted, staring at the male figure lying on the bed. *Zeită! What did I do?* I could see the rise and fall of his back while he breathed, so I knew he wasn't dead, but I didn't recognize him.

I stood there frozen, trying desperately to remember what had happened, but nothing was coming to mind. I wasn't sure what to do. My clothes were in a heap on the floor close to the bed. I tiptoed to retrieve them and back tracked into the bathroom. I stole one last peek to make sure I hadn't disturbed him, then closed the door softly and locked it.

I couldn't hold it any longer and I threw the clothes on the floor, rushing to the toilet to relieve myself. I washed my hands and picked up my clothes. They were completely different from what I remembered wearing last, sporting lots of leather and a Metallica sweatshirt. I quickly put them on, feeling around for my phone; I was relieved to find it in my pocket. Luckily, it still had some battery life. It was 9:16. *Holy crap! I lost a whole day?!* There were missed calls and texts from Vi, asking me where I was and hoping that I was safe. I dialed Vi's number and put the phone to my ear. It only rang once before I heard Vi's shrill voice.

"Nadia! Where the *hell* are you?! Are you hurt?" Vi asked, sounding beyond agitated.

"Vi!" I spoke over her. "Vi, I think I'm losing my mind! I don't remember how I got here, and I woke up in a bathroom with blood on my face! There's this guy lying unconscious or something—"

"Wait, what? Bathroom? Blood on your face?" she asked. "ARE YOU HURT?! Did he do something to you? Call the cops!"

"No, no, Vi." I took a deep breath. "I think I'm fine. I just don't remember anything."

"Where are you?"

"I don't—" As soon as I started to tell her that I wasn't sure, an address popped into my head. I repeated it to Vi.

"What the *hell*? How did you end up all the way on the Upper East Side?"

"I don't know; I don't remember," I said again, groaning.

"Okay, okay. We will figure it all out. I'm on my way to you. Just...stay in the bathroom; I'll be there as fast as I can."

I clicked off and started pacing. *How did I end up here?*

Who is that on the bed? What did I do? My mind filled with the possibilities of how I got here: *Did I pick him up from the bar? Did we have sex? Oh no! What else did we do?* I stopped pacing and played with the ring on my finger, finally throwing my hands up, exasperated. Being locked up in the bathroom was driving me crazy, so I decided to wake up the mystery guy and demand some answers. I opened the door and tiptoed around the room, looking for a weapon to protect myself. I wasn't entirely sure how this Strigoi thing worked, and I wanted to be prepared just in case he wasn't receptive to my questioning.

I spotted a crystal camera trophy on the bookshelf in the far corner of the room. I quietly made my way over there and grabbed the trophy, then turned to look at the guy. *I can't believe this is happening.* I walked towards him, watching him breathing deeply in his peaceful slumber. He was topless, lying on his stomach, snuggled underneath the blanket. He had a golden brown complexion, like honey, and a toned back.

The crest tattooed into his left arm looked familiar to me. It was a tattoo of a dragon in front of an ankh. The dragon had black stones for eyes. I could feel its origin tugging at the corner of my mind, but no matter how hard I tried, I couldn't place it. I shrugged and studied his face, noting how attractive he was. *Well, here goes.* I readied the trophy with my right hand and shook him with my left.

"Hey!" I said firmly, "wake up!" He didn't stir. I tried again, shaking more vigorously. "Wake up, wake up!" Still nothing. *Zeită! He really is unconscious!* "Hello?" I was using both hands now, but no matter how firmly I shook him, his slumber was impenetrable. I sighed and stood up, feeling defeated. *I hope Vi hurries up.* My eyes widened. *I hope we don't have to take him to the hospital!* I gave him a second look before deciding to explore the rest of the apartment. I figured I would be able to find out who he was, and hopefully some clue as to how I'd met him.

The rest of the apartment was contemporary and neatly kept. I found nothing out of the ordinary in the kitchen, living room, or guest bathroom. I kept searching, but still didn't find anything. I scrunched my face up in frustration. *I need help...*

I walked to the other side of the apartment, chanting silently. *Wolves and faeries, dragons and ghosts; help me find what I need most. Answers to questions are what I seek; as I will, so mote it be.* As I headed closer to the second bedroom, I felt a pull. I'd walked inside. He'd made the room into an office. I bypassed the stacks of paper on the desk, feeling drawn to the bookshelf that was cattycorner from the desk. It was home to a lot of antique-looking books, each more intriguing than the one next to it. I turned around to make sure I was still alone before I picked up a very interesting black leather-bound book.

As soon as my hands touched it, I *knew* I was somehow connected to it. Waves of energy were streaming from the book, making it feel alive. The leather was worn and the pages were browning with age. I carefully flipped through them, but some of the corners still broke off in my hand. It appeared to be a journal, written with a quill pen in Old Romanian, and a lot of the text had faded.

Some of the pages had intricate diagrams, pictures, and maps. I saw drawings of eerie fanged creatures in various stages of transformation. On the following page, one word stood out to me: *Strigoi*, Vampyre. I attempted to read it.

Third day before nones, April, 1494.

Third day before nones? What the heck does that mean?

The change of a newly awakened Vampyre is gradual...sharp as a nail...eyes like that of a hawk, hearing sounds from great distances and smelling just the same...

I looked up at the ceiling. This has to be a joke, right? But

I returned my attention to the book and kept reading.

You see with new eyes and clearer sight. Only when visited by the Hunger, do your eyes look like that of the devil. The Hunger—insatiable and excruciating. This is her current situation, poor child. But this was her choice, to be turned...to aid in the defense against this evil. I just hope that we survive...

The rest was unreadable. I began pacing. I wondered who this "she" was. I grew agitated. Me? A Vampyre? How would that even happen? This journal had listed all the symptoms, but was it real? I plopped down in the swivel chair, feeling like I'd just stepped into a movie. *Zeită, what am I going to do?*

I could feel Vi outside of the building. *How can I feel her from all the way up here?* I looked at the book in my hands and considered taking it. *Oh man, but that's stealing!* I shook my head—I didn't have time for moral dilemmas. I had to take it; somehow, I knew it belonged with me.

I rushed to the kitchen, looking for a bag to put the book in. In my mind's eye, I could see Vi walking down the hallway. Luckily, it didn't take long for me to find a brown paper bag with handles. I quickly ripped off the sweatshirt I'd been wearing and used it to gently wrap the book, then placed it carefully in the bag. I created mental blocks so I wouldn't hear Vi's thoughts, and noticed it was much easier to do than before. I raced to the door and opened it.

"Vi," I exclaimed. "I'm so glad you're here!"

Vi gave me a tight hug and then pulled back, searching my eyes. "Are you okay?"

I ushered her inside the apartment and began rambling. "I think I'm going crazy, Vi! Something's happening to me!"

"What do you mean?"

"I'm hearing thoughts and can smell things." I didn't mention the fangs—I didn't want to sound crazier than I already did. "I don't remember anything after you dropping me off yesterday. Next thing I know, I woke up in a bathroom and there's this guy passed out in the bed. I think I hurt him or something!" I was getting worked up.

Vi's demeanor immediately changed, and she smirked at me. "Relax. I'll tell you what happened." She put her hands on her hips. "We went out last night and I think you had too much to drink. You met this guy and...you know." She wiggled her eyebrows suggestively.

"What? No way!" I slapped her on the arm. Now that Vi was here, I was calming down. "Wait, we went out last night?"

"Yeah. I'll tell you about it on the way home. Now, show me where this guy is."

I grabbed her hand and dragged her down the hall to the bedroom. "He's on the bed. I hope he's okay."

"Trust me, honey," she replied, giggling. "He's fine."

She still didn't believe me, but I knew nothing like *that* had happened. I glanced back, giving her an evil look. As we walked closer to the room, I could see the bed was empty.

"Oh no, where is he?" I ran to the bed, throwing the comforter on the floor. "I left him here!"

Vi took my hand to stop me from tossing the sheets. "Nadia, unless he's a bug, I doubt he's in there." Just then, we heard a flushing sound, followed by running water. We turned towards the bathroom. The door opened and there he stood in his boxers, scratching his head. *Damn. He's even cuter than I thought.* He had green eyes and a sly smile. Vi stiffened and I gave her a sidelong glance.

"Oh, hey," he greeted me. "You're still here? I thought you left." Then his gaze shifted to Vi. "Viviana, what are you doing here?"

"Rian," was all she said.

My head flipped back and forth between them. "Vi, you know him?"

She shrugged. "I've seen him around," she said shortly.

She took my hand. "Come on, Nadia, we better get going."

"Huh," I said, pulling my hand from hers. "I'm not going anywhere until you guys tell me what happened last night!"

"You don't remember?" Rian asked. I shook my head.

He walked towards his bed, then stopped and turned to me. "You are definitely helping me make this." He smirked and then sat down.

"Sorry," I mumbled.

He waved away my apology. "I'm just playing with you. So, about last night. We met at Relik," he began. "I noticed you when you walked in, and practically had to wait in line to speak to you." I scoffed at him—none of this sounded like me. "We spoke for some time before you told me you were going to return to your friend at the bar."

"I don't remember seeing you there," Vi said accusingly.

"I didn't want to be seen," Rian responded swiftly, his eyes never leaving me. She huffed and closed her mouth, biting back any retort she had.

"But how did we end up here?" I asked.

"Ahh. After you left me, I kept my eyes on you—from a distance." He picked at a piece of lint on his sheets before continuing. "I saw this guy with his hands all over you. At first, I thought he was your boyfriend, but there was some-thing...off about him. When you left the bar, I gave myself ten minutes before I would go after you." I was somewhat flattered by the fact that he seemed to have been watching over me. Vi's shoulders tightened, suggested she was feeling otherwise.

"Enough with the heroics, Rian. Just get to the point."

"Ooo, touchy, touchy." Watching them made me feel like I was in the middle of a sibling rivalry. I rolled my eyes. "Naturally, I only waited seven minutes. Then I went out to look for you and there you were! You walked right up to me and told me to take you home."

"No!" I was horrified.

"Yes. You were so cute I couldn't refuse, and I'll tell you," he said, getting up and walking closer to us, "you're into some freaky shit." My eyes widened and I threw my hands over my mouth. *Oh please, oh please tell me I didn't sleep with him!*

Vi huffed, crossing her arms over her chest. "What are you talking about, Rian?"

"Your friend here was practically eating me up," he replied. Vi gave me a curious glance, searching my eyes. Then she turned her attention back to Rian and her eyes hardened. "She marked me up nicely," he said, pointing to his neck. It was red and irritated but didn't have any visible marks. *Zeită! Was that his blood? This can't be happening.* I was in shock.

"But we didn't...do anything, right?" I asked, embarrassed.

"No, no. Not yet." He winked, causing me to blush.

Vi's mouth thinned into a hard line. She took my hand again. "Stuff it, Rian. Come on, Nadia, let's go." This time, I didn't fight her; I was too ashamed to stay there any longer.

"Aww, so soon?" The look that Vi gave him was scary. I was surprised; I had never seen her act like that before. "Okay, okay," he surrendered, then looked at me. "It was a pleasure meeting you, Nadia." *Those eyes...*I found myself blushing again and had to look away.

"Nice meeting you, too," I mumbled. I had to get out of there. I waved as we walked out. Vi didn't say anything else to him. The further I got away from him, the clearer my head became. It was more than enough for me to focus on Vi's behavior.

"What's going on?"

"I don't trust him," she answered simply.

"Why not? How do you know him?"

"I don't want to talk about it." *Strange.* "Let's just get you home and refresh your memory of last night, okay?" I nodded, letting the subject drop. We walked down the hallway in silence. I could see waves of annoyance coming off of Vi, and it was starting to bother me.

"Hey, hey." I stopped her. "Thanks for coming to get me." She looked at me and then smiled; I knew that made her feel a little better.

"Anytime."

By the time we made it to the car, the curiosity about what happened the night before almost had me bursting at the seams. As we settled in the car, I blurted, "Vi, what happened last night? The last thing I remember is you bringing me home from lunch because my stomach hurt." Now that we were in the car, Vi sighed and relaxed. She started down the street.

"A couple of hours after I dropped you off, I texted to check on you but you never responded, so I thought you were sleeping." I nodded. "You called me around eight and told me you 'needed to go on the hunt'. I just translated that as you wanting to find someone to hook up with. I was excited because I really wanted to take you to Relik, and the way you were feeling earlier, I wasn't sure if we would be able to do that. I knew this would be a perfect way to end the night. You know?"

"Naturally." I smiled; Vi loved going out.

She ignored me. "Anyway, I packed some potential outfits and headed over. When I got to your place, your door was unlocked." She didn't mention anything about the handle. I wondered if Mamă had fixed it after I passed out—unless I just imagined breaking it? Thinking of her, I realized I hadn't seen her since before we left yesterday. *I wonder where she was last night.*

"By the way, I told your mom that you slept over at my aunt's place."

"Thanks! I owe you one."

"Don't mention it. Anyway, "Vi continued, "I walked in and heard you call me. So, I went to your room to look for you. You walked out of the bathroom—" she paused. I was studying my hands and looked up at her.

"What? Keep going," I insisted.

"Well, um." She hesitated. "You were naked."

"No way! Really?" I was slightly self-conscious—for me to walk around naked, especially with my door unlocked, was unusual for me. And yet, at the present moment, I didn't feel uncomfortable with it. I went back to studying my hands. They looked younger and paler; my nails had grown too.

"Not only that," Vi continued, "your skin was flawless. I swear even the scars on your knees were gone." I thought about my childhood scars—I hadn't noticed they were gone.

"Hmm," was all I said. I rummaged through Vi's glove compartment until I found a note pad. Searching through her cup holder revealed a pen. I wrote down all that she'd told me thus far. A cop car whizzed by, sirens blaring.

"I blinked and you were standing right next to me. You scared the shit out of me! Then you started laughing, which by the way, was not funny." I smiled. It was slowly starting to come back to me.

"After scaring the bejesus out of me, you said, 'Do not fear me, I will never harm you'." She shook her head. "You had a thick accent, too. It was so weird; I thought you had already started drinking. You smiled at me, then went inside the bathroom again, I guess to take a shower. I went to the kitchen to get a drink because the whole day with you so far was bizarre. That's when I heard the song."

"What song?" I asked as Vi turned on Eighty-Fifth Street.

"At first I thought it was your iPod or something but there was no background music. That's when I realized you were singing." I snorted.

"No way was I singing."

"Swear! It was so beautiful, but I couldn't understand it."

"What do you mean?"

"It was in Romanian. Something about the moon and the night. I didn't know you were fluent in Romanian."

"...I'm not."

"Could have fooled me. What was the song anyway?"

The moon and the night...I sat there thinking about it for a few seconds, and then it came back to me.

"Crească din nou pentru noaptea este a mea. Eu merg pe străzi a cordere a de timp. Luna este închis dar mintea mea. Este luminous câştige puterea mea di noaptea," I finished beautifully, surprising myself. I didn't sing for others often and the fact that I sung even for Vi was a shock to me. The song came so naturally; it was like I wrote it myself.

"Yes, that was it," Vi said. "What does it mean?"

"I rise again for the night is mine. I walk the streets claiming time. The moon is dark but my mind is bright. I gain my strength from the night."

"Wow! Where did that come from?"

I shook my head. "Hell if I know."

"That's so weird. You probably just heard it from your mom or something."

I shrugged. "Yeah, maybe. I'll figure it out." I sang it again silently to myself, willing a memory of its origin to come to me, but I got nothing. I sighed. More unanswered questions. I looked out of the window; we were in Hell's Kitchen, heading down Ninth Ave.

"So what else happened?" I prompted.

"I was rummaging through your closet when you came out of the bathroom wrapped in a towel, looking like a swimsuit model."

Once again, I snorted. "I doubt it."

"I'm serious!"

"Yeah, whatever." That was too hard for me to believe.

"Anyway, you were still humming the song. You went to your closet and pulled out a black mini dress with fishnet sleeves. You threw it on the bed saying it was for me. I don't think I could have picked out a better outfit for myself!" I could just imagine Vi's delight. "You went back in your closet and came out wearing a leather corset, with hip-hugging leather pants. You had leather bands on your wrists with spikes, and your hair was in a high ponytail. My jaw dropped! Where did you get those clothes from?"

"I have no idea," I mumbled, looking down at my outfit, the same one Vi had described; I was just as puzzled as she was.

"Well, when you figure it out, you have to take me there."

"Sure thing."

"Anyway, you went to the mirror to do your make-up, then you stared at your reflection. You said, 'desăvârşit' and I agreed; your outfit was definitely perfect for Relik. Then you walked out of the room, saying something about needing to not lose control. When I was done getting myself together, we left."

We were on Fourteenth Street now and almost back at the condo. I was trying not to get impatient. I still wanted to know who I'd fed on and how I ended up at Rian's apartment. I sighed.

Vi continued. "It was crowded when we got there, but people made a path for you. The bouncer didn't ask for your ID. He seemed to be in a trance and he let you through, no problem. I was just like, 'Wow, okay.' You walked in and stood there surveying the place with a smirk. It seemed like everyone in the club flocked to you—guys, girls; it was like you commanded the attention of the room."

I couldn't picture any of what Vi had just told me actually happening. First of all, I couldn't get in *anywhere* without being IDed—I blame it on my baby face. Secondly, the whole "commanding attention" thing was just absurd and didn't sound like me at all. I'm not shy, by any means, but I don't "command" attention unless I'm asking for it. However, as soon as she said it, memories of last night came back to me.

"I started to feel awkward," Vi admitted, "so I said I was going to get a drink. You just walked around mingling with people."

"I'm sorry, Vi. I didn't mean to make you feel uncomfortable. None of that sounds like me at all."

"I know it wasn't intentional. You just seemed so different; I didn't know how to handle it."

"I'm sorry," I repeated.

"It's okay. I'm just glad you're safe." She sounded relieved. Then her tone completely changed. "When I came back from the bar, you were gone! I asked the bartender if he saw you and he said that you left with some guy." Vi shook her head. "Don't ever do that to me again! Do you know how worried I was?!"

"I know, Vi. I don't know what came over me last night; I didn't mean to make you worry." I wasn't sure what else to say, since I *literally* didn't know what had come over me last night. "I guess I did drink too much," I added, hoping that would be acceptable to her. It seemed to be enough. Vi took a calming breath.

"Yeah, we have to teach you some self-control." She winked at me and I gave her a small smile. I was certain it wasn't alcohol I'd drunk last night.

∞

Vi dropped me off and made me promise to call her later. As I was walking towards the lobby, I felt a tickle across my mind. I looked over my shoulder at a group of people waiting to cross the street. I thought I saw familiar brown eyes staring at me, but when I blinked, they were gone. I shrugged and then headed upstairs to my condo. Mamă wasn't home, for which I was thankful. I decided to use the time to review the notes I had taken, and clear up some more of the fuzziness. I put the bag in my closet and lit the white candle on the side table. Sitting on my bed, I closed my eyes. Nefi settled next to me before I traveled deep into my subconscious mind. I plucked the memory and brought it to the forefront of my mind, allowing myself to remember.

There is a man eyeing me wickedly. Even if I couldn't read his mind, his intentions would still be clear; his vile thoughts are making my stomach churn. He's the perfect candidate for what I have in mind—I have waited too long to feed, and I don't have the time to be picky.

I sashay to the bar and lean over seductively. I order water, and ask the bartender to put it in a shot glass. He does so without comment. I guess requests like this are quite common. After taking my 'shot', I order another. I feel pin-pricks of negative energy before the man physically touches me by placing his hands on my hips. I resist the urge to move away from him. Instead, I push my body closer to him and rest my head on his chest. Turning to face him, I wrap my arms around his neck.

"Hey, baby," I greet him in a smoky voice, slurring slightly, giving the impression that I am somewhat tipsy.

"Sexy," he responds. He leans close and whispers in my ear, "I've been waiting for you all night." His breath smells of whiskey and stale cigarettes. Disgusting.

"Aww, baby. Did I keep you waiting long?" He smiles mischievously.

"Too long." He orders me a double shot of Patrón. The bartender looks at me and I shake my head slightly, but enough so he knows to stick with water. I thank him when he hands me the glass and down the contents in one draught. Placing the now-empty glass on the bar, I stumble slightly. I feel eyes on me,

and look over at the very attractive guy with a tattoo on his left arm that I spoke to earlier. I am intrigued by him, but I return my attention to the man in front of me as my belly starts to rumble again.

My new "friend" takes my hand and leads me outside. His aura is blacker than the night and I'm amazed no one else can see it. We silently walk down the street until he turns me towards an alley. The smell of urine and garbage is so strong, I gag. Distracted by the smell, I don't see him take out a blade. He rounds on me, pushing me against the brick wall.

"You were really popular in there," he says with a sneer. He presses the knife against my throat with an evil gleam in his eye. I give him a mock look of fear. "You stupid bitches are all the same." Maintaining his grip on the knife, he uses his left hand to unbutton my pants. He unzips his and continues, "You always go out, dressing like whores, begging for us to buy you drinks." Spittle flies from his mouth. "Then you cry like babies after we treat you like the little sluts you are. Well, not tonight." He angrily tugs at my pants. "No, not tonight." He curls his lip. "If you make a sound, I'll slit your fucking throat!"

He falters when I don't give him the reaction he's expecting. "Pull your pants down," he orders. I don't move. He adds pressure to the knife and asks, "Are you deaf, you dumb bitch? I said pull your fucking pants down!" Still I don't oblige. Instead I look him square in the face and smile, pushing against the knife with enough pressure to draw blood.

I feel his uncertainty, and before he can react, I push the knife aside and grab his wrist with my left hand. At the same time, I grab his throat with my right hand and spin around, pushing him against the wall. I move with such lightning speed that he doesn't have time to process what's happening until it's too late. His eyes widen and he drops the knife as his hand slams into the wall.

Glaring at him with red eyes, I say mockingly, "You *pull*

your *fucking pants down."* I tighten my grip on his neck, cutting off any screams, then carefully tilt his head to the side. A small growl escapes me, and with fangs bared, I sink them into his flesh. The salty taste of his sweat and fear are masked by the iron flavor of his blood. He tastes like whiskey and the alcohol in his blood starts to go to my head.

The pain I have been experiencing all day begins to recede. All too soon, I pull myself away from him and let out a contented sigh. Though slightly dizzy from the whiskey blood, overall I feel good. He is noticeably paler and looks at me in complete horror. I stare deep into his eyes and enter his subconscious, trying to erase all memories of me, but I can't concentrate long enough. Instead I go for the art of manipulation and tell him to stop preying on girls; it is easier to insert a command than to erase a memory. I add that if he ever mentions this, I'll come back for him. It seems to work; he nods his head vigorously. I redo my pants and leave the alley.

I stumble slightly—I need clean blood. Right on cue, the attractive guy with the tattoo races out of the club. He looks relieved when he sees me. I walk up to him and look deep into his eyes. "Take me home?"

He grins. "To my place or yours?"

When I returned to the present, I ran to the bathroom and vomited in the toilet. The combination of almost being sexually assaulted and feeding from someone made my stomach turn. I swished some water around in my mouth, and then brushed my teeth. *How did I know how to feed? How did I know when to stop? How is any of this happening?!*

My mind raced with all the questions swirling through my head. The whole thing seemed to come so naturally to me, and yet I hadn't been taught anything. Mamă wasn't Strigoi. I didn't know much about Tată, but I doubted he was one either. I took a deep, calming breath, deciding a shower was necessary. My phone rang from the bedroom—I knew it was Mamă, but I couldn't speak to her right then. She was worried; I could sense it even from a distance. I took another deep breath and turned the water on as hot as it would go.

This is crazy! What am I going to do? I stepped inside, relishing the sting of the heat against my skin. I instantly relaxed, and began washing away the makeup from the night before, all the while wishing I could wash away the memory seared into my mind.

CHAPTER SEVEN

BRAN, WALLACHIA 1480

I lurked in the woods, peering through the trees at the tavern before me. I had knowledge from our spies that much of the Order frequented this place. It was pouring rain, which made it easier for me to hide by muffling any sounds and limiting sightlines. I was drenched with water, but the weather reflected my foul mood. I'd travelled all night and well into the day, hiding within the trees, to get to this city, and I wasn't leaving until I got what I'd come for: vengeance.

During my journey, I decided to take out all the key players, picking them off one by one until I got to Mihnea. I chose to start with Raz—the team leader and knight who killed Luca. I could see him through the window, drinking ale and palming the bum of the whore, Ileana, who was sitting in his lap. He was laughing at something one of his companions said, and raised his mug in a toast.

A growl sounded at the back of my throat. How dare he sit there enjoying the company of friends when only days before he'd slaughtered an innocent babe and countless others with no remorse? Luca would never know the taste of ale or the feel of a woman's touch. I would stop at nothing to avenge him and the people of both our villages.

I watched the scene intently, waiting for the poison to take effect. I'd paid Ileana generously to keep Raz entertained, and to pour the poison mixture into his mug whenever she brought him a refill to mask the taste. I provided her with the poison ring and specific instructions on how to administer the mixture in just the right amounts. She was more than happy to complete the task—she had her own vendetta against this lot.

Raz and a handful of his knights were known to be rough with the women. Ileana, who was younger than I, had left the tavern more than once bloodied and bruised. She told me of a time that she was unable to work for days because she needed to heal. I pursed my lips together, growing impatient. *Come now!*

As Ileana stood up, Raz slapped her on the bum with force. She winced but still managed to put on an inviting smile. He downed the contents of his drink in one gulp and smirked at his companions before taking Ileana's hand. He stumbled, and laughter filled the tavern. She held him up to stop him from landing on his face and he slapped her away, embarrassed.

Ileana clenched her jaw and flared her nostrils. She glared at Raz, but he took no notice as his steps became more unsteady. He flopped to the floor and the patrons nearby howled with mirth. This time, he didn't turn away from Ileana's help, and she practically carried him up the stairs behind the bar.

It is almost time. I smiled mischievously, and slowly made my way towards the back entrance of the tavern. I allowed Ileana time to have her way with him—a woman's scorn can be a dangerous thing. I slipped inside the tavern unnoticed and easily blended into the shadows. As I climbed the stairs, I tried to find their scent, and listened intently to discover what room they were in.

As I passed a door, I encountered a strong feeling of uncertainty and apprehension. *This is it.* I sent word to Ileana that I was outside and more than ready to get started. I heard soft footsteps and the door opened, revealing a young girl with a sandy complexion. She quickly ushered me inside and closed the door behind me before casually strolling towards the body lying on the bed.

"I did as you instructed—he went down only moments before you arrived."

"You've done well."

Still near the door, I observed Raz carefully—he was free of his armor, but still dressed, and his eyes hardened at the sight of me. The hemlock had weakened him, and eventually would cause paralysis. Although Raz's body was still, his mind was unaffected, and he was well aware of what was going on around him. His eyes began moving frantically between the both of us, and it was only a matter of time before his muscles would become unusable. I had to make haste before then if I wanted to see my plan successfully carried out. Ileana faced me and asked, "May I do one last thing, Your Highness?"

I nodded. "Do what you feel must be done."

Light from the candle reflected off the blade she pulled from her pocket. His eyes widened. As she approached him, I could feel an increase in his fear at the uncertainty of what was to come. She slowly unfastened his trousers, twirling the blade in her hand.

"Before we part, I would love a memento," she said, pulling his trousers down to his ankles and exposing his bits. "After all, we've shared many unforgettable moments," she added sarcastically.

His breathing quickened and he started to perspire. I leaned against the wall and crossed my arms in front of my chest—Ileana was handling this very well, and I enjoyed watching her toy with him. I smiled as he grunted when the blade moved closer to his shaft. It slowly grazed him as Ileana spoke. "Bid him farewell."

Ileana began peeling the skin from his prick. *The mind can be very cruel*, I thought. Raz psychologically registered pain even though he lacked the sensation to feel what was happening to him. He watched in horror as layer upon layer of skin was taken from his most prized possession. He cried out and the sound angered Ileana, who glared at him.

"Be silent and enjoy the moment," she whispered venomously.

Most humans are sickened by gore and I was impressed at her tolerance. Tears leaked from his eyes as she carved her initials into his shaft. My nostrils flared at the rich smell of his blood, and I licked my lips as she began slicing into his bollocks. Dark crimson blood soaked the sheets underneath Raz, and I could barely contain my hunger.

Finally, I pushed myself off the wall and sauntered towards Ileana, who was dangling a bollock in front of his face, taunting him. The tears came faster, and still he could do nothing. I took the piece from her hand and glowered at Raz as I bit into it like a piece of fruit. I drank the small amount of blood it offered and placed the empty sac into his limp hand. The risk was minimal—the small amount of poison in his blood wouldn't affect me. His breathing slowed as his anxiety made the poison work faster.

I rushed to him and grabbed his jaw, my face inches away from his. I frowned. "Shhh. Not so fast, miscreant. Your death is to be slow—this I can promise. You will regret the day you joined the Order; the Gods will see to that."

His crying reduced to whimpers, like a lost puppy. I turned towards Ileana. Taking the blade from her hand, I licked the blood off and brought it to his face. I pressed the knife under his ribcage and slowly pushed against it, piercing his skin. The blade sliced with ease, and I didn't stop until I'd punctured his spleen. I pulled the blade out, and blood started flowing from the wound. If his dying organs didn't kill him first, then blood loss would do the deed just as well.

"This is for Luca and all the others of our villages that your lot have massacred. May you feel their pain tenfold," were my last words to him. I turned away from him and handed the blade back to Ileana. "I am satisfied by what my eyes have seen. You are free to do what you please." She leered at him in anticipation. "Just promise to make it slow," I added.

She bowed her head, "Aye, Princess—he deserves nothing less." I said nothing, walking towards the door to take my leave. "You need not worry about the others downstairs—they, too, have sipped a juice of death of my own creation."

I stopped and grinned, pleased with her. As I started back downstairs towards the tavern, I could still hear the babble of the patrons and clanking of mugs on tables. I was ignored as I walked through, and was almost to the door when a loud sob caught my attention. A patron complained about his wife's infidelities, while his companion nodded sympathetically.

He picked up his mug to take another sip and jumped at a yelp from the back. A wench gasped, and stepped away from a knight whose face landed on the table. No sooner did the ale in his mug settle, than another fell. One by one, the remaining knights slumped from their chairs, dead. The patron stopped weeping and regarded his companion with wide eyes.

"If nothing else, thank the Gods that you're not among *them*," his friend said, pointing to the dead knights.

"Aye," he agreed and picked up his mug, chugging the ale.

Some of the men eyed their mugs suspiciously and poured the contents onto the tables before taking their leave. Slowly, the atmosphere returned to its former jollity, and I smirked as I strolled outside. I started down the path, keeping my eyes peeled for something to feed on. I would have taken a knight, but their blood was tainted and no longer pumping. I passed several small beasts, but nothing large enough to sustain me. My thoughts flipped to Ileana. *She is brave and has much anger—that could be of use.* I was considering taking her under my wing when I heard something shuffling ahead of me.

I crouched low and crept to the tree line. Making no sound, I continued forward, focused on the flashes of movement I could see through the trees. As I reached the source, my eyes brightened as I recognized what I saw. There, happily feeding on grass, was my beloved Fyuree. She nickered at me as I approached. Tears of joy filled my eyes; I had been unsure that she had gotten out alive.

"You have come far, girl," I commented, rubbing her muzzle. Sensing a familiar presence behind me, I stiffened. "Who else survived?" I asked without turning to face my new companion.

"Jeniviva is with Nic. We were able to get most of the children to safety, and a handful of the Witches, but were unable to save many elders, including the Seer, Una, and..." He didn't have to finish his statement—I was well aware of Mother's death.

I finally turned to Fabian, gaze filled with resentment. "This is your fault." He said nothing, and that angered me. "This could have all been avoided had we just acted instead of sitting on our asses, twiddling our thumbs."

He stepped closer to me. "I know that I cannot say anything to take away your pain, but Ecaterina is with the Gods now."

"But she *shouldn't* and she *wouldn't* be if we didn't take the coward's approach. The Order destroyed our homes and brutally murdered my and Jeniviva's family—there is no more 'waiting for the right time' or 'planning'. The time to act is *now*." He was silent, and I asked, "Why are you even here, Keeper?"

"To try and reason with you. You have others who need you. Be wise and do not act out of grief. Come with me." He held out his hand.

I looked at it with disdain. "Come with you *where*? Our home has been *destroyed*."

"We have set up camp in Hârșova and the others are awaiting your arrival."

I didn't respond right away, thinking about what the Keeper had said. "Prithee take Fyuree back with you—she will only slow me down." I gave her one last pet before turning on my heel and starting back down the path.

"Antanasia, prithee," he pleaded, but I was determined to make the Order pay for their crimes.

"I will travel to Hârșova when I've completed my tasks." I ran, partly expecting Fabian to try and stop me, but he did not.

∞

I followed the red fox and her kits through the forest, waiting for the right time to attack. They were small beasts, so I would need to feed off all of them for it to be worth it. I frowned—I didn't want to kill them, but I couldn't see any other way. One of the kits caught the scent of a shrew, and started tracking it in an effort to show he could hunt for himself.

The shrew scurried closer towards the tree that I was hiding in and burrowed into its hollow. The little fox approached and sniffed the base of the tree in search of the creature. I shifted my weight and the fox stiffened. Just as he looked up, I landed on him with an audible thump. He whimpered before I snapped his neck. I sunk my teeth into his throat, ignoring the fur as I began to drink.

I heard a low growl behind me and turned to see the other kit stalk closer. She jumped in the air towards me. I threw my fist out, and she crashed into a tree before slumping to the ground. A loud shriek sounded as the mother fox appeared. She sniffed her dead babe, lying against the tree, then looked up and saw me with her other kit in my arms. Her lips curled up and she crouched, poised for an attack.

I jumped to my feet. The father charged at me and I staggered, caught off guard. I yelled as teeth pierced my midsection. The mother came at me and I kicked out, trying at the same time to throw the father off of me. I threw a number of punches, my fists connecting with his head, and eventually he released his grip on me. He shook his head to clear the stars while the mother came after me again.

I decided to meet her head on and raced towards her. It was easy for me to overpower her, and I snapped her neck in a single motion. She fell dead at my feet. The father hunched back on his hind legs and cried out to the heavens. Guilt swam through me and I wanted to ease his pain. *I had no choice.* In his despair, he didn't sense me sneaking behind him. I snapped his neck as well. I fed from him and then stared at the still, furry bodies scattered around me. I sighed and lowered my head, resting against a tree. Between recent events and feeding, I was exhausted.

"It is alright, you know." I jumped up at the sound of a man's voice, turning to face him. He wore a plain cloak, making it impossible for me to determine where he was from. He was of average build, had short, dark hair, and piercing blue eyes. "You seem to be new to feeding on animals; you must have had your Ritual only days ago," he said. I narrowed my eyes at him, and he smiled. "Yes, Princess, I know who you are. You put on quite a show back at the tavern—very impressive."

"Who are you?"

"Best be on your guard around here. You never know who you may encounter," he said, walking closer to me.

"You have left my question unanswered." I stood my

ground.

"It appears I have."

As we began circling each other, I eyed him skeptically. "What do you want?"

He stopped walking and rubbed his chin, looking upwards in thought. "What do I want? I want my own castle and servants. I want a never-ending supply of blood without having to hunt for it. I want my king to be breathing once again, and those who killed him to be dead. But most of all," he approached me, smirking, "I want the reward I will get for presenting your head to Mihnea." I growled and took a step back, bracing myself for battle. The stranger laughed. "Come now, Princess. No need for a fight. Perhaps he will spare you."

"If you know who I am, then you must know that going to Mihnea is the last thing that will happen."

No sooner did the words leave my lips than I charged at him. When I was close enough, I twisted my body and delivered a kick just below his ear. He spun in the air before landing on the ground. Had he been human, that would have knocked him out from the lack of blood to his brain. As it was, he lay still for only a moment. The stranger reached over and massaged his neck, growling as he turned to look at me. He charged at me, his hands around my throat in an instant. I clawed at them.

"Do not waste time, Princess. I have decades on you— you could never defeat me."

I ground my teeth together and slammed down on his forearms, breaking his hold on me before head-butting him. He dropped me, grabbing his nose, and I kicked his legs out from under him. "Are you quite certain?" I asked close to his face.

He grabbed my hair—his tight grip pulling strands from my scalp. He smashed my head into the ground and I tasted the earth. I felt several teeth loosen and the cartilage and bone in my nose break. "Yes," he whispered in my ear.

I scrabbled desperately behind me, seizing his thumb and pulling it back towards his hand until it snapped. He clenched his jaw, and his grip loosened enough for me to roll away. I staggered up, holding my face. Blood dripped through my fingers and onto my overcoat as I struggled to breathe. He ran towards me and punched me in the cheek, breaking bone and sending me spiraling through the air. I smashed into a tree and slumped to the ground.

My nose and mouth were already healing, and he kicked me in the abdomen. As he kicked me again, I coughed up blood. He lashed out at my face, re-breaking my newly healed nose, and my head cracked against the tree. I flopped to the ground, blood pouring from my mouth. I closed my eyes as my vision darkened. I could feel the heat of his breath on my ear, and my necklace grew warm just as he began to speak.

"When you both are finally reunited, tell your fool of a mother that Brây—"

I opened my eyes and my hands flew to either side of his head. They grew warm and light seeped through my pores. It felt as though fire was shooting from one hand to the other. As my necklace grew hotter, my hands would soon follow.

"You feel pain." The energy between my palms made my hands throb, and I sent it into Brây. The scream that erupted from his throat made my ears bleed. He sunk to his knees with my hands still on his head. When I blinked, he was dressed in unfamiliar clothing. Tears formed in his eyes as he spoke in a foreign language. The tone of his voice made him sound pathetic and it angered me. "You insult me and my Mother but expect mercy?"

I sent more energy into his head and his shrieking rose an octave. I bit into him and ripped out a chunk of his neck, spitting it on the ground. His blood dripped down my throat, burning on the way down. I hissed, letting go of him, and his hands flew to the hole in his neck. Blood spurted out, showering us in red. Brây crawled away from me, his breathing ragged. I glared at him.

"So much...power..." he sputtered, blood trickling from his mouth. I shook my head, clearing it of confusion as he reappeared in his old clothing. Blood stopped flowing from his throat as the wound began healing.

I walked to him, ready to strike again, and he cringed. "You fear me now? Good."

As I pulled my foot back, Brây held up his hand. "What are you?"

I cocked my head to the side, frowning at him. "What is this you ask? You know what I am."

"I knew not of your power. You will be a valuable asset to the Order." He spat out blood, smearing crimson in the dirt.

"I care nothing for the Order," I responded, growing impatient. "Or for you," I added. I kicked him in the head and he spat out several teeth. "You were not on my list, but I am willing to settle if it means reducing the Order's numbers."

As I moved to stomp on Brây, he caught my foot, throwing it to the side. Completely unbalanced, I fell to the ground. I rolled out of the way just as he leaped to follow up on the attack. Jumping to my feet, I gasped as a figure soared through the air and tackled Brây. He grunted loudly, landing face first in the dirt with Nic on top of him. Before Brây could react, Nic violently twisted his head and snapped his neck.

"I did not need your help," I huffed.

Nic moved off of Brây's limp body and ambled over to me. "Perchance, but what kind of man watches idly while his lover fights senseless battles?"

I glared at him, throwing my hands on my hips. "Did the

Keeper send you?"

"Nay, my father did not send me, though I do agree with him." He stepped closer to me and took my hand. "We are concerned about you; you mustn't seek out trouble."

I snatched my hand from his. "*Seek* out trouble? *He* approached me," I pointed to the body, "Wanting to deliver my head to Mihnea!"

"That does not explain what took place at the tavern."

I held my head up proudly. "Raz and his bandits deserved what they got. I'm sure the Gods would agree with me."

"The Gods would want you to go for the head of the snake, not the body. Killing off members of the Order leaves you exposed. Is that not how this one found you?"

"The Order brought devastation to our doorstep! They are a problem that I intend to eliminate once and for all." I turned my back on him.

"My love—"

"I thought you of all people would support my decisions."

He grabbed my shoulder and turned me towards him, frowning. "I wholeheartedly support you, Antanasia. But you are not behaving wisely."

I slapped him in the face. "How dare you! They brutalized and murdered Mother! They destroyed our home!"

"Aye, and it pains me as well, but you cannot travel alone hoping to kill them all without a plan."

"Killing them *is* the plan," I said stubbornly. "You understand nothing—you have never lost your mother."

Nic furrowed his brows. "Haven't I? Mine is a member of the Order."

I softened my gaze and sighed. "It is not the same..." I responded as tears rolled down my cheeks.

He held my face in his hands, wiping away tears with his

thumb. "Alas, my love. The Order did not slay my mother, but they took her from me all the same." He gazed into my eyes. "If nothing else, think of Jeniviva—you made her a promise. Should anything have happened to you, you would have lied."

Nic pulled me in for a hug and I sobbed into his chest, embracing him tightly. I let go of my anger and allowed myself to mourn for all that had been taken from us: villages and people that I had known all my life, including Una, the Seer, and Mother. He was right of course—I was being reckless. The death of Mother left me feeling lost and hollow. I sniffled and looked up at the sky. *Why did you allow this to happen?* I closed my eyes as Nic kissed my forehead, and I hiccupped. I pulled away, glancing at him through swollen eyes.

"I did not realize how much I needed that," I said, wiping my nose with my hand.

"You hold on to too much—always have."

I nodded in agreement. "I thank you."

"Unnecessary. I will always be here for you, until my last breath."

I shuddered. "May that day never come."

He smiled at me and took my hand. "Do not fret—the Gods need me around to reel you in should you decide to go on a rampage again."

I playfully hit him in the arm. "Bastard." He laughed. A thought occurred to me as I looked at Brây's body. "Should we not burn him?"

Nic followed my gaze, deep in thought. He sauntered towards the body and pulled out his dagger. Squatting down, he took his blade and sliced it through Brây's neck, severing his head. As he walked back to me, he wiped the blade on his trousers and put it back in its sheath.

"There." He smirked and took my hand. "He will not be cause for concern any longer." He gently tugged on my arm and we commenced on our journey towards Hârşova.

CHAPTER EIGHT

NEW YORK, NEW YORK 2015

The shower eased some of my nerves, but my mind was still reeling. Even though I knew Mamă had more expertise than I, I still wasn't ready to speak with her just yet. I didn't know what to tell her or where to start, and I didn't want her to think I was losing it. I knew I would have to call her soon or she would confront me when she got home from work.

Time, I thought to her, *Give me time.*

Instead, I decided to see what answers lay within. I was determined to figure out how I'd known what to do. How did feeding come so naturally to me, even though no one in my family was a Vampyre?

I dried off and walked back into the room naked. It's always best to be natural when really communing with your Higher Self, as there are no other energies distracting you. I turned off my phone and grabbed my candles from my sacred chest. Mamă taught me that black was for protection, removing negativity and confusion, and revealing truth. White was for both Lord and Lady, warding off doubts and fears, revealing truth, and meditation; it could also be used as a substitute for any color. Setting my candles in a circular pattern on the living room floor, I started to focus my mind on the answers I sought. The circle was about nine feet in diameter; big enough for me to sit in without burning myself.

After arranging my candles, I went back to my chest for a

stick of nag champa incense. I loved the way it smells and it always got me in the mental state needed for deep meditation. Finally, I grabbed my lighter from the drawer in the kitchen. Once back in the living room, I lit the incense. I closed my eyes and inhaled deeply, letting the scent fill me. I opened my eyes and waved the stick in the air while walking the perimeter of my circle.

"Incense, air of high refine, purify this space of mine. Cleansed and purged be this place, that I have chosen as magickal space." I walked the circle three times, repeating the chant. Upon completion of my third circle, I felt ready. I placed the incense in the holder and sat cross-legged in the center of my circle. Nefi dashed to my side and nestled there. I smiled, then rested my hands on my knees and closed my eyes. I took a deep breath and let it out slowly to clear my mind.

I started breathing in a pattern of inhale, count to four, hold for two, exhale, count to four and hold for two. Repeat. With each breath, I felt myself getting more and more relaxed. I continued counting my breaths until I drifted off into a familiar place within myself. I opened my mind, acknowledging the visions that appeared. I gently pushed the irrelevant thoughts aside, seeking only answers to my new condition. The rich scent of earth wafted across my mind, and I followed it until I found myself in a forest.

I am sitting at the edge of a pond, dressed in a gown with a low front opening that laces over a kirtle. The hem creases upward, revealing the rich fabric of my kirtle skirt. I lean over and gaze into the water. My eyes widen at my reflection. I stare at my golden-amber eyes, but they are set in a different face. The brows are straighter and the lips are more rounded. I furrow my brows and lean closer to the water's surface.

'What do you see?" I look up at the woman who speaks to me. Although she asks me in Romanian, I understand her per-

fectly. She is beautiful, with features similar to those the water reflected back to me—she is my *Mamă* and I smile at her.

'Nothing," I respond. She returns my smile, then looks at the person beside me. I follow her gaze and my heart swells at the young man I see. We have a deep, intimate connection; although we are young, he is my lover. He takes my hand in his, rubbing his thumb across my knuckles. The three of us look down at a doe that is lying calmly as if in a trance. There are bite marks on its neck; my *Mamă* and my lover are teaching me to feed from an animal, for which I am thankful.

The doe was drinking from the pond when we found her. My lover glamoured her to be at peace. I look at the doe and feel the familiar ache in my belly. My canines lengthen to fangs and I bend over to sink my teeth into the animal's neck. I can smell pine on her hide from the nearby trees, and her fur carries a light coat of sweat from her morning frolic. My lover rubs my back encouragingly as I drink, and I am overwhelmed by the love and appreciation I feel at his touch.

Soon, my lover places his hand on my shoulder, indicating that I should stop. With a last swallow, I sit up, regarding him. He nods at me, and I look deeply into the doe's eyes, connecting with her. I mentally thank her for her nutrients and let her know that she is free to go. Her gaze clears, and the doe immediately stands up and prances away. I am proud of my achievement. *Mamă* and my lover both smile brightly at me.

Then my lover and I tense, sensing something nearby. An arrow soars by and we jump to our feet. While my lover runs towards the archer, I motion for *Mamă* to follow me in the opposite direction. We zigzag through the trees, branches and dry leaves crunching underneath us. *Mamă* is much slower than I and soon falls behind. I am overcome with trepidation seconds before I hear *Mamă* fall down. Halting, I turn around and run to her. She is tugging at an arrow that's lodged deep in her thigh. I know it's risky for me to stay, but I can't leave *Mamă* here. I reach down and try to help her remove the arrow.

'You must go!" she yells at me tremulously.

'Mother, I can at least carry you," I protest.

'Nay! I will only slow you down!"

'But..."An arrow flies past my head.

'Go now, Antanasia! RUN!" Tears well in my eyes as I give her one last look and turn away from the woman who bore me. I run as fast as I can, but an arrow grazes the side of my arm.

"Ahh!" I cried out, breaking my trance. My eyes snapped open. My heart was racing and I focused on trying to slow my breathing. Tears were rolling down my cheeks and my eyes darted around the room; I knew I was in my condo, but the smell of dry leaves was still so fresh in my nostrils. I placed my hand over my right bicep where the arrow had scratched me. The area was tender and my skin was hot and throbbing.

I had never experienced such a strong Vision before. I looked down at my necklace. *Maybe this helped...*I didn't understand what the Vision meant; if anything, I had more questions than ever. *I've never had past Visions before; what year was it? Am I related to that girl? Why were they being hunted?*

I almost cried again thinking of Antanasia leaving her Mamă behind. *Wait a moment—Antanasia...that's my middle name!* Nadia Antanasia Gabor. I had never given much thought as to where my middle name came from, always thinking it was just a name Mamă liked. I wondered why Mamă hadn't told me it was from our ancestor. I took a deep breath and counted to seven to clear my mind. As I cleaned up my tools, I thanked my Higher Powers for allowing me to receive the Vision, even though I was left confused by it.

I was in my closet getting dressed, with my mind all over the place. It was challenging, but I was slowly starting to come to grips with the fact that I was experiencing an Awakening and becoming Strigoi. But the list of questions was ever-growing: how was I becoming a Vampyre? How would this Change affect my life? Could I still be around people, or hang out with friends? And what about my body being taken over last night? That was a scary thought. I sighed and played my thumb over my ring, trying to figure out my next move. My eyes flittered to the brown bag in the corner of my closet and I felt the pull of the journal. Now in the privacy of my own home, I could take my time looking through the book and hopefully find more answers.

I grabbed it and lay down on my bed to get comfortable. I started turning the pages, some legible and others so far gone I couldn't tell what was originally on the page. Something caught my eye: the crest—it was similar to the one that Rian had tattooed on him, except instead of an ankh, it was a cross. I ran my fingers over the picture, then stopped to read. I couldn't translate all of it, but what I was able to read gave me the chills.

...The Order is getting stronger...have killed...must go in hiding...find the host...prophecy...evil...rise again...world is destroyed...

The jumble of words made little sense to me, but it felt like a warning. I snapped the book shut. My head was starting to hurt and I needed to get some fresh air. I wasn't sure where to go at first, but anywhere was better than being home, and I found myself walking a few blocks towards Best Buy.

As I walked into the store, I noticed that it was easier for me to block out all the unwanted thoughts. This made me smile; for the first time since my birthday, I felt like my mind was my own. I ambled over to the music section, browsing through the CDs, and picked up a Red Hot Chili Peppers CD. I turned it over to view the tracks and nodded in appreciation. *This will do.*

I spent the next ten minutes leafing through more CDs, and had a handful of them when my senses tingled. I looked up and felt a blush creep across my cheeks. Rian was heading towards me, wearing dark blue straight-leg jeans and a short-sleeve light green shirt. *Zeită, he is so yummy.* I involuntarily bit my lip. Immediately, I remembered the night before and looked away, wishing that I could disappear.

"Hey there," he greeted me.

"Hello." I smiled nervously.

He chuckled and said, "Are you feeling any better?"

"I am, thank you." I had to look away from him, so I focused all my attention on the CD rack, counting every paint chip on the battered metal. Anything to stop myself from looking at him.

"I'm glad." He walked closer to me. "You know, I've been thinking about you a lot since you left."

"Oh...oh really, now?"

"Yes."

I blushed deeply and my heart rate increased. *What is he doing to me?*

I took a chance and faced him. "And why is that?"

"Well, we didn't get to finish our conversation last night." He took my hand. "And I'm really interested in learning more about you."

His gaze trapped me for a moment before I was able to respond. "Like what?" I asked slowly, taking my hand from his.

Rian took a step back. "Come." He held out his hand. I hesitated to take it. "I'm not going to hurt you. Besides, I think we know who the dangerous one really is here." He winked and I wanted to run and hide. He had a point: I *did* spend the night with him unharmed, leaving *him* with marks even if I didn't remember it. If I really was Strigoi, I would be more than capable of defending myself. I relaxed a little.

"Fine," I said finally. "But let me pay for these first."As I walked to the counter, a thought occurred to me. "What are you doing down here, anyway?" I asked. Considering that his apartment was uptown, I had a hard time believing he'd come all the way down here just to go to Best Buy.

His response was instantaneous. "I was actually on my way to the New Museum when I thought I saw you walk in here. And now, I think it would be a great idea for you to join me."

I crossed my arms over my chest. "Oh, is that so?" I tried to remain cynical, but I failed and found myself grinning slightly. I was impressed that he was going to an art museum, and it piqued my interest.

"It is so." He smiled back. I bit the inside of my lip as I finished paying. We walked outside and he turned to face me. "So, what do you think? Care to join me?"

I was so glad that I couldn't hear other people's thoughts right then, because my mind was chaotic enough. If I was being honest with myself, I would love to spend more time with Rian...and actually remember it. Plus, I could use this opportunity to fill in the blanks of what we'd talked about last night and learn more about the crest.

Scrunching my nose, I looked away and sighed, feigning boredom. "I guess so. I didn't have any other plans, anyway."

"Excellent." He beamed.

I pointed at him. "But this doesn't mean anything, mister."

He held up his hands. "Yes, ma'am, don't hurt me...again." He laughed.

"Oh, shut up," I said smiling.

Once I allowed myself to relax, I could appreciate Rian's fun energy; it was nice to be around. We started walking down Broadway.

"So, what did we talk about last night?" I asked.

"That's right—you don't remember."

"Don't remind me," I grumbled.

Rian put his hand on my arm, stopping me. "Hey, no worries." He lowered his voice and whispered, "Unfortunately, there have been a few times when I've drunk too much. But I promise you, nothing happened." He smiled reassuringly.

I bit the inside of my cheek and nodded. "Okay. So, what did we talk about?" I repeated as we started walking again, making a left on Prince Street.

According to him, we'd talked about where we were from, where we grew up, and what school we went to, as well as other basic information.

He was a little older than I, at twenty-one years. He was born and raised in Texas, but branched out to attend SVA for photography. Rian admitted that his parents weren't too thrilled about him pursuing photography, claiming that it wasn't much of a career. I enjoyed that he was into the arts—it was a part of me I couldn't satisfy since I'd started pursuing law; I just didn't have the time anymore.

When we arrived at the museum, Rian sweetly paid for both of our tickets. I admitted to him that I had never been there before. He smiled at me and told me he hadn't either. We started with the Triennial exhibition, discussing our opinions on each piece. I thought that the exhibit was very different, using sound, dance, and comedy in addition to the usual artistic media. There were a lot of collections from international artists. The exhibit was compelling and led to a deep discussion of social media and societal, like our sense of self and our identity in a time where our culture places so much emphasis on how we should be and act.

Next, we walked through Jim Shaw's exhibit and it was mind-blowing. I loved the abstract and surreal pieces and how he combined traditional categories in a single exhibit. We found ourselves talking about history, politics, and theology—about Shaw's unique perspective on these topics mixed with mild historical accuracy. When it came to politics and theology, I really wasn't fond of having those conversations with anyone, and yet it was a pleasant discussion with Rian. I found myself smiling the whole time as we walked through Barbara Rossi, Wynne Greenwood and my absolute favorite of the day, Histories of Sexuality.

After the museum, we shared appetizers at Father's Run, which was known for its duck wings and waffle fries. While I had him at the table, I thought it would be a great time to ask him about his tattoo.

"So," I started after swallowing a fry, "what does the crest on your arm mean?"

"It's my family crest," he answered without hesitation.

I eyed him skeptically. "Well, what does it mean?" I asked again, admiring the details in the dragon.

"Overall, it stands for protection and guardianship. The dragon is a symbol of strength and wisdom."

"It's very interesting. I feel like I've seen it before," I said, trying to remember; I knew the journal wasn't the first time I'd seen it.

"Perhaps you've seen something similar—dragons are a common tattoo." Well, I knew there was a history to it, if only I could translate the rest of the journal. I didn't ask any more questions, deciding that I would do my own research when I got home. If he noticed his book missing, he didn't mention it, for which I was grateful. The rest of our meal time was spent talking about places we'd like to travel and things we'd like to see. There was a lot we had in common. We finished eating and he surprised me by offering to pay for the whole meal.

"Are you sure? I don't mind splitting it," I said.

He dismissed my offer. "It's my pleasure. Just promise me that we can do it again sometime." He gave me a charming smile and I melted inside. *How does a stranger have this type of effect on me?*

I smirked and said, "I'll think about it."

"I can live with that."

We exchanged numbers and went our separate ways at the door. I walked home giddy as a little girl with her first crush. When I got inside my condo, I still had a smile plastered on my face. I'd had a pleasant afternoon with Rian, and I admitted to myself that I was very interested in him. I blushed at the thought. Walking to my room, I tossed my CDs on the bed. Mamă wasn't here yet, but I had a feeling she would be home soon. My good mood dissolved at the thought—I knew I would have to talk to her, but I wasn't sure where to start. I had so many questions to ask her; there was so much I didn't know.

When I felt Mamă walking down the hallway, I sighed, still unsure how to bring the situation up to her. But I needed answers. I met her at the door.

She greeted me with a question. "Nadia, what's going on? Ce s-a întamplat?" Concern was etched into her face. I hugged her tightly; just hearing her voice eased my nerves. I stepped back.

"Nothing's wrong, per se. I just haven't been feeling like myself lately. I thought I'd meditate to get some answers and—" I paused. "Mamă, who's Antanasia?" Her eyes widened in complete shock.

"You had a Vision of Antanasia?" I couldn't place the emotion in her voice, and that made me nervous.

"Yeah. Who is she? Why didn't you tell me I was named after her?" Mamă looked down and shook her head.

"No," she whispered, "You can't." Then she looked at me, her voice rising in fear. "You can't have her! Leave her alone!" she yelled, grabbing my shoulders tightly and shaking me.

"Ow! Let go!" I broke away from her. "What the hell is wrong with you?!" I'd thought I was going crazy, but maybe

I wasn't the only one. She looked away from me.

"I had hoped," she started, "I had hoped that the necklace would save you..."

"What are you talking about?"

She sighed deeply and answered my question with one of her own. "What did you mean when you said you weren't feeling well?" I eyed her suspiciously before responding.

"I..." I paused. I wasn't sure how to describe my symptoms without sounding crazy. I tried again, "I thought I had food poisoning or something because my stomach hurt so badly, I had a splitting headache, and I—I blacked out last night," I admitted. Mamă sucked in her breath, looking stricken. I started picking at my fingernail. "I think I know what's happening, but it's too unreal for me to say it aloud."

"No, no. My poor fiică." She gazed downward. "I'm so sorry," she said in a hushed voice. I stepped towards her, growing concerned.

"Mamă, what's going on?" She took a deep breath.

"Let's sit down." *Uh oh. That's never a good sign.*

I hesitated before following her to the couch. Once we were settled, she turned to me and grabbed my hand. She glanced at the ring, but didn't comment.

"We never got to finish our conversation yesterday," she began slowly. She opened and closed her mouth a few times. I was witnessing something I had never seen before: Mamă was speechless.

"Mamă, what is it?"

"I just don't know where to start..."

"What are you talking about? Just start where you left off yesterday." I wracked my brain, trying to remember the last thing she told me. "You were starting to tell me about the Order," I reminded her.

She shook her head. "There's no time to continue from there. The bottom line is—" she stopped and sighed, running her hand through her hair. "I've been trying to prepare for this conversation for the past nineteen years. When nothing happened on your eighteenth birthday, I had just hoped...I was giving you the necklace as a precaution, but then I saw your golden-amber eyes and the door handle..."

I furrowed my brows and blinked a few times. "I'm sorry," I said abruptly. "You've been trying to *prepare*?"

"Well, I knew there was a chance that—" I cut her off.

"Wait, you knew?"

Mamă hung her head. "Yes."

I blinked and looked at her like I was seeing her for the first time. "You knew and you didn't tell me?" I asked, my voice strained.

"Nadia, there's a lot to explain..."

"But you knew and you didn't tell me," I repeated, still trying to grasp that concept. "Why not?"

"I wanted to, but I didn't know how." I wouldn't hear any of it.

"Well, I don't know. How about sit me down and start explaining that I was going to Change!"

"It wasn't that simple..."

"I can't believe you knew and you didn't tell me!" I yelled incredulously, no longer sitting. She winced at my tone. My disbelief quickly turned to anger.

"Fiică, I tried—" she attempted again, but I spoke over her, pacing.

"This *crazy* shit's been happening to me! I've been hearing voices and smelling *everything*! At first I thought I was losing my mind, but then today I realized I was experiencing an Awakening." I paused, and my voice softened. "Though I'm not sure how," I said to myself. Then I rounded on her. "I can't believe you knew! You've been lying to me my whole life!" I felt like I had been slapped in the face. She stood up, reaching for me, but I pulled away.

"I was trying to protect you," she said in a small voice.

"*Protect* me? You don't think becoming Strigoi is something I would need to know? Did it just *skip* your mind for nineteen years?!"

She looked away, ashamed. "It's complicated."

I held my hand up and shook my head. "Stop. Just stop it," I sneered at her. I felt so betrayed that I was at a loss for words. Grabbing my phone, I headed to the door. "I have to get out of here," I announced.

She followed me. "Aștepta, wait! Nadia! Undete duci?"

Without facing her, I said, "Away from you."

She stopped. I knew my comment stung, but I was too hurt and upset to care about her feelings. I slammed the front door behind me and stomped down the hallway, down the stairs and out to the street. I headed towards the subway, unsure of my destination, fueled by my anger. Hopping on the R train, I rode it a few stops before getting off. I stormed down the block, still fuming, lost in thought. The farther I walked the more trash I saw. Eventually, I found myself in front of Petey's, a shady billiards hall located in a seedy area of the East Village.

Anyone with their wits about them avoided it at all costs. *Guess today, that's not me.* Arguing with Mamă had left me so frustrated; I just wanted to take my mind off of it. My stomach growled painfully and I screwed my eyes shut. *Fuck!* I lightly pressed my fingers against my temples. From the outside, I could hear the heartbeats and thoughts of the patrons inside. I headed in, still unsure of what I was doing here, wrinkling my nose at the smell of stale cigars and old booze. There were only a handful of people, for which I was thankful. Most of them didn't pay me any attention. However, I didn't go completely unnoticed.

Damn! Look at that ass, thought one person.

I would love to get into THAT, thought another.

I rolled my eyes and tried to shut out the thoughts; I wanted my mind clear. It was difficult though; someone had a very strong opinion of me. The bartender gave me an appreciative once-over as I sat down on the stool. He finished wiping the counter with a filthy rag, then walked over to me.

"What can I get for you?"

"Bud," I responded without hesitation. He didn't move right away and I could tell he was deciding whether or not to card me. He thought better of it and gave me a curt nod before shuffling away to fill my order. Now that I was left alone, my psyche was bombarded with questions.

Why would Mamă keep that from me? What is she trying to protect me from? Who was she yelling at when I told her about Antanasia? Who is Antanasia? How do I control my hunger? Do I need to find a donor? I made a face at the thought. My beer made a *clunk* on the bar, bringing me back from my contemplations. I started to pass the bartender a few bucks when he shook his head.

"Compliments of the gentleman over there." He motioned to a guy standing near the pool table. He was much older, I guessed in his thirties—cleanly shaven, of average height and build with piercing blue eyes. But I doubted he was a "gentleman," if his thoughts were any indication. I suppressed a shudder and weakly smiled at him. He was twirling his cue, eyeing me suggestively. I held my beer up to him in thanks, and turned back towards the bar. I took a long swig and placed the beer onto the bar top, hiding my distaste as my admirer came to sit next to me. I turned to acknowledge him.

"Thanks again," I smiled. He held up his glass in a toast.

"You're more than welcome, sexy." I clunked my beer against his glass and took a sip. He watched my every move. I could smell his arousal, and I made a face as the new scent tickled my nose. "Not a beer drinker, honey?" he asked, inching closer to me. I wanted to move away, but I stayed by his side. My stomach growled again and he tilted his head, expression unreadable.

"Oh, beer is fine with me," I responded. "But I may need something stronger." It was a true statement; I had chugged most of my beer and wasn't feeling anything.

"I think that can be arranged." He nodded at the bartender and then looked back at me. "Come play a few games with me," he offered

"Why not." I followed him to the pool table. While I was picking out my cue, he went to retrieve my drink.

"Now, here's a big girl drink," he said, handing me the glass. I thanked him and took a sip, almost gagging at how strong it was. There was another taste underneath the alcohol, but I couldn't place it. He laughed at my expression. "Too strong?"

"Whoa—it's definitely up there." He laughed again, and then started setting up the game. We played a few rounds, and I surprised myself by making some decent shots. My admirer, whose name was Barry, watched me like a hawk. It was slightly unnerving, but I didn't think about it too much. My appetite was increasing to dangerous levels. I noticed that I was having a hard time reading Barry's thoughts and that my head was getting foggy, which I credited to my drinks finally kicking in.

I leaned into him, mumbling that I had to go to the bathroom. He nodded and told me not to keep him waiting long. As I made my way towards the bathroom, I saw the bartender giving me a sympathetic look. I couldn't tell what he was thinking, and I realized I couldn't smell the bar anymore either. *What's going on? My senses get stronger when I'm hungry, not weaker.*

The bathroom was single occupancy. After knocking, I walked in and took a deep breath. Looking in the mirror, I saw that my eyes were completely red now. It hit me then that my eyes turned red when I was really hungry. *Uh oh.*

What if Barry noticed? I was wondering how I wasn't attacking every living being in sight when a light knock sounded on the door.

"Just a minute," I said to the person on the other side.

"I came to check on you," Barry explained through the door. I rolled my eyes.

"Aww. How sweet of you." I opened the door and he gave me a hard smile.

"May I come in?"

I hesitated slightly; something felt wrong, but my mind seemed to be having trouble connecting thoughts. "I was just about done," I began. He stepped closer to me, closing the door behind him.

"But I insist." His eyes flashed black so fast I thought I had imagined it. Before I could react, Barry had me against the wall with his hand around my throat. Surprised, I scratched at his hand, trying not to panic. *Oh no! What's happening?*

"Who are you?" he hissed, fangs bared. He increased the pressure on my throat before loosening his grip for me to answer.

"Let go." My voice came out garbled. He tightened his grip again and brought his face close to mine, glowering at me.

"Who. Are. You," he repeated. Then he tossed me on the ground. My head banged against the wall, sending a sharp pain through my skull. Stars danced in front of my eyes. I stood up quickly, ready to defend myself. *Holy shit!*

I was terrified about being confronted by another Vampyre, and even more so at the fact that I wasn't able to sense him. I thought back to the fogginess and then it clicked: he'd drugged me. *What am I going to do? Does he know that I'm a Vampyre too? How many of them exist?*

"My glamour failed, which it never does," he said as we

started circling around each other. "You drink more than the average woman. You have a heartbeat and yet your eyes are red. Who are you?" I stopped circling, immediately annoyed, and crossed my arms over my chest.

"Who are *you*?" I shot back stubbornly. "Besides a disgusting piece of shit." His eyes narrowed. The thoughts I'd heard before I was drugged made sense to me now. "You take advantage of women by getting them drunk or drugging them. If that fails, you glamour them?" I smirked. "Well, I guess your personality leaves much to be desired. No wonder women don't want you."He snarled and lunged at me. I dodged his attack and he crashed into the wall, breaking several tiles. He turned around quickly, his eyes black. "Uh oh. Did I go too far?" I asked.

He rushed at me again. I reacted a second too late and his fist sank into my gut. It carried enough strength to cause serious damage, and had I been merely human, I would have needed immediate medical attention. As it stood, I crumpled to the ground with the wind knocked out of me. I recovered fast enough to block the kick aimed at my face. I grabbed his foot and pushed his leg up toward his head with all my strength. Barry flipped over himself, crashing onto the floor. We stood up quickly and faced off.

By now, I was ravenous. Adrenaline coursed through my veins. I passed the mirror as we circled each other again. My eyes were black and my fangs were visible. My mind was getting fuzzy—it felt different than the drugs, like I was inside my body but not in control of my actions. My vision dimmed and then cleared. I started speaking in Romanian in a voice that didn't belong to me, but I could understand most of what I was saying. Before Barry could blink, I charged into him, and we collided into the wall once more. I put my hands on either side of his head.

"Te simti durere." *You feel pain.* My hands grew warm and bright. I sent the energy into Barry, who made an ear-piercing scream. He clawed at my hands, scratching them up, but I felt nothing. He fell onto his knees and I followed, still grasping his head.

"Stop! Please," he begged.

My stomach tensed up and I seized his neck with my fangs, ripping a chunk out. He shrieked and dropped like a rag doll. His blood burned my mouth, and I started screaming too. Barry's eyes bugged out and his hand flew to the gaping hole in his neck. Blood was seeping through his fingers as he crawled as far away from me as he could in the tiny bathroom. Considering the damage we had done, there really wasn't anywhere for him to hide. There was a violent knock on the door.

"Hey!" yelled the person on the other side.

We stopped screaming, realizing the attention we were drawing, we glanced at the door as another knock sounded. Barry was gasping. His shirt was stained with blood, as was mine. The handle turned forcefully.

"What's going on in there? Open up!" The person threw himself against the door. Barry and I frantically looked around for a method of escape, but there was none. The door came crashing in, landing on the floor with the bartender on top. The room was small enough when it was just Barry and me. Now with a third person, there was barely enough space to breathe. A few patrons took a peek inside the bathroom. New screams filled the air as they ran away from the scene: two monsters covered in blood.

"Barry," the bartender said, getting up and dusting himself off. "What the hell—" he stopped. Barry and I stared back at him, eyes black and fangs bared. Barry's throat was completely healed and the blood had started drying. I was panting and famished.

"What...what," the bartender stuttered, looking between Barry and me. His facial expression would have been comical if the situation were different. As it stood, I needed to get out of there. Barry made the decision for me. He scowled at me and hissed before he ran out of the bathroom. I heard people screaming and stools being flipped over as the remaining customers tried to get away. I narrowed my eyes at the bartender with my nostrils flared.

"Lebada Neagra." *Black Swan.* Once again, the voice that spoke didn't belong to me, and I remained trapped inside my body. "Permiteți acest comportament în unitate dumneavoastră?" *You allow this behavior in your establishment?* I growled, and he stumbled back towards the wall, tripping over debris. I slowly walked closer to him.

"I...I," he sputtered. I closed the gap between us and curled my lip at him.

"Esti patetic," I spat.

I took a deep breath and inhaled his scent. My stomach tightened but I ignored the pain. I gave him a sly smile, further exposing my fangs, then snarled and quickly sunk my teeth into the bartender's soft flesh. He tried to fight me off, but his attempts were feeble compared to my Vampyre strength. I closed my eyes, savoring the taste of his blood. I pulled and pulled, his blood flowing freely into my mouth and melting away my hunger.

He was a Black Swan, a human who was friendly and familiar with Vampyres; I remembered reading about them. At least he wasn't a Fledgling—Vampyre in training. They don't fully Turn until they've fed at least once. I was disgusted that he would enable Barry's sick habits in hopes of one day becoming a Vampyre. I was so irritated at this prospect and at Barry's escape that I wanted to drain the bartender. But I could almost feel the tap on my shoulder telling me to stop.

I eased up and wrinkled my nose at the smell of urine coming from him. I glanced at his pants and saw dampness running down his leg. The bartender was frightened and trembling. I released my hold on him and he slumped to the ground. Stooping so that we were face to face, I saw tears forming in his eyes. I pitied him. Almost.

I bit my thumb and wiped my blood over his neck wounds, which healed instantly. Looking past his irises until I was in his mind, I removed the image of me. But I didn't want to erase the whole scene entirely. I wanted him to be reminded of what could happen if he didn't change his ways. There was a seed of doubt already planted in his mind about his aiding Barry. I fed that seed until it blossomed into overwhelming guilt. It was so much that he needed to confess in order to sleep peacefully tonight.

The fuzziness evaporated and my mind cleared—I was no longer a prisoner inside my own body. I stood up and made my way to the sink to wash the blood off of my face and hands. Looking in the mirror, I noted that my eyes had returned to their golden-amber color. I was shaking violently, the contents of my stomach threatening to come up. *What is happening to me?* *Zeită, I was almost assaulted...again. How was I able to defend myself?* I glanced at the bartender. He was sobbing as he shakily took out his phone to call 911.

I rushed out of the bathroom into the now-deserted bar. I picked up a jacket that had been left behind and put it on, zipping it completely. Even in Manhattan, the amount of blood I was wearing would raise eyebrows. I walked briskly to the subway. My senses prickled and I stopped before walking down the stairs; someone was watching me. I glanced over my shoulder, but didn't see anything. I frowned and quickly thudded down the stairs just in time for the train.

CHAPTER NINE

SĂTIC, WALLACHIA 1480

The sky was growing brighter as a new day approached, and Nic and I took our time in heading back to join the others. Now that I had come to my senses and was no longer vulnerable, there was no rush for us to return. We walked down a path through the woods, just outside of Sătic—only a day's journey from where Mihnea sat on the throne in Târgovişte. I sighed and gripped Nic's hand tightly. I wanted nothing more than to run to Târgovişte and end this war for good, but I resisted.

Nic looked at me with concern. "What ails you?" he asked.

"I am just frustrated. To be so close and yet refrain from heading towards Mihnea...it is challenging."

He rubbed his thumb across the back of my hand. "Worry not—I am here to remind you to stay on task."

And to that, I smiled. *Aye, you are.* He surprised me by sweeping me into his arms and planting a kiss on my lips. His tongue danced with mine, and I was breathless once our lips parted. As he released me, I felt flushed. I had to take several breaths before I could speak.

"You must behave."

He eyed me wickedly, moving closer. "Why must I?"

I pushed him away but there was no force behind my action. "I have been delayed long enough."

"But my eyes have not laid upon your beauty in days."

"Jeniviva is waiting for me..."

"Jeniviva is under the care of my father and the other elders," he responded swiftly. Nic tugged on my arm and I bit the inside of my lip to stop myself from giggling.

"Nic, go away."

"I will do no such thing." He wrapped his arms around me and spun me in a circle. I threw my head back and laughed heartily, feeling as free as a child.

"Put me down! That's an order!"

But I loved every moment of this. It was the first time in days that I had not a care in the world. It was just me having fun with my beloved, and I didn't want it to ever end. He stopped spinning and looked at me with his eyebrow raised.

"An order, you say?"

"Aye."

"As you wish, my lady." He put me down and started walking away. I exhaled and rubbed my abdomen; it was cramping from all the laughing. I tried to step forward, but Nic rushed back and held me against a tree. Bark pressed into my back. He gave me a mischievous smile. "I take no orders from you. Did you actually think I would listen?"

I wrapped my arms around his neck and ran my tongue across his bottom lip. "I had hoped not."

Nic growled and kissed me with an urgency that I eagerly returned. The love I felt for him was beyond my comprehension, and we shared these feelings through our deep connection. I let out a contented sigh as his kisses ventured beyond my lips. Nic didn't get very far before I felt my senses tingling, and he lifted his head to look over his shoulder.

Someone approaches, I thought to him. I was instantly on guard—the way things had turned out lately had taught me to always be prepared. This new person was close but still hadn't appeared in our field of view. We stepped away from the tree and listened intently. I relaxed when a breeze flew by carrying a familiar scent—and then I grew confused. *What is he doing here?* Nic raised his eyebrow, but didn't stop me when I walked towards the path. I could see Cristian atop his horse, Aurel, wearing bright green trousers and heading towards us around the bend.

Nic appeared behind me. "Is that your Swan?"

"It is."

"The way you spoke of him, I always thought he was a woman."

I grinned. "He might as well be, but there is no cause for concern, my love. He is rather fond of *you*."

He cocked his head to the side. "Of me?"

"Oh, very much so."

"How? We have yet to meet."

"Some time ago, he laid eyes upon you, and hasn't forgotten the sight."

I was interested to see how this interaction would play out. *I am expecting it will be quite humorous.* As Cristian rode closer, he finally noticed us and waved cheerfully.

"Greetings, Princess!"

He navigated his horse to the side of the path and stopped next to us. As he glanced at Nic, his cheeks flushed. I snorted and approached his horse, rubbing his muzzle as Cristian jumped to the ground. I gave him a hug and kissed his cheek before turning towards Nic.

"Nic, this is Cristian. Cristian, meet Nic."

"Pleasure," said Nic, and held out his hand.

Cristian gulped audibly and shook it, still unable to speak. Nic guffawed and I smirked as Cristian smiled nervously. I could understand his behavior—Nic was a sight to behold, with his raggedy brown hair and smile that lit up my world; it was easy for him to stun the humans. However, I was not used to seeing Cristian so timid, and it was entertaining to watch. He cleared his throat.

"The pleasure is mine." With that one sentence, he

seemed to revert back into his old self. "Forgive me, I don't encounter many Vampyres and have yet to meet others of my kind who possess such elegance."

I snorted. "Don't build him up."

"I rather like this Swan of yours," Nic commented.

I rolled my eyes and ignored him. "What brings you this way?" I asked Cristian.

His cheerful mood evaporated and he looked at me with somber eyes. "Papa is at peace now. I am traveling to Câmpulung to inform others in our family and invite some to return with me to help in the shop. It is a difficult time, but I must remain strong to support Mama and Adelina."

I grew alert. "I don't understand—we just spoke days ago and he seemed in good health."

"Aye, we thought so too..."

"What happened?"

"I am uncertain. He seemed to grow weak the last several days, and needed me to work more. Upon sunrise yesterday he did not wake. Myself and others in our village built a pyre, and we bid him farewell at midday."

I thought back to when I'd last seen Dragoş and how he gifted me with the peasant knife. *He knew of his impending death, mayhap?*

"And how does your mother and Adelina?" I asked.

"I worry for Mama; she and Papa have known each other since they were babes—his death has put a hole in her heart. Our neighbor is caring for her until my return. Adelina has shown great strength, though I fear she has not properly grieved."

Nic placed his hand on Cristian's shoulder. "We will aid you in any way we can."

He nodded in thanks and I threw my arms around him in another hug. News of Dragoş passing only rekindled the sadness I felt for Mother. My eyes watered and I sniffled, but I refused to let the tears fall. I finally released Cristian and he furrowed his brows, concerned.

"What ails you, Princess?"

I inhaled deeply. "I understand your loss."

Nic explained what I could not—how Mother came to her demise, and the destruction of our village. Cristian grew angry.

"First the child's village and now yours! We have to attack!" I smiled at his use of the word 'we'. Though I admired his spirit and was grateful that he wanted to help on our quest, I would never allow him to put himself in danger without proper training.

"I shared those exact sentiments, which is how I came to be in Sătic. But Nic and the Keeper are right—we should plan appropriately before making our move." I looked at Nic and he smiled encouragingly. Cristian nodded, but said nothing. I rubbed his cheek and smiled at him. "I appreciate your concern, but come. Let's go to your family—Nic and I will accompany you on your journey."

"Shouldn't you be returning to the others?"

"There is time enough for this," I replied, and looked at Nic for confirmation. He nodded in agreement.

Cristian grinned and said, "That is most appreciated." Then he furrowed his brows at me. "But I am the only one with a horse, and must make haste."

"I understand."

"Then, would I not arrive before you?"

Nic and I both laughed. "My dear friend! Do not underestimate our speed! We may arrive before you."

Cristian looked doubtful. "We shall see. Let's make a friendly wager?"

"You're on!" Nic jumped in. "Ten thalers to the victor."

"Agreed," Cristian said, and they shook hands.

Once again, I rolled my eyes. *Men.* "But first, we must feed," I said.

Cristian's eyes widened and I could sense his apprehension. I took his hand in mine and squeezed it reassuringly. "Worry not. Surely, you don't think we would *both* take from you? We will feed from another, or a creature." He sighed and instantly relaxed. "Unless," I added, eyeballing Nic, "you would like *one* of us to feed from you?" I winked as Cristian reddened and shook his head vigorously. "Very well. Off you go, and *should* you reach Câmpulung before us, we will see you upon our arrival."

Cristian mounted his horse and bid us safe travels before taking off down the path and out of sight. I turned towards Nic and found him staring at me.

"What is it?"

A breeze flew in between us and he closed his eyes as it ruffled his hair. Then he took my hand and kissed the back before focusing his hazel eyes on me. "You are a sight to behold."

I smiled sweetly and said, "As are you. Come, my love, let us feed so that we can aid Cristian."

"Aye, so that we are triumphant in our wager."

"*Your* wager." And to that, he laughed.

We made our way through the trees, in search of whatever creatures lurked in the woods. Now that I was physically able, I preferred to feed off of animals if I could. It wasn't long before we spotted a brown bear near the river foraging for food. We remained out of sight until we were sure it was alone—having to battle more than one would be quite a task.

We watched it for several minutes, monitoring its behavior and communicating telepathically, deciding the best way to attack. Its size led me to believe it was male, and he was more than enough for the both of us to be satiated without killing him. I slowly walked towards the water, intentionally making some noise to alert the bear of my presence; I didn't want it to be completely alarmed which would make it more defensive.

The bear caught sight of me as I approached. He stood on its hind legs, several heads above me, and sniffed the air. I maintained some distance, but heard him growl the closer I got to the water. I stopped walking and remained still—we both watched each other, uncertain of what the other would do. The bear growled again and began swinging its arms wildly. I caught sight of Nic on its back, with his fangs lodged into the bear. He was dodging the bear's arms as the animal attempted to remove him from his back.

Now distracted by Nic, the bear didn't notice me charging towards him. I delivered a swift and powerful kick just below his jaw line. The bear groaned loudly and fell to the ground, dazed. He attempted to stand and I quickly gazed into his eyes, telling him to relax. At once, the bear stopped moving and lay there in a dreamy state.

Having fed slightly when he first attacked, Nic smiled at me and watched as I bit into the bear's neck. He had an earthy taste, and when I closed my eyes, I could picture his travels through the woods and see him feasting on berries. I opened my eyes and saw Nic drinking just a little more. I took several deep gulps before I felt satiated. After we were done, we left the bear resting near the water. By the time he returned into himself, we would be gone.

Nic and I raced through the trees, hunting each other and making a sport out of it. Having just fed, I felt revived and free. As we neared Câmpulung, we still saw no trace of a horse and rider. I heard a horse snort and turned to see Cristian riding in shortly after.

Nic approached him as he dismounted his horse. "It appears that we have arrived before you." He smirked.

"Only just," Cristian responded.

I shook my head at the both of them. "I will settle this—it was a tie."

"I can live with that," Cristian said.

"But—" Nic started.

"Hush now, love." I smiled and turned to Cristian. "What will you have us do?"

He bowed his head. "You are too kind, Princess. I am going to fetch Aurel a bucket of water and then make my way to Sorina—my nana. Prithee feel free to join me."

And with that, Nic and I followed Cristian and Aurel a short distance to the stables, where there were quite a few beautiful horses resting. While he retrieved fresh water and food, I walked around giving attention to the others. I suddenly missed my Fyuree and was impatient to return to her. *I hope Jeniviva has been caring for her as well as she deserves...*

Soon, Cristian was ready to go to his nana's. I was somewhat nervous: what if I was recognized for what I truly was? In wanting to help my friend, the thought hadn't occurred to me until now. Only certain villages knew of my identity, and it was imperative that it remain that way until the time was right.

There is no cause for worry, love. Our mission is widespread; you have more allies than you believe you do.

Nic's reassurance put my mind at ease, and I felt more confident by the time we reached Sorina's home. But that quickly faded once I laid eyes on her. She lived alone in the house—a stern, dumpy woman with grizzled hair and eyes that seemed to look right through me. Her gaze made my skin erupt in goose bumps. She was silent for most of the encounter, but her gaze spoke volumes. She looked at me like I was the vilest person she had ever seen. I was not easily alarmed, but I couldn't wait to escape her presence. Cristian and the others in his immediate family were the complete opposite of this woman—there was no way they could possibly share the same blood. *Then again, look at me and my father...*

Sorina had a tapestry hanging on the wall with a familiar cross and dragon embroidered into it. She also had several candelabras around the room, made out of precious metals and encrusted with rubies—something commonly seen in royal households. They had to be gifts, but from whom? My eyes traveled back to the tapestry. I shot Nic a nervous glance, and his eyes told me that he was thinking the same: mayhap there were no allies here? I knew deep in my soul that Cristian had no ties with the Order, but was it possible that his kin did?

"Nana," Cristian began, "I'm afraid I have terrible news." He took a deep breath and I took his hand in mine. Sorina saw this and narrowed her eyes. "Papa is gone." Cristian's voice trembled, and I squeezed his hand as tears ran down his cheeks.

Sorina was silent at first. "Is he now." I glanced at Cristian, and Sorina sighed. "I guess I will have to inform Alin," she said, referring to her youngest son.

She said nothing as she walked past us, and I frowned. We took our leave, and I felt much better as soon as I stepped out of her house. I was concerned for Cristian—I had never encountered a mother who lacked sympathy for such a loss. Nic placed his hand on Cristian's shoulder and I wiped away his tears. He gave me a weak smile, then sighed.

"Let me show you around," he offered, and we followed him. "I grew up here before we relocated to Chilia many years ago."

"What was the reason for moving?"

"To put as much distance between us and the mad king as possible. But Nana refused to move; she has been here since she was a babe. It upset her that Papa left and they haven't had much communication since then."

That could explain her lack of emotion when hearing of his death. Even still, I couldn't imagine not wanting to be involved in my son's life—if I had one.

"I have tried many times to help mend their relationship," Cristian continued, "but Nana felt that Papa was being disloyal. I am only here out of respect."

"That is unfortunate. Family needs to stick together; sometimes, that is all you have."

He merely shrugged. "So, care to see the village?"

I held out my hand. "After you."

We followed Cristian through the village until we arrived at a small grammar school. I smiled as a group of younglings ran by, chasing each other and laughing merrily. After experiencing such loss, it was pleasing to witness such life as this village held. I soaked up their energy like a sponge in water, and any doubts I had were removed. Nic took my hand and I found him smiling as well.

"This is where my studies were held," Christian said.

"It is lovely," I said, still watching the kids.

"Easy for you to say, you did not learn here." I laughed at his remark and he smirked. "There isn't much else, besides other dwellings. Perhaps we should go to the market? I am starting to get an appetite. I am uncertain of how much time my nana and uncle will need."

"Prithee do—I am anxious to see the rest of this village where you were raised." We passed several houses and a large cathedral before we found ourselves in the open area of the market square near the center of town.

"I wonder if he is still here," Cristian whispered to himself. "Ah, yes, over here. Theo bakes the best rolls in the region," Cristian said gleefully as he led us to a booth containing a variety of baked goods. A little boy ran past, and I smiled before closing my eyes and inhaling deeply; the smell emanating from the baker's stall made my mouth water, and I walked ahead of Cristian to get a better look at what the vendor had to offer. Cristian soon stood beside me on my left with Nic on my right.

"This smells heavenly," I commented.

"Aye, my lady," the vendor said, "I guarantee you have yet to taste bread such as mine." He took a small piece from the nearest roll and handed it to me to sample. "This is made with honey that I have cultivated on my own land."

I took the bread and smiled, bowing my head in thanks On placing the bread in my mouth, I was consumed by the sweetness of honey. The bread itself was light and had a slight crunch, and I could somewhat taste the yeast. The flavor had me yearning for more.

"That is indeed very delicious. I may have to bring some back with us."

"It is like I said!" Cristian said.

"Care to try a piece, sir?" The vendor asked Nic.

"Aye, thank you."

Nic gave thanks as the vendor handed him a sample. He chewed it slowly, savoring the flavor, and I could tell he was as pleased with it as I had been. It was then I noticed how quiet he was. While Cristian gathered his bread, I pulled Nic to the side and tapped into our connection. *Why so silent?*

He frowned and looked around suspiciously. *I feel that something is not right.*

I hadn't felt anything since leaving Sorina's, but I had allowed myself to become distracted by my surroundings. I tried to shut out the bustle of the village, and opened myself to that something more. *There!* Underneath the sounds of the lively village, I could sense another's tenacity—it was impossible to ignore, though I couldn't place where it was coming from. It grew stronger and immediately I was alert. I scanned my surroundings, but could find nothing unusual. Cristian turned to us with a basket of various breads.

"Are you not getting anything?" he asked us.

"Aye." Nic shuffled back to the vendor. I remained where I was, eyes peeled for the slightest threat.

"Princess?" My eyes flashed to Cristian. "What is it?"

"I am uncertain, but I feel that we must leave soon."

"You are free to leave any time you wish," he replied. "I will be fine on my journey back to Chilia."

I looked deeply into his eyes and said, "I cannot leave you; I think it is best for you to come with us."

Cristian opened his mouth to respond when a shout made us look across the square at another booth. A female vendor was chastising a youngling who had attempted to steal an apple from her fruit stand. She waved an angry fist at him, and then returned the fruit to the pile with the others. Terror seized me as someone roughly bumped into me. I turned around to face Cristian just as the bread fell from his hands and he slumped to the ground.

"Cristian!"

I fell to my knees and gathered him in my arms. His breathing was labored, and I felt the warmth of his blood seeping into my gown. Nic appeared by my side almost instantly.

"What happened?"

"I know not! Oh, Cristian, Cristian!"

I looked at Nic, horrified. I had no choice but to expose myself to save him—there was no way I could allow my dearest friend to die. I returned my gaze to Cristian. Even as I worried what to do, I could sense him slipping away. He raised his hand towards my face and tried to speak, but all that came out was blood. As I was about to bite into my wrist, I felt Nic's firm grip on my arm, stopping me.

I glanced at him with a mixture of anger and confusion, but his eyes were not on me. I followed his gaze and fear gripped me. The villagers in the square had us surrounded and were staring at us with loathing, even the younglings. My breathing quickened, and I looked back at Cristian, whose eyes were slowly closing.

"Nic," I said, voice wavering, "I have to save him."

"It would be of no use, child." I lifted my head towards the voice and my eyes met Sorina's. "It is a special toxin of my own making—your blood will affect it not. I give thanks to Nai, whose swift movements made him undetectable, just as they did in Chilia."

A little boy stepped out of the shadows, twirling a blade and grinning maliciously. I instantly recognized him as the one who'd run past while we were buying bread. I gasped as his appearance changed and he stood before us a grown man. *A Shifter!* Shifting was a rare Gift for a Vampyre; I only had knowledge of four in existence, including this new one. I held Cristian tighter, feeling the last of his life slipping away, and I went hollow inside.

I took a deep breath and regarded his nana. "Why?" I shook my head, holding back tears. "Why would you do this to your own grandson?"

She laughed shrilly. "He was no grandson of mine—a traitor, perhaps, just like his papa—but no grandson. His mother and sister would have met the same fate had they been home that glorious day."

"I don't understand."

She stepped closer, looking down at me with hostility in her eyes. "His papa moved them because he refused to join the Order and see it for the great organization that it is. If he were to ever come back, it would be the last thing he did."

I furrowed my brows and looked down at Cristian's body, puzzled. *Cristian wouldn't have returned if he had knowledge of this, would he?*

"He had no knowledge of this, of course," she continued, answering my unspoken question. "It is unfortunate, really. If his papa wasn't such a coward, this might not have happened." She stopped for a moment, thinking. "Or mayhap it would have, as he was engaging with the enemy all on his own, letting you feed from him," she finished, disgusted.

I gave Cristian one last look, mentally asking the Gods to

watch over his soul. Then I rose to my full height to face her, with Nic close by my side. The anger that I'd tucked away earlier now came back full force, my necklace heating against my chest as I growled. I could feel Nic tensing, preparing for a fight.

Once again Sorina laughed. "You dare think you can defeat all of us, Princess?"

My eyes went from one face to the next, assessing each one's strength; we were badly outnumbered. Distracted by Cristian's death, I hadn't realized that they were closing in on us. *What are we to do?* I asked Nic.

Take out as many as we can, he answered simply.

I smirked and felt my eyes darken, nodding in agreement before addressing Sorina. "I never turn down a challenge."

CHAPTER TEN

NEW YORK, NEW YORK 2015

Although I felt rejuvenated, my mind was unsettled. Being upset at Mamă took a lot of energy, and yet I couldn't let it go. She *lied* to me. To make matters worse, I was scared of what had happened to me at the bar. If *whatever* it was hadn't taken over my body and helped me fight, Barry could have killed me. And what had that mysterious presence been, anyway? Nothing made sense to me anymore, and I had nowhere to get answers.

Before I could figure anything else out, I had to get cleaned up. As I walked down the hallway, everything that had happened whirled around in my mind. It was almost comical how nineteen, which isn't as significant as eighteen or twenty-one, had gone from pointless to overly eventful. When I reached the door, I was mindful to turn the handle gently so I didn't yank it out this time. I went to my room and stripped down before running to my shower; I couldn't wait to remove the stench of blood and sweat. As I rinsed the soap off, I visualized all the negativity and confusion washing away as well.

Drying off, I noticed how smooth and clear my skin looked; there wasn't a blemish in sight, and the scars from my childhood adventures were gone. I wondered if I would stay like this or continue to age like I had been. *Ugh. More questions.*

My jeans were crumpled on the floor. I pulled out my phone from the pants pocket, surprised the device had survived the battle. I saw there were a few missed calls from Mamă. My phone started ringing—she was calling again, but I sent her to voicemail. I wasn't ready to speak to her just yet. What I needed was some normalcy. It was a little after eight and I had work the next day, but my brain was too wired for sleep. I decided to call Vi and see what she was up to.

"Hey, honey, how are you feeling?" she answered.

"Ehh, I'm alright. I got into an argument with Mamă earlier."

"Seriously? About what?"

I sighed. "It's a long story and I really don't want to get into it right now. She keeps calling, but I can't bring myself to talk to her right now."

"I know you're mad, but give her a chance. I'm sure she has a good explanation for whatever it is she did."

"Yeah, I guess. I really just want to get out of here and forget about it for a while." I stopped, thinking. "Let's go somewhere, to make up for yesterday."

"What do you have in mind?"

"I'm thinking we see *Last Man*. I've been meaning to see that movie for a while."

"I'm down. Want to grab a bite, too?"

I laughed. "No thanks; I already ate."

"Alright. Well, I'm going to get something real quick. Meet me at my aunt's place."

"Sounds good."

"How are you getting here?"

"I'll drive to save time. The train takes too long, and I should *try* to get some sleep tonight."

"You could always call out tomorrow."

I looked at my phone in mock horror. "No way! The office would cease to exist without me there."

Vi laughed. "Fine, fine. Well, you can park in the garage,

but make sure you tell them you're there to see me. That way it's free."

"You got it." We agreed to meet at 9:30 and clicked off. That gave Vi time to eat and both of us time to get ready. I walked to my closet, still wrapped in my towel, and pulled out almost everything in it before I felt satisfied with my outfit. After throwing my hair into a messy bun and applying some mild makeup, I wrote a small note for Mamă, saying that I was with Vi and left it at that. I might be upset at her, but I didn't want her worrying about me. Then I grabbed the keys and headed to my car.

I blasted Red Hot Chili Peppers as I started up Tenth Ave towards the Upper West Side. I loved Vi's aunt's apartment; it was in a luxurious building and had floor-to-ceiling windows, allowing terrific views of the Hudson. If it weren't for the fact I had work the next day, I would be sleeping over there tonight. Luckily for me, traffic wasn't bad, so it only took me about thirty minutes to get there.

After parking my car, I walked back outside, deciding to wait for Vi there. I began feeling uneasy and looked over my shoulder, half expecting to see someone there. I wasn't trying to be paranoid, but I couldn't shake the feeling that someone was watching me.

Antanasia.

I swung around, *feeling* more than hearing my middle name. Turning my head to the right, I saw a familiar-looking man leaning against a wall across the street. He was about five-nine with shaggy brown hair. I furrowed my brows as it clicked where I'd seen him before: *He was on the corner of my street when Vi picked me up from Rian's apartment. Why is he following me?*

I locked eyes with him, and was immediately assaulted with Visions and memories that were not my own. I saw him in battle, fighting in armor, surrounded by fire; I saw him helping a little girl ride a horse; I saw him walking on a path with another woman at his side. There were so many images—too many to comprehend. As soon as they began, they stopped, and I hadn't realized I was walking towards him until I heard Vi's voice behind me.

"Nadia, where are you going?" My trance broken, I turned around to address Vi.

"Nowhere—just thought I saw something." I looked behind me, but the man was gone. *Where did he go?*

She shrugged, coming down the remaining stairs and looping her arm through mine. "I'm glad we're getting out."

"Me too." *You have no idea.*

"Just promise me one thing."

"Anything."

"No funny business," she ordered.

I laughed, saluting her. "Scout's honor."

She smiled at me. Although it was getting later, it was still a beautiful seventy-two degrees out, and the walk to Eighty-Fourth Street was enjoyable. My thoughts drifted towards the guy I'd just seen; I had a nagging feeling that I knew him from somewhere. I felt like I needed to speak with him, and that he could help me somehow. *Weird. Most importantly, what were those Visions I had? It felt like I'd been there before—beyond déjà vu.* I shook my head and shivered.

"Have you," Vi swallowed deeply. "Have you spoken to Rian?"

"Oh," I gave a small smile, blushing. "Yes, I have. Actually, we kind of hung out this afternoon."

"What?" She stopped walking. "How did that happen?"

"Well," I looped my arm through hers to keep her moving. "It was strange, really. I went to Best Buy and he just happened to be in the neighborhood."

She eyed me skeptically. "Rian doesn't 'just happen to be' anywhere."

"What's your issue with him? We had a really good time

today, and he was really sweet."

"I just don't trust him, okay?"

"Why not? Why won't you tell me how you know him?"

"Let's just drop it."

"Fine." I wasn't sure why Vi was acting like this, but I didn't feel like getting into an argument with her, either. Having one with Mamă was enough. We were almost at the theater and I decided to change the subject. "Since we're talking about guys, what's going on with Adrian?"

Just like that, Vi was off in lala land reminiscing about Adrian. When we arrived at the theater, I blanched at how expensive the tickets were. *This movie better be fucking fantastic at $15!*

I was pleasantly surprised that I had more control over all the thoughts that were swimming in the air; in fact, with a little concentration, I was able to block out all outside thoughts for a longer period of time. We made our way to the concession stand, getting in line behind a dark-haired woman. She turned around and I was surprised to see Jeni, our waitress from the day before. *What are the odds...*

She smiled sweetly and greeted us before asking how I was feeling. I felt like there was more to her innocent question than she was letting on.

"Better, thanks for asking. I think it was a stomach bug. I'm not one-hundred percent myself yet."

"You will be one-hundred percent soon. You have to let it run its course," she replied matter of factly.

"Yeah..." She gazed at me so intently that I grew uncomfortable and broke eye contact. There was something about her that I didn't understand, and it bothered me. Or maybe I did understand, and just didn't want to be honest with myself. Sensing my discomfort, Vi turned to Jeni.

"So what are you going to see?" Vi asked, covering for my awkwardness.

"*Life of An Assassin*," she said brightly. I recognized the title; it had just been released last week, and I'd been dying to see it. *Next time.* She didn't strike me as the type to watch something like that; she seemed too...delicate for a movie with such violence. *Goes to show you that appearances are often misleading.* I was about to ask if she was here alone when a guy came up to her side. *He's the one from earlier!*

"Hello," he greeted us politely. His voice was smooth and he had the same accent as Jeni.

"Nicolae," Jeni said, "This is—" she looked at Vi. It occurred to me that we had never introduced ourselves. *How embarrassing.*

"Viviana," she responded, gazing at Nicolae in awe. He *was* really attractive, with a boyish grin and riveting hazel eyes. He took her hand and politely kissed the back. Her face reddened and I rolled my eyes. *Give me a break.*

"Nice to meet you, Viviana." He shifted his hazel eyes to me. His gaze was so familiar, I felt like I was experiencing déjà vu. "And you are?" he asked.

"Nadia." Whoever this guy was, I refused to let him affect me like he had Vi. He took my hand in his to kiss it, but I shook it firmly, then let go. He grinned.

"Nadia, what a beautiful name. It means 'hope'."

"Yup," I agreed. I could feel Vi staring at me, wondering why I was being so standoffish. To be honest, I wasn't sure why, either. I was attracted to him—I'd be a liar to deny that, but it bothered me that I couldn't figure out how I knew him or what those Visions meant. A part of me wanted to ask him about it, but I thought better of it—this wasn't the time for such a conversation. *Then when?* His gaze lingered on me for a second longer before he turned back to Jeni.

"How do you all know each other?"

"We met at the restaurant Jeni works at," Vi answered quickly. She looked at Jeni and asked, "Is he your boyfriend?" I rolled my eyes again—leave it to Vi to get right to the point. Jeni and Nicolae glanced at each other before they burst out laughing. Vi giggled nervously, confused by their exchange, but I already knew the answer before Jeni responded.

"No, no," she said. "Nicolae is a good friend, actually more like family to me."

"Oh!" Vi's face reddened. "I'm sorry."

Nicolae looked at me again. "No need to apologize."

I avoided his gaze—the weight of it was starting to make me uncomfortable—and gently tugged on Vi's arm to get her attention.

"We should get seats," I suggested. She looked at me as if seeing me for the first time.

"Oh, yeah." She returned her gaze to Nicolae and said, "Nice meeting you. I hope you enjoy your movie. See you, Jeni." I simply smiled at Jeni and mumbled a goodbye to Nicolae.

Jeni smiled and said, "You too." Nicolae was looking at me, his expression unreadable. Vi and I made our way towards the theater.

Ne vom întalni din nou, a voice said in my head. *We will meet again.* I paused and turned around to look at Nicolae, wide-eyed; I knew it was his voice in my head. *How? I have my blocks up...*Both he and Jeni were staring at me intently. I quickly spun around and continued walking.

Who are they? What do they know? Maybe I was wrong and Nicolae *could* help me. We found a couple of seats near the back of the theater. The previews started as we sat down. Vi continued talking animatedly about Nicolae while I drifted off into my own thoughts. *How did he do that? How does he know me?* I let out a frustrated sigh—I needed some answers.

The movie sucked me into all the action, and provided me with a much-needed distraction from the craziness that my life had become. All too soon, it was over and I was brought back to reality. I found myself searching for Nicolae as Vi and I exited the theater. To my dismay, he was nowhere to be found. I frowned at the fact that I cared, his last statement echoing in my head: *We will meet again.* I wondered what he meant by that. I was convinced that he knew something about me.

Vi and I were discussing the movie as we started our walk back towards her aunt's apartment when I shivered and stopped walking—something wasn't right. Vi gave me a questioning glance.

"What is it?" she asked.

"I don't know," I answered, looking around. "I feel like we're being followed."

Vi began looking around too. "I don't see anyone."

I nodded; I didn't see anyone either, but I *knew* someone was there. Determined to find the source, I listened intently.

"Let's just go," Vi said, tugging on my arm. "You're scaring me."

She was on the verge of panicking, and her fear was an unpleasant smell. I didn't want her to freak out, so I let her pull me along. We only had a couple of more blocks to go before we reached her aunt's apartment building. My senses were on high alert, and I kept my eyes peeled and ears perked for anything unusual. I could see the building about three-hundred yards away. The energy I felt was stronger, and I knew that whoever was watching was very close. I looked over my shoulder, but still saw no one.

"Come on," Vi pleaded. "We're almost there." Just then a strong breeze whipped past us, carrying a musky scent. When it had passed, so did the sense of being watched. I furrowed my brows and looked at Vi.

"What was that?" she asked me.

"I was wondering the same thing."

Vi shuddered. "Let's get inside." I nodded in agreement. We rushed upstairs to the apartment, but it didn't make me feel better. The windows and open view that I usually appreciated made me feel exposed and vulnerable. I turned to Vi.

"Actually, I'm going to head home and attempt to get some sleep."

"Oh, yeah. No problem." She smiled and we embraced tightly. "Call me tomorrow?"

"Sure."

"And whatever it was that happened, try not to be so hard on your mom."

I sighed, nodding my head. "You're right. It's just...I've got a lot to think about."

"I'm sure. Well, if you need to talk about it, text me."

"Thank you," I said sincerely.

We hugged one last time before I took my leave. Pulling out of the garage onto the empty street, I was still uneasy, but I didn't feel the presence this time. I knew I wouldn't feel comfortable until I was in my own space. On the drive home, I listened to Les Nubians to ease my mind, but my thoughts were troubled. *Who is Barry? What are Jeni and Nicolae really up to? Who are they anyway? Who was following us?* All these thoughts were starting to give me a headache.

I shifted gears and instead wondered if Mamă would be awake when I got home, waiting to speak with me since I had been ignoring her all evening. But when I pulled into our garage, I could sense that she was in a deep sleep, and for that I was thankful. At this point, I was exhausted and didn't have much energy for discussing what had happened earlier. Nefi meowed at me, and I put food in her bowl before heading to my room to get dressed for bed. I looked at the clock on my bedside table. *Damn, it's almost one a.m.! I hope I can wake up for work.* To be safe, I set two additional alarms on my phone. After changing clothes, I brushed my teeth and crawled into bed. I was asleep before my head hit the pillow.

∞

Water splashes loudly as I run through the stream, and back onto land. I stop running and steal a look behind me. I hope the water has washed away my scent, allowing me time to find him. A shudder runs through me and I continue running. I hope they have not harmed him. A branch snaps behind me, and I push myself even faster. They were not thwarted by the water. I hear the whistle of the arrow releasing into the air seconds before it reaches me.

"Ahh!"

I sat up in bed and put my head in my hands. *Damnit, I can't do this anymore; I have to find out what this means.* I guessed my subconscious wouldn't let me rest until I understood the meaning behind this nightmare. Nefi meowed and began kneading her claws into my blanket. I scratched her head as she purred.

"What do you think it means?" *As if you could answer me.* I looked at the clock and noticed I had woken up only ten minutes before my first alarm was set to go off. Sighing, I threw the covers to the side, spooking Nefi, who jumped off and hid under the bed. I walked to the closet and pulled out my outfit for the day, throwing my knife on the bed next to my clothes before going to take my shower to make sure I remembered to bring it.

As I walked into the kitchen, I had a sudden flash of déjà vu as I watched Mamă pour two mugs of coffee. She handed one to me.

"How are you feeling?" she asked cautiously.

I took a deep breath. "I'm feeling stressed and confused," I said honestly. Putting the mug down, I ran a hand through my hair. "Someone *attacked* me yesterday! I spoke in a different voice and used some weird magick! Can you please,

please tell me what's going on?" I pleaded.

Mamă sucked in a breath. "Oh, fiică!" She ran to me, throwing her arms around me. "I'm so, so sorry! Are you hurt?" She looked me up and down, checking for injuries. "Who attacked you?" she demanded.

"I don't know! Another Vampyre. He asked me who I was because I had a heartbeat, but I don't even freaking know my damn self!" My temper was rising, and I took some deep breaths to calm down. Mamă didn't respond right away. When she did, she sounded grave.

"You have every reason to be upset with me, fiică. I shouldn't have kept this from you, and I'm sorry," she repeated. She took my hand and led me to the couch. We sat down and she gazed deep into my eyes. "You come from two very powerful families, and your bloodline has made you a target."

"But I don't understand. Why would we be a target? We've never done anything to anyone. *I've* never done anything to anyone..." I trailed off.

"I know, fiică, I know. Long ago, your ancestor started a horrible war, killing tens of thousands of innocent people. When he was killed, his son vowed to avenge his death and continue his legacy—he made it his mission to destroy everything we hold dear."

"I don't understand—what does this have to do with me? This doesn't explain what's happening."

She lowered her head, thinking of how to word her response. "It was prophesized that the strongest Vrajitoare in the world would Awaken to possess the powers of her enemies, so that she could defeat him and save all of humanity."

"Defeat *who*?"

She hesitated. "Mihnea—Dracula's son."

I blinked, staring at her in disbelief. I stood up and sighed. "You've lost it." I started towards the door. "I don't have time for this—I have to go to work."

"Wait!" Mamă rushed to me. "You have to believe me!"

I turned around, fast. "No, Mamă, I don't! You expect me to believe that *Dracula's son* is trying to destroy the world and *I'm* supposed to stop him?! Do you know how ridiculous that sounds? Dracula isn't even real, Mamă!"

"Nadia, you have to listen to me—"

"I will *not* listen to this! If you don't want to tell me the truth about what's going on, fine! But to make up some crazy story is just childish!" I shook with anger. "How could you do this to me?" I pulled the door open and stepped out.

"Nadia, please! Don't leave; it isn't safe!" She was yelling down the hallway. "The ring makes it easier for them to find you! I'm telling the truth, fiică. I'm trying to help you!" A couple of doors opened as our neighbors poked their heads out to see what the commotion was about.

I stopped walking and turned to face her. "You need to help yourself." I closed my eyes and rubbed my temples; I was starting to get a headache. "Mamă, I think it would be best if I stayed with Vi to mull things over."

"But—"

I held up my hand, shaking my head. "No. I can't deal with this." I clapped my hands together underneath my chin and pointed them towards her. "I'm going to work right now, and afterwards, I'll come pick up some things." I started walking down the hallway again.

"Fiică, fiică!" she yelled, but I ignored her.

I was fuming as I walked to the subway; I couldn't believe Mamă would do that to me. I was looking forward to working today because it would provide a much-needed distraction from this morning's incident. Before I walked down the stairs to the train, I strengthened my mental blocks—I didn't want to get bombarded with other people's shit right now. I spent the whole ride reviewing what Mamă had told me. *Is it possible she was telling the truth?* I shook my head, twisting the ring. *No.* It was too absurd.

My phone pinged, pulling me from my thoughts, and I saw a text message from Rian. I smiled sheepishly and bit the inside of my cheek as I opened it: *Good morning, beautiful.*

Good morning ☺

I waited anxiously for a response, but didn't have to wait long.

What are you up to?

I told him I had to work, and he suggested that we meet up afterwards, if I was open to it. I *would* like to see him, but wasn't sure how I would feel once I was done working. I told him I would let him know.

I put my phone away as my stomach growled, and I remembered that I'd rushed out before eating anything. When I got off the train, I made a pit stop to Dunkin Donuts to grab a ham, egg, and cheese on a croissant. I finished the sandwich before I got to the office and immediately wished I had ordered another. I brushed off the crumbs and opened the door, being greeted by Darius' honey scent. He looked up at me from his desk and smiled brightly.

"Good morning."

"Good morning," I said, walking to my desk. "How was your weekend?"

"It was nice! I went to Connecticut to visit my sister. We went to the aquarium with my niece—I can't believe how big she's gotten!"

"Yeah, they grow up so fast," I agreed as I turned on my computer. "That sounds like a good time—I'm glad you enjoyed yourself."

"Thanks. But now I want to hear all about your weekend, birthday girl."

"Oh, it was filled with...excitement." *That's putting it mildly.* I gave Darius the Vampyre-free version—our dinner on Friday, seeing Gabby and Vi, and going out to Relik together.

"I've been hearing good things about that club. Did you have fun?"

"Yeah, it was a good time." *Considering.*

"Very cool; I have to check it out." He turned to his computer and continued typing.

Let's see what's on the agenda for today. I opened my inbox and checked the email from Mr. Dalca. "The Boss Man's in meetings all day," I said to Darius, smiling.

"I saw that. Isn't it awesome? Office to ourselves!"

"That is awesome—now we can relax a little." But as I continued reading my email, it dawned on me that relaxing wasn't part of my agenda. Mr. Dalca had left me with lots of tasks to complete, including phone calls, research, and filing. I sighed. "Never mind. There's a crap ton to do."

"Well, think of it this way: it'll make the day go by faster."

I nodded. "Good point."

The office became silent as we each started working on our assignments. I was getting into a flow when my phone went off with a message from Gabby.

Want to do dinner later?

Hell yeah! Where to?

She picked a Mexican restaurant about a fifteen-minute train ride from here. I was excited to spend some quality time with Gabby—it would give us a chance to really catch up about what had been happening throughout the years. I was just about to get back to work when my stomach growled loudly. My eyes widened and I stopped typing.

Darius giggled. "Well, it *is* lunch time."

I gave him a small smile, but I was uneasy. Food wouldn't satisfy me; this was a different kind of hunger. I bit the inside of my lip. *What am I supposed to do?* I had to think of something, fast. I didn't want my hunger to get to the point where it was uncontrollable. Plus, I couldn't walk around the office with red eyes.

"What are you getting today?" he asked me. I looked at him, considering my options as my stomach cramped up again.

"I'm not sure," I said.

"Well, let me know and maybe we can go together."

All I could do was nod. I hadn't thought of what I would do in this situation, and I wasn't sure how to get what I needed. I looked at Darius again, letting his honey scent envelop me. *Could I? But it's Darius—he's my friend! Well, it's not like I'll drain him...*I felt like I had an angel and a devil on my shoulders and both were arguing with each other. Another pain went through me and I made a decision. I just prayed I could do the glamour right.

"I'm going to get some coffee," I announced.

Darius raised his eyebrow at me. "Alright."

Zeită, how am I going to do this? What if this backfires? I walked in the break room and took a deep breath to calm my nerves. *Trust yourself*, I repeated in my head. I began rummaging through the cabinets as though I were searching for something.

"What are you looking for?" Darius asked.

"Do you know where the sugar is? I thought there was some out here, but I don't see any."

"Yeah," he responded, and I could hear the scrape of his chair as he stood up. "Here—let me show you." Darius walked into the break room and went to the cabinet closest to the fridge.

"Oh, is that where it is," I asked, feigning ignorance. He giggled and grabbed a box, turning to hand it to me. "Thank you," I said and caught his eye. I focused all my energy into my gaze.

"No problem..." He started fading.

Another cramp wracked through me. It took me a minute

before I was able to fully enter his subconscious, and I had to push aside the doubt that my glamour wouldn't work. I kept concentrating, and soon he wore a faraway expression. I quickly planted the thought that he had gotten me the sugar and gone back to his desk to keep working. *Zeită! I can't believe I'm about to do this.* But I didn't waste any more time thinking about it; it was necessary until I could find another way.

Closing the distance between us, I took a deep breath. I started to lean into Darius' neck, but stopped—it made me uncomfortable, reminding me that I was invading his personal space. Drinking from his wrist would be more impersonal, I decided. I picked up his arm, which was hanging limply by his side, brought his wrist to my mouth, and pulled my lips back. My canines lengthened and I slowly bit into his skin. He winced. Still connected to his mind, I made Darius think he had gotten a paper cut on a stray sheet when he was trying to take a file from the cabinet. I closed my eyes as the first drop of blood hit my palate. It was like sweet nectar, and I drank until the gnawing in my belly faded away.

"You really should be more careful when feeding," said a familiar voice.

I gasped, and looked up to find Nicolae leaning against the doorframe, studying me. Unfortunately, it was enough to break the trance, and Darius started coming back into himself. *Oh no!* He looked at me in utter confusion—he hadn't noticed Nicolae yet because his back was to the door.

"What happened?" he asked.

Thinking fast, I said, "You came in here to get a Band-Aid for your cut, remember?"

He nodded slowly. "Oh, right. Girl, that hurt."

"Yeah, those paper cuts can be brutal," I said, grabbing a Band-Aid and handing it to him. *Just go back to your desk*, I silently pleaded.

"Apparently. Looks like you have one on your lip," Darius said, pointing to my face. My eyes widened as I wiped my finger across my lip. I looked at the drop of blood on my thumb. *Crap.* I stole a glance at Nicolae, who was smirking. Narrowing my eyes at him, I quickly turned my attention back to Darius.

"Well, look at that. I'll be okay, though. Thank you for the sugar. Why don't you take lunch first—I'm still undecided." At that, Nicolae chose to laugh, and Darius twisted his head to look at him.

"Who are you? When did you get here?"

"He's nobody, and he's just leaving," I answered for him. This time I pushed Darius out of the room. "Go, take lunch. See you when you get back." He started to protest but I had already closed the door. I rounded on Nicolae. "What are you doing here?"

He walked closer to me. "How about we talk about why you were feeding off of your colleague."

I took a step back, bumping into the counter. "I...I couldn't—" I stopped as a thought occurred to me. With Darius waking up, I hadn't had time to process the fact that Nicolae wasn't freaking out about what he'd just witnessed, or that he seemed to know what I was doing in the first place. I frowned. "Wait, how do you know what I was doing? How did you get in here without me hearing you? *Why* are you here, again?"

He waited patiently until I was done. Smirking at me, he closed the distance between us, reached up, and wiped a drop of blood off my lip that I'd missed earlier. His hand remained in the air as he gazed into my eyes.

"Frumoasa." *Beautiful.* Once again, I was overcome with the feeling that I knew him from somewhere. The look he was giving me was intense, but I couldn't read it. I blinked a few times and looked away, breaking the connection.

"Answer my questions," I demanded.

He dropped his hand. "As you wish. I know a lot about you, Nadia—"

I cut him off. "What are you talking about? You don't know anything about me. I just met you for the first time last night."

"Was that truly the first time?"

I started to protest, but in my heart I knew that I had met him before. His face became still when he realized I had come to that conclusion. He reached for my right hand and lightly touched my ring. It grew warm under his fingertip.

"I remember the first time I saw this ring," he said softly. *What? He's seen the ring before? Is he the one that gave it to me?* Just as quickly, the moment had passed and he moved away from me. "Actually, I'm here to deliver this to my father," he said, holding up a thick manila envelope.

"Your father?" I was puzzled.

"Yes, I believe he is your boss."

My eyes widened. "Mr. Dalca is your dad?"

Now that he mentioned it, I could see the resemblance, especially in the eyes. *Zeită. Nicolae is Mr. Dalca's son and he just caught me feeding. He isn't freaking out; why isn't he freaking out? What does he know about the ring? What does he know about me?*

"Crezi prea tare—you think too loudly," he commented, rubbing his temples. "You need to work on that."

My eyebrows became part of my hairline as my eyes widened more. Then I crossed my arms over my chest and narrowed my eyes, annoyed. *I need to work on that? This just started happening to me! Jerk!* He flinched as if I'd hit him, and I softened my gaze.

"Mr. Dalca's not here," I said. "He's in meetings all day."

Surprise quickly flashed across his eyes. He held up the package. "Can you please see to it that he gets this when he returns?"

"Sure thing." I took the package from him.

"Multumesc." He smiled sweetly and turned to leave.

"Wait!" I called out to him. Nicolae stopped in his tracks and faced me with a questioning expression. "How do I know you? How do you know about my ring? Did you give it to me? Why have you been following me?"

His eyes filled with sorrow. "Nadia, I—" his phone rang, cutting off the rest. He checked the caller ID and made a face as he answered. "Ce s-a întâmplat?" As he listened to the response, his demeanor changed. He tensed as he asked, "What?! When?!" He was quiet once more, listening intently. "Stai aici! Stay there! I'm on my way!"

Nicolae hung up and rushed to the door. He gave me one last look, then ran through the door so fast he appeared to be a blur. I blinked rapidly, staring at the door. *I wonder what happened.* Highly curious, I considered following behind him. Whatever it was sounded serious. I shook my head. *Don't be silly, Nadia. You barely know him. Besides, it's none of your business.* Still, I couldn't help but feel somewhat concerned. I did have one answer though: Nicolae was obviously Strigoi.

I made my way back to my desk just as Darius returned from his lunch break. He sauntered over to me and stood there with his hands on his hips. Still embarrassed about feeding on him earlier, I couldn't look him in the eyes.

"Well?" he asked, smirking.

"Well what?"

"Spill it!" He threw his hands in the air. "Who was the hottie?" He pulled his chair over to my desk and plopped into it.

I laughed. "Believe it or not, that's Mr. Dalca's son."

Darius' jaw dropped. "No way!"

I nodded. "Yes way."

"He is delicious. How do you know him?"

"I don't *know* him. Vi and I ran into him at the movies last night, but he came to give Mr. Dalca a package."

"Whatever, girl. You guys had some serious vibes going on in there," he said, cocking a thumb at the break room.

"I don't know what you're talking about."

Darius blinked at me, then shook his head. "You're weird." He wheeled back to his desk as I laughed. "Did you decide what you were going to eat?"

I bit the inside of my cheek nervously. "I, uh, ate while you were gone. I ran to the deli next door real quick," I added. He nodded, but wasn't really listening—he had gotten back to work. I let out a breath. I was really going to have to find a different way to feed. *But more importantly, I need to figure out how I know Nicolae.*

CHAPTER ELEVEN

TĂRGOVIȘTE, WALLACHIA 1480

As Nic charged at Nai, I raced towards Sorina, determined to make her pay for the murderous acts against her own family. Immediately, the villagers closed their ranks around Sorina. Before I could reach her, Sorina was lost in the crowd and I was being attacked from all sides: kids were throwing stones while the adults were trying to bludgeon me with shovels. From the looks of it, Nic wasn't faring much better. I lashed out at the closest person I could reach, taking his head in my hands and snapping his neck.

I winced as one of my attackers hit me in the head and quickly spun around, sending a powerful punch through his chest. He flew backwards, landing on the ground and out of the fight. At the same time, something stabbed white-hot into my side. I wrenched the dagger free; blessedly, the blade was made of something other than silver, allowing the wound to heal in a short time. A woman tried to kick my legs out from under me, and I stabbed her with the dagger. Although I was armed and blocked many of the attacks, there were still too many people for me to take on, and soon the sheer weight of their bodies pressed me to the ground.

Reaching to the back of my mind, I remembered a protection spell that the Seer had taught me. I closed my eyes and a warmth began inside me, my necklace vibrating against my chest as the heat traveled all throughout my body. I visualized a white light erupting from the heat in my chest and surrounding me. My eyes snapped open, and I caught the gaze of a middle-aged woman holding a dagger.

Reflected in her eyes, I could see the fire in mine; as each second passed, I sent her the heat growing inside of me. She dropped her dagger and fell to the ground screaming. The skin on her arms shriveled and began to peel off in flakes. Those around her stopped attacking me and turned their eyes on her, startled. They wrinkled their noses as the smell of burnt hair and skin danced into the air. A man standing nearby quickly began tending to her.

"What is this magick?"

"Stop it!" Someone spat at me.

I felt others' eyes on me, their scents dripping with fear, and smirked when they ran away.

"Monster!"

The woman's screams died as she went into shock. As the trance among the villagers was broken, the beatings started again. My head was thrown to the side, and my arms flew to my head as I once more blocked punches and kicks. I saw Nic, drenched in sweat, tearing through his own group of attackers trying to get to me. I cried out as someone stabbed me with silver—a hideous burning spread from the wound, and that fueled Nic to reach me faster.

Someone kicked me in the head and I spat out blood. I wanted to pull the blade out, but my hands were being held down. Squirming as the poison from the silver made its way through my system, I tried to access my inner power once more, but I couldn't concentrate through the agony of the silver swimming through my veins. When I felt another blade enter my side I screamed louder, and my vision blurred. Just as I was about to give in, I heard a whoosh and the weight on my arms lightened.

My eyes fluttered open and I saw a couple of people soaring through the air. Nic grunted and punched another who was holding me down before pulling the blades from me. Immediately, I could feel my body pushing out the poison, and the pain began to recede. My attackers backed away as Nic picked me up in his arms.

"What are you doing!" Sorina shouted. "Kill them!"

A couple of villagers approached us, but hesitated as Nic growled at them. He pushed past them and began running towards the outskirts of the village.

"Stop them! They must not escape!"

Nic stumbled and fell to the ground. I flew from his grasp. My wounds were almost healed but my sides were still tender. I looked up to see Nic reaching for a dagger in his leg with Nai standing over him, smirking. Fear gripped me as I crawled over to Nic.

"Worry not. There is not poison on the blade—the Order has many plans for you." He crouched until his lips were a touch away from Nic's ear, then whispered, "They are to take their time with you, before delivering you to Mihnea. I hope your humans are worth dying for." He scowled at me and stabbed Nic in the neck. Nic screamed shrilly, causing the hairs on my arms to stand on end.

"Nay!"

I reached out to Nic, but wasn't close enough. Nai pulled the blade out and blood spattered all over him. In one swift movement, he stabbed Nic again and Nic slumped to the ground. I grew hysterical—*how do I get out of this and save him?* Closing my eyes, I dug deep into myself. I'd started to grow warm when Nai grabbed a fistful of my hair, pulling tightly.

"Magick not, Princess, and take heed. You are savior to no one." I ground my teeth and reached around to untangle my hair from his hand. Nai's hold on me tightened, and I winced in pain. His breath brushed against my ear. "You will never see victory."

Then his hand was gone. As I turned to face him, I caught

a glimpse of links of mail armor and heard them clink together before the pain blocked out everything else. I tried to rip the armor off my head, but the silver seared through the skin of my hands. Excruciating pain blinded me, until my throat grew raw from screaming. My head flopped to the ground and my eyelids fluttered. The last thing I saw was Nic bleeding out on the dirt. Then my vision went dark.

∞

I heard a squeak near my ear and winced as I felt the little teeth of a rat nibbling on me. As I moved my head to the side, the rat scurried away. Peeking through heavy eyelids, I gazed at my surroundings. It was dark—the only light coming from a torch outside my cell, which cast eerie shadows on the cobblestone walls. I could see moss growing in the crevices of my prison. Shifting my weight as I sat up, I felt more moss underneath me in a depression created by the bodies that had lain there previously.

The air held a scent of suffering and death, and a shiver ran up my spine at the shackles dangling from the walls. In the corner, I noted an iron chair covered in spikes with restraints on the armrests. Underneath it was a dark stain, and I shuddered at what it could be.

Where am I?

I stood up and groaned as I stretched, feeling sore and stiff.

How long have I been here? I hope Nic is alive...

As I walked towards the bars of my cell, I could feel the heat emanating from them an arm's length away. *Silver.* I let out a frustrated sigh and ran my hand through my hair. I spun around in a circle, looking for another means of escape, but saw nothing but cobblestones. *How do I get out of here?* Footsteps sounded down the hall, and I moved closer to the bars to see who was approaching without burning myself.

The footsteps ceased and I heard the clanking of a key in a lock. The door scraped open and there was a shuffling of feet as the prisoner moved away from the door. I inhaled deeply as the sour stench of the prisoner's fear entered my cell.

"Let me go," he said, and the guard merely grunted in response. The prisoner yelped and I could hear the sounds of a struggle before the prisoner spoke again. "Nay! Stop!" There was a loud smack and the prisoner went silent; the guard must have knocked him out. Softer noises filled the space. My mind swam with different possibilities of the heinous acts being committed in the cell near me—even as a Vampyre, that prospect made me nervous.

Another smack sounded. "Awake!" ordered the gruff voice of the guard. The prisoner groaned but said nothing. His fear heightened, and I stumbled back as it suddenly overwhelmed me.

"Nay!" He was breathing heavily as he started to panic. "Prithee! Untie me!"

The guard snickered. "I think not."

"I will tell you anything you want to know!"

"Indeed you shall." I heard the creak of a lever turning. "Tell me where they are," the guard demanded.

"Stop!"

"Answer me!"

The prisoner screamed shrilly and the sound turned my blood to ice. "I know not where they are! Prithee, release me!" he pleaded.

"You dare lie to me? Were you not involved with the others set on destroying Mihnea?" He turned the lever again.

"I lie not! I had no knowledge of their attempts on his life!" I could hear the tears in his voice as it grew shaky. "Release me, release me."

"I do not believe you."

"I swear...to the Gods...that I speak only the truth," he whimpered. "Prithee, I have a daughter—I am all she has..." There was silence for a moment as the guard seemed to contemplate his words. But the prisoner's relief was short lived as the creaking lever started again, and he cried out.

"You should have thought of her before you decided on your traitorous acts."

"Nay! I will talk! Turn no more!"

"The time has passed," the guard replied simply.

The screaming that followed reached a deafening octave, then there was a popping noise that made me shiver. As soon as it started, the screaming ceased and was followed by a thump. All was silent, and then the guard gave an audible huff. I heard him moving around the cell and guessed he was cleaning up what was left of the prisoner.

I need a means of escape!

I heard the cell door open, then shut. The clunk of footsteps disappeared down the hall, and I breathed a sigh of relief. I inspected my cell more carefully, determined to find *anything* that could help. My eyes raked up and down the bars, and I wondered how strong they were.

Inhaling deeply, I reached out to take the bars in my hands. I could feel my skin sizzling before my fingers even wrapped themselves around the bars. Pushing past the pain, I tried to pull the bars apart. I began sweating and was only able to separate the bars about an inch more before the burn of silver overwhelmed me.

My screams filled the dungeon and I yanked my hands away, the skin on my palms starting to blister. I bit my lip to hush my screams, tensing up as the pain continued to flow through me. I prayed to the Gods I had gone unheard, but I learned otherwise as footsteps pounded down the stairs.

"What is the cause of such racket?" came the same gruff voice as before.

I mentally cursed myself as the footsteps grew louder. I took a step away from the bars as a beast of a man appeared, covered in blood and holding an iron rod.

"What do we have here?" he asked. I cocked my head to the side and frowned, confused by his physiology—he was Vampyre, but at the same time, not. *His eyes are red with Hunger, yet his heart beats?* I had never encountered such a making before. "Aye, Princess. I have started the Change, the Curse flows through my veins, but I have yet to fully Turn—not until I've fed."

He smirked, flashing baby fangs, and I crinkled my brows. *So, this is how the Change works for those who are turned...*He slapped the rod into his palm. It had a ball on the end with several holes in it: a lead sprinkler. Molten metal was poured in one end and rushed to the other side where they could be poured onto a victim—in this case: me. He glanced down at my hands, still smirking.

"Tried to escape, I see." He moved closer until his face gently pressed against the bars. My eyes widened. *Silver does not harm him!* "There is no escape." He took a step back. "You are pleasing to the eyes. Tell me what I wish to know and you shall remain that way."

I approached the bars as close as I could without burning myself and glared at him.

"Nay, it is time for you to release me," I sneered, looking deeply into his eyes, attempting to enter his subconscious. He said nothing and instead stared at me in return. Then he threw his head back and laughed deeply.

"Your glamour has no affect on me." He stepped closer, and I could smell his rancid breath. "Bless the Gods that my Vampyre side is stronger than my measly human one."

I glowered at him and said, "That may very well be, but you are not Vampyre enough to defeat me."

He threw his arm out and I screamed, covering my face with my hands. My skin felt like it was melting, the burn piercing through each layer until I felt it in my bones. I found my hands covered in blood from the melted skin and I glanced through my bloody fingers towards the beast. He was rushing to fill the sprinkler with molten silver from his miniature crucible.

I rushed at the bars, flinging my hands through them, and the beast snarled as I clawed at his face. My nails cut deep and blood started dripping from the slashes.

"Cunt!" I was only at the bars for a second before I fell back, gripping at my arms. I clenched my jaws and watched as my skin started to heal from the blisters. "You'll pay for that," he spat.

His wounds hadn't started healing, and I wondered if his human half was stronger than he believed it to be. I thought of how to use this to my advantage, but there were no obvious weapons around.

Gods help me—what can I do?

My face was almost fully healed. I held my necklace as I ran to the far corner of the cell, thinking of what magick could assist me. I watched the beast as he yet again began filling the sprinkler, then reached for a key to unlock the cell door—I needed to act fast.

I can send him pain, mayhap?

As the beast unlocked the door and slowly walked over to me, I tried to focus all my attention on sending him painful energy, but I was unsuccessful. With each step he grew closer, sneering at me with blackened teeth. I continued to step back until I was against the wall, trapped.

"Nowhere to go, eh Princess?" He flung his arm out quickly, and once more I screamed as the molten silver melted through my skin. I threw up my arms to cover my face as more silver showered down on me. As I sunk to the ground in agony, I could hear his laughter over my shrill voice. "It appears I can defeat you after all," the beast said.

I growled as a surge of anger spiked through me, but the sting from the silver made it impossible for me to move. He spoke again, but I was unable to comprehend his words. Time ticked on and he continued to fling molten metal on me until the bones of my hands and arms were exposed.

Are the Gods so cruel that they would allow me to perish in such a way?

Tears rolled down my cheeks from the pain and thoughts of failure. After what felt like a century, the showering of silver stopped and I heard the shuffling of his feet as he moved away from me. I looked up to find him rushing to re-fill the rod and the next second I charged at him. I placed my hands on his head, attempting to subdue him, but the beast was stronger than I had anticipated. He flung me off of him with ease and slammed me into the wall.

I didn't stay down for long. Scrambling up, I pushed against the cell door. The fool had left it unlocked, and soon I was running down the halls of the dungeon. I could hear his clumsy footsteps in pursuit behind me. The beast was strong, but his speed did not measure up. Soon I no longer felt his presence behind me. I slowed down to a walking pace and looked around. This area was much darker than where I had been held captive, and an eerie chill filled the air. An iron scent floated towards me and I wrinkled my nose. I could hear the faint sounds of struggling, and followed them to another cell. I gasped at the sight before me: there was my beloved Nic, battered and bruised, struggling against the manacles that held him. His left eye was swollen shut and there was blood dripping from his split lip. He was surrounded by so much blood, I was surprised he was able to move at all.

"My love!" He stopped fighting and stared at me with his good eye. I raced as close to the bars as I safely could without burning myself.

"Antanasia? How did you escape?"

"The great brute made the mistake of opening my cell to attack me, and I was able to push past him. He was not fast enough to follow me." My expression saddened to see him in such a state, and I reached out to grab the bars.

"Nay! Don't!" Nic called out. I froze. "I don't want to see you hurt by the silver, not for me."

"But—"

He shook his head. "There is not much time, you must listen to me. We are under the castle."

"But how do you have knowledge of this?"

"Nai believed me to be unconscious, but I was not—I observed the hidden entrance."

"Good news. I shall get you out and we can leave together."

"Nay! Leave me!"

"You have lost too much blood—you speak nonsense."

"Antanasia, you are the one Mihnea wants; you are the one meant to protect us—you must escape without me while you still can; I will find my own way."

I couldn't speak for a moment—how could I leave him there? His open eye widened, and before I could open my mouth to speak, I felt a presence behind me.

"There you are." I spun around and came face to face with the brute's fist. It felt like it packed the power of a thousand men, and I saw stars before slumping to the ground. As I spit out a loosened tooth, I heard Nic address the beast as he stood above me.

"You will regret that." His voice was dripping with menace.

The beast guffawed and gripped my hair tightly in his hand. "You threaten me behind the bars of your prison?"

My vision began to clear just as the beast pulled my head back and dumped the contents of the sprinkler on my head. My screams pierced the air, reverberating off of the cobblestone walls. He lost his grip on me as my hair melted off of my scalp, landing on the ground in heaps. He watched as I writhed around in pain, screaming with my hands on my head, picking at my scalp as it peeled off my skull.

Nic was straining against the chains that held him, cutting his skin, blood running down his arms. I felt like the molten silver was melting through my skull and staining my brain. Slumping to the ground, I started to black out from the pain. My eyes fluttered closed.

"Get away from her!" Nic yelled at the beast.

"Speak again and I shall kill her on the spot." I heard nothing else from Nic, but from the clank of chains I could tell he was still trying to break free. The beast spoke again but I wasn't able to comprehend what he was saying—I couldn't think and I started to slip away into unconsciousness.

Antanasia! Stay with me...

Nic's voice was the last thing I heard.

∞

It was the squeaking that woke me first, followed by one or two bites. My eyes popped open, and I could feel the cold damp stone underneath me. My head felt raw, and when I shifted my weight, I could hear the scurrying of the rats around me. I sat up quickly, my hands flying to my head. I winced at the tenderness of my skin—my hair still hadn't returned, though I could feel the stubble of new growth. I whipped my head to the side, following the sound of all the squeaking.

It was a mound of rats, all feasting on the remains of some poor soul. I frowned and crawled towards the body, grimacing at the aches and pains that ailed me. A few of the rats ran away, but the others refused to let me interrupt their meal. Rats' affinity for blood made me wonder if *they* were real Vampyres in tiny, furry bodies. I took pause—underneath all the blood were the tattered remains of green trousers. It hit me that these creatures were feeding off of my dear Cristian.

"Ahh!" I yelled, startling them. I charged at the mound, reaching for as many of those little bodies as I could and chucking them against the wall. My body reached high temperatures as I let the energy build. The injustice of seeing Cristian's body covered in rats fueled my rage. The next few rats I touched burst into flames in my hands, and the cell filled with their squeaks and squeals.

A few of the rodents fought back; though I suffered many bites, I didn't let that deter me. My hand flew from one side to the other, swiping at the creatures and sending them soaring through the air. Angry tears rolled down my cheeks as I thought of Cristian's warmth and friendliness. I thought of Adelina and his mama, now without a brother and a son, and I shook my head, blinded by tears. I stopped attacking the rats and sat back, completely distraught. Why were the Gods punishing me? What deed had I done?

"These humans are our food and you spill tears for them?" asked a stern voice from behind me. I spun around and saw a tall young woman standing just outside my cell. She looked slightly older than I, and was dressed in an elegant coat, fitted trousers, and black boots.

"He was more than 'food'! He was a dear friend!"

She raised her eyebrow. "You fed from him often?" I said nothing. She smirked. "You want me to believe that you cared for this human, but the truth is he was merely sustenance for you."

I glared at her, my anger growing. "Who are you?"

She gazed intently into my eyes. "You know who I am."

I said nothing at first, instead focusing on her gaze and her face. I took note of her coppery hair and the shape of her eyes, boring into mine.

"Nay," I said in disbelief, shaking my head. "This cannot

be..."

"Aye, it can." She stepped to the cell door and pulled out a key with a gloved hand. She unlocked and opened the door, and I stood up as she walked into my cell.

I frowned. "But Mother..."

She delicately held my face in her hands. "You look so much like her." Turning my head to the side, "More than I."

I snatched my head from her hands. "I refuse to believe these lies. Mother would have told me if I had a sister. Especially one as maniacal as you."

She dropped her hand and took a step back. "She tried to keep you safe from our world—there was no reason for you to know about me. As for the fun, she had no idea it was me; how could a woman be capable of such madness?" She picked a ball of lint from her glove. "Nay, she believed the acts to be those of our brother."

I shook my head. "But I have seen him! We all have seen him! You speak lies."

She threw her head back and laughed. It was a shrill sound that made the hair on the back of my neck stand up. "Darling Antanasia—your innocence is sweet. It was my twin you saw, but *I* am Mihnea. *I* am the mind behind everything." She crossed her arms. "Our brother is too dumb to lead this empire. *I* am the true heir of our dear Dracula."

"But...why? Why do this?" With that one question, her mood changed: as though a flame had been blown out, she was immediately cold as ice.

"*Why?*" Mihnea stepped towards me once more and her gaze chilled me to the center. "Why," she repeated. "Should the humans not pay for their acts against our father? Should they not suffer for what they did to him?"

"He was insane. His death was a blessing."

She slapped me and my head snapped to the side. "You are pathetic! He was a god—he cared about preserving our kind, and knew that the humans were only good for our survival or to do our dirty work. I will see to it that his death was not in vain."

I massaged the sting from my jaw and glared at her. "You are crazy."

Mihnea shrugged. "Mayhap I am, but you are also of my blood—it runs in you, too. Together, we would be unstoppable; we could rule the world."

I moved close enough to smell her breath. "You murdered innocent people, including our Mother and Cristian. I will *never* work beside you." I spit in her face. "I will stop at nothing to make sure you don't succeed."

Mihnea growled and wiped the spit from her skin. She punched me with enough force to spin me into the air, and I landed in a heap on the ground. "You will not be around much longer to do anything about it." She gave me a mischievous smile and called out behind her. "Nai!"

The same Vampyre that killed Cristian stepped into the cell and looked at me, intrigued. "A shame for one as pretty as her to die," he commented, his green eyes boring down on me.

Mihnea frowned and hit him on the arm. "Quiet! Get any information you can, then get rid of her." She grabbed his collar and pulled him to her, kissing him roughly. "And make it painful."

He bowed his head. "As you wish, my love." Mihnea took leave without another glance, and I stood up as Nai approached me. He reached towards me. I stood my ground, flaring my nostrils at him as he wiped the crimson liquid from my split lip. "Mihnea can be quite unreasonable. If you tell me something useful, she will be merciful, mayhap."

I moved my head away from his touch. "I have nothing to say."

"It seems you are as difficult as your sister." He gently rubbed my arm. "I like a challenge."

"Do not touch me."

He moved with lightning speed to stand behind me. I could feel his breath on my neck as he said, "This doesn't have to be painful. Just tell me the location of the remaining Brotherhood."

I threw my head back, smashing it against his nose. "Never," I spat, circling away from him.

Blood rushed down his front from his broken nose. He calmly placed his hand against his nose and twisted, setting it back into place. As the blood slowed to a trickle, he said, "That was uncalled for." He swung at me and I flew into the air, crashing into the wall. He moved too fast for me to react, and in the next second he was standing over me. Shaking his head at me, he said, "It's a shame that it must end this way." He bent down and whispered in my ear, "You could have been better than Mihnea, mayhap."

He took my head in his left hand and smashed it into the ground. I felt my nose and several teeth break, and had to spit out blood and teeth to stop myself from choking. My head met the ground once more, and I saw stars. Picking me up by the head as though I weighed nothing, he tossed me into the bars of the cell. I cried out as the silver burned through my tattered clothes and then my skin. Slumped on the ground, I tried to sit up and scoot away from the bars, but my muscles felt like goo. I looked up and involuntarily trembled as Nai walked closer to me.

His eyes softened only just. "There are more pleasurable reasons for me to make a woman shiver." He rubbed his finger across my cheek but I was too weak to move away. "I wish this was one of those moments."

A shadow flew over me. Nai sailed through the air and landed on the ground in a heap. Nic stood over him, breathing heavily. He looked to be in even worse condition than before, covered in more gashes and bruises, but he radiated a fury that I hadn't seen in a long while.

"That moment will *never* come," he seethed. "And you shall never lay a finger on her again." His foot met Nai's face with such force that his head snapped back with a loud *crack*. I believed his neck to be broken, but all Nai did was cough up lots of blood—his strength was impressive. Nic punched Nai, and said without facing me, "Run, Antanasia. The exit is close by—get as from here as possible."

This time, Nic didn't have to tell me twice, and I rushed to my feet and out of my cell. I stumbled slightly as I tried to stop myself from passing out. There was a slight humming from the silver bars that lined the walls of the dungeon. Some cells were occupied, the prisoners in chains, iron maidens, or attached to racks. I believed some of them to be well beyond death, if the scent was anything to go by. *How many of these people suffered, only guilty of being human?* I choked back a sob.

Just ahead, I could see what looked to be daylight on the cobblestone floor, and my adrenaline pumped. A few yards away, I noticed bodies on the ground. As I grew closer, I could see two guards with their heads lying several feet away. *Nic's handiwork.* I ran past them, flying up the stairs, and found myself in a side courtyard with more stairs not too far from me. Still on high alert, I continued running up the stairs. I slowed down when I entered an elaborate hallway. There were high ceilings and archways, and torches on the stone walls. The windows were large enough to fit through, and the breeze carried the scent of waste.

My ears picked up the sound of hurried footsteps and muffled voices, and I hid behind a tapestry hanging from the nearest wall. I held my breath as a cluster of guards rushed past me and thudded down the stairs towards the dungeons. Making sure they were a good distance away, I left my hiding spot to search for a way out of the castle. I was as quiet as inhumanly possible, ears open for the slightest sound. Only a few moments went by before I felt the presence of another.

"You do not go down easily—I admire that." I turned and faced Mihnea, her expression unreadable. She jerked her hand to her head and massaged her temples. "But you are causing much delay. I should have known never to send a man to do a woman's job."

Before she could attack, I jumped into the air and kicked her in the chest with as much power as I could muster. The sight of my murderous sister seemed to reenergize me, and before she landed, I had my hands on both sides of her head. I had prayed for this moment for years. My first thoughts were of our Mother, how her life had been unfairly taken away before her time. Her death made worse, not only by how it was done, but by who had been in charge of it. I thought of Jeniviva's family and my dear Cristian. I sent all of my grief into Mihnea—I wanted her to explode with the pain I was feeling.

She screamed and gripped my wrist hard enough to break it. I lost focus as pain reverberated up my arm. Mihnea used the distraction to slam her head into mine before sending a powerful kick into my abdomen. I crashed through a doorway and into the Great Hall, splitting a table in two as I landed atop it. I rolled out of the way just as a dagger lodged itself into the table where my head had been only seconds before.

Without thinking, I grabbed the dagger with my good hand, my skin immediately burning away as it touched the silver blade. I clenched my jaw and threw the dagger at Mihnea. It wedged deep into her thigh and she fell onto one knee, snarling. Holding my broken wrist in my good hand, I walked towards her as she struggled to remove the blade.

She began to speak, but I had grown tired of hearing her voice. Before a single word left her mouth, I lifted my leg and kicked upward into her jaw. Mihnea's head snapped back and blood flew from her mouth. She sagged to the ground, but I knew she was still alive, though she remained unmoving. An arrow whizzed by my head, and I heard the sound of another one being nocked.

Without looking behind me, I took off running through the Great Hall. More arrows flew past me as I maneuvered in between the chairs and ran through a doorway into a hall. I looked left then right, choosing to head in that direction. As I sped down a flight of stairs, I could hear the whizz of arrows and thudding footsteps chasing after me. I reached the landing, startling the guards patrolling the hall.

"Stop her!" someone yelled behind me. The guards raced towards me, one closer than his partner. Another set of stairs loomed before me, and as he reached for me, I leaped over his head and tumbled down the stairs. I caught sight of the castle door. That sight gave me added motivation. I barreled into the door in my haste to reach it, grabbing the wooden bolt and tossing it to the side as though it were nothing more than a splinter.

Looking back, I saw that the guards were almost upon me. Adrenaline rushed through me as I went to crank open the door. I ground my teeth together, turning the lever as fast as I could. Even for a Vampyre, it was heavy. I heard the guards' footsteps and the clanking of armor as they reached the ground level. I gave the lever a final crank, and slipped through the small opening just as a guard approached me brandishing his sword. He sliced my arm before I made it all the way through the door, and I grimaced.

Once through the gate, all I could see were clouds floating over a sea of forest. I stole a glance behind me and bolted through the trees, feeling relieved to be back in my element. The guards were yelling behind me, scrambling to catch up. I picked up speed, stray branches scratching me and twigs digging into my feet. Ignoring the pain, I continued running on a downward slope. *Clank, clank, clank* sounded behind me. One guard tried to flank me and lost his footing, rolling down the mountain into a tree. He struggled to sit up.

I ran past him as the ground leveled out, and took a moment to figure out which way to go. I cut left, listening closely to see how near the rest of the guards were. Now that they were on even ground, the arrows started coming at me again. One soared over my head and I ducked and started to stumble. I threw my hands out to stop my fall, and pushed myself back up on my feet. Before I could take another step, I was thrown off my feet. As I sailed through the air, I could hear Mihnea barking out orders to her guards.

"KILL HER!"

I crashed into the side of a cliff, leaving a visible dent in the rock before slumping to the ground. I had no idea who threw me, but they had some power behind them. The impact left me dazed and I could feel the cracks of broken ribs. I wheezed and coughed up blood. I could hear the footsteps of my attacker approaching, and only rested for a moment before getting up and taking off through the trees again. My arms pumped by my sides as I increased the gap between myself and Mihnea. At least I thought I was increasing the gap. I heard the sound of a bow being drawn, and cried out as a silver-tipped arrow pierced my back.

CHAPTER TWELVE

NEW YORK, NEW YORK 2015

I was a block away from the restaurant when it hit me that I hadn't eaten any solid food all day; I guessed the little bit of blood I was able to get from Darius had been enough to sustain me. My phone went off, signaling a text. It was from Rian, and I smiled. My fingers flew across the screen as I let him know that I was having dinner with Gabby.

That's too bad. Maybe another time, he sent back. I saw Gabby standing outside and called out to her. She turned and waved. There were a bunch of people waiting outside the restaurant.

"It's really crowded for a Monday night," I commented.

She shrugged. "It's Manhattan—it's always crowded."

I giggled, nodding. "Touché."

She smiled at me. "It smells so good; I can't wait to eat. They said about ten to fifteen minutes—is that okay?"

I looped my arm through hers. "Of course, darling." I said in a British accent. She snickered at me, and we grabbed a menu before sitting to wait on the bench near the wall. We began flipping through the entrées. After a few minutes of considering, Gabby sighed.

"This all sounds yummy. I don't know what to choose," she said.

"I think I'll go with the beef burritos."

She nodded. "I'm leaning towards the chimichangas."

"Mmm. I may have to take a bite of yours."

She smirked. "Did you not eat today?"

"No, I did—I'm just being greedy." We laughed and stood as Gabby's name was called.

I took in the décor as I walked inside. All the walls were brick and had sombreros or paintings of daily Mexican life. The tables had candles and the recessed lighting was turned down low. There was soft mariachi music playing in the background. Combined with the rest of the décor, it gave the restaurant a cozy feel.

It was gone the moment I sat at the table. A chill ran through me so deeply that my skin broke out in goose bumps and the hairs on my arms stood on end. I shuddered and rubbed my arms. Gabby gave me a questioning glance.

"Are you okay?" she asked.

"Oh, yeah. Just got a little chilly, that's all." I gave her a reassuring smile, but I felt extremely uncomfortable and found myself looking around the restaurant. I caught a glimpse of raggedy brown hair, but the dim lighting made it difficult to see clearly. Gabby lightly touched my arm and I brought my attention back to her. "I'm sorry, I thought I heard my name."

"It's fine. I just want to make sure that you're okay."

I gave her a genuine smile. "No, I'm good, Gabby. Seriously." I tried to put the sensation to the back of my mind, but it wasn't easy. *Someone is watching me.* Our waitress came over and introduced herself, then took our drink order. "Thank you for inviting me to dinner tonight. I've been dying to have a moment to catch up with you."

"Yeah, man. Definitely. But we will need a lot more dinners for me to tell you all of what I've been up to," she said, picking up the drink menu.

Another chill ran through me, this time accompanied by a slight tugging sensation in the back of my mind. I stiffened and stared straight ahead, on high alert. Luckily, Gabby didn't notice. The tugging became stronger, like someone was trying to unravel my mind. It was then that I realized I was under a psychic attack.

Thankfully, Mamă had taught me ways to protect myself just in case. I immediately strengthened my blocks until I could no longer feel the intrusion. Glancing over my shoulder, I looked around the restaurant, but I didn't see anything unusual. *Who's there?* I thought to no one in particular.

"What are you looking for?" Gabby asked, bringing my focus back to her.

"I—nothing." I pulled the drink menu from her hand and shrugged. "So, are you going for that margarita?"

Gabby looked at me, unconvinced, but said, "Nah, I think I'll pass."

She sat up straighter as our waitress returned with our food. It smelled and looked delicious, but I wasn't really in the mood to eat. Regardless, I took a forkful and commented on how good it tasted.

Dinner was delightful, now that I was more in control of my heightened senses and wasn't hearing everyone's thoughts and emotions.

Gabby and I talked about everything—from my upcoming semester, to her job and family, to us making traveling plans later in the year. I didn't mention anything about my recent changes—it felt good to just enjoy her company without thinking about all the new Vampyre stuff I was going through. Every so often, I felt the intruder trying to catch me off guard, but my defenses were strong.

What is going on? Why is someone trying to penetrate my thoughts? Who is it? More questions for my ever-growing list. I thought about Mamă—the only person who could give me insight. I hadn't given much thought to our argument since it happened, but I was starting to wonder about what she had said.

It was nearing the end of dinner; Gabby and I both declined dessert, and soon our waitress came back with the check. Although I offered to pay a few times, Gabby refused to let me.

"Can I at least get the tip?" Even that took some coaxing before she agreed. Although I was being treated for my birthday, I hated having people pay for me. After gathering our belongings, we stood and made our way to the exit. I felt another chill, and this time I was able to pin point where it came from: there was a brunette woman staring at me from outside the restaurant. When she caught me looking, she turned and walked the other way. *Who was that?* Gabby and I walked outside and I watched her pull a key from her bag.

"You got a car?"

"Just a rental. I'll be doing a lot of traveling outside the city while I'm here. Do you want a ride home?" she offered.

I shook my head. "No, thank you. It's a beautiful night; I think I'll take my time getting home."

"Sounds good," she said, nodding. "Let me know when you get home."

"Will do. Thank you again for dinner." I leaned in to give her a hug.

"Anytime. Let's do it again sooner rather than later."

"Agreed. Have a good night!" I waved as she sat behind the wheel, and then started walking towards the subway, pulling out my phone to call Mamă and let her know that I was on my way home. I felt bad about how hectic things had become the past few days. I planned on apologizing and promised myself I would be fair—I had to give her a chance to explain everything to me. I didn't like the strain my Awakening had caused on our relationship, and I needed to make it right.

I was scrolling through my favorites to find her contact when I accidently bumped into someone as I pressed "Call". I turned around to apologize and continued walking towards the subway. It rang three times and then went straight to voicemail. I left her a quick message and hung up. It was 7:30; it would take me about twenty-five minutes to get home—if the train was on time. I shrugged. *Guess I'll see what happens when I get there.*

I walked down the stairs, digging into my bag to find my Metrocard. I was lost in thought as I strolled down the second set of stairs to wait for the train. There were a few people on the platform, indicating that the last train had left a short time ago. I walked down the platform towards a bench and sat down. I was beginning to pull out my book to occupy myself when my ears perked up at someone whistling an eerie tune. A man was walking slowly in my direction, swinging a key chain. He sat down next to me, and I wouldn't have given it a second thought if it weren't for the fact that he was the one I'd accidentally bumped into only moments before.

He continued to whistle the creepy tune and I frowned. Without looking up from my book, I tried to read him to see what his intentions were. I was surprised to find that his mind was heavily guarded; so far, I'd found most people didn't have any defenses at all. What set my alarm bells off even more was that he didn't have a heartbeat. *Where is the train?* He continued to whistle the tune and played with his key chain.

I turned the page to keep up appearances, but internally I was willing myself to relax. *Come on, come on, train.* Hurry up! It felt like hours before I heard the train's horn blast and put my book away, watching the cars zoom by. As it slowed to a stop, I stood up. The whistler stood as well, still sending that song into the air. I gripped my bag tightly and waited. As soon as the doors opened, I bolted. I could feel the man running behind me.

I got evil looks as I pushed past people who were trying

to get off the train. I even knocked some bystanders over, resulting in lots of angry yells and curses thrown my way. Once on the train, people jumped out of my way as I raced past, throwing open the doors that separated the cars. I heard the familiar ding signaling that the doors were closing. The train lurched forward as it started to slowly roll down the tracks. I lost my balance and stumbled into a passenger. The car was fairly crowded, but that quickly changed when the door slammed open behind me and the whistler hissed before sprinting towards me at an unearthly speed.

Passengers started yelling and some jumped out of his way, while others tried to run in the opposite direction. There were some unfortunates who didn't move fast enough; he flung them against the walls. I didn't stick around to see what other havoc he wreaked. Instead I pulled open the next separating door, shattering the glass and startling the couple closest to the door, who yelped and practically climbed up the wall to get away from me. I sped through the car, feeling the whistler close behind me.

The train slowed to a stop and people clamored to get off. I darted off the train into the crowd, hoping to trick the whistler, and then ran down the platform to the last car. Glancing behind me, I didn't see him; I got back on the train. The doors closed behind me and I hunched forward, trying to catch my breath. As the train started moving, I looked over my shoulder onto the platform, but I still didn't see him. *Hopefully I lost him.*

I stood up and looked around the car. There were only five people occupying it with me. Suddenly, I realized I felt lighter. *Shit, my bag.* I was sure it had already been claimed by now. *Oh well. At least I didn't have anything crazy important in it.* I didn't have much time to think about it—I felt a chill, and the car door slammed open on the whistler. He was about ten feet from me, his black eyes gleaming as he walked slowly towards me. I started backing up towards the door, and the passengers looked back and forth between us. He growled and they started screaming. I wracked my brain trying to come up with my next move, but I was already on the last car. *Damn.*

My back hit the door and he gave me a sly smile, exposing his fangs. With nowhere else to go, I stood there and waited for the attack that I knew was coming. Sure enough, he broke into a sprint towards me. I flew out of his way, landing on a seat as he barreled through the last door. Glass shattered everywhere. The five passengers were forcing themselves through the connecting door on the opposite side of the car, and soon I was alone. I jumped off the seat and stared at the door, wondering if he'd fallen onto the tracks. Cautiously. I walked towards the broken door and looked over the threshold. I looked left, then right, frowning when I didn't see him.

I straightened up, and was about to head back into the train when a pair of feet greeted my chest. The kick sent me flying backwards, and I crashed into a pole. I felt my spine snap and cried out at the sudden pain. My assailant swung into the car from above, and I realized he'd been hanging from the roof of the train. He was covered in blood from cuts that had already healed, and his clothes were tattered. The crack in my spine had temporarily paralyzed me, but I could feel my back also slowly starting to heal.

He raced towards me, hands out as if he was going to grab me. When he got close enough, I used all the strength I could muster to kick him in the stomach. I winced as he soared through the air and crashed into the wall. The car rocked back and forth on impact. My spine was almost completely healed, and I used the pause in action to stand. I faltered slightly as the train stopped. My assailant was already on his feet and coming at me again. I could see people looking at us from the platform outside the car, clearly able to see our altercation. Some backed away from the train while others ran through the turnstile. I could hear the passengers who'd witnessed our fight from other cars shouting as they left the train.

As the doors closed and the train started moving again, I decided to go on the offensive and attacked first. I did a skipping roundhouse kick to his head, quickly followed by a side kick aimed at his midsection. He grunted and fell backwards into the wall, lip bloody. I was about to deliver another kick when he grabbed my foot and twisted it, forcing me to kneel to the floor. He punched me in the back of the head, and I lurched forward face first on the linoleum. I heard a crunch and felt wetness as my nose started bleeding.

I lifted my head, but didn't recover fast enough. He stomped onto my freshly healed back. I screamed out as excruciating pain shot through me. I was completely stunned and unable to move. He kneeled down on one knee and whistled the eerie tune in my ear.

"I've been waiting a long time to meet you." He sucked in a breath and shook his head. "Such a shame you won't live long enough for us to get better acquainted."

I felt warmth against my chest and realized it was coming from my necklace. As the warmth spread over my body, I felt the pain recede. I growled and flipped over, head-butting him in the jaw. Jumping to my feet, I moved to stomp down on his head, but he rolled out of the way. The train slowed to a stop once again, and I wiped away some of the blood that had dripped from my nose. When the doors opened, a cop rushed on and instructed us to freeze, holding up a taser. We both turned to look at him.

"What the hell..." He scrunched his eyebrows and unintentionally lowered his taser. "Your eyes..."

My assailant used this distraction to rush the cop. No amount of training could have prepared the cop for the whistler's speed. The taser flew from the cop's hand as the two of them slammed into a seat, and the cop went limp. Just as the doors were about to close, another cop ran on and tried to tackle my assailant. I ran to grab the taser from the seat as the whistler threw the second cop into the wall. Before I could reach the taser, I heard a third cop open the sliding door.

"Stop right there," he yelled, pointing his taser at me. I slowly lifted my hands in surrender. The whistler gave an otherworldly snarl and we both looked at him.

"Enough with the interruptions," he spat.

He charged towards the cop, moving unnaturally fast. The cop fired at him but missed, and the whistler punched him in the jaw. I heard a loud crack as his head snapped back, and he slumped to the floor. I gasped and covered my mouth with my hands. *Zeită! He killed him! I have to stop him before he hurts anyone else!*

I went for the taser one more time, but I wasn't fast enough. My assailant kicked it under the nearest seat. I backed away from him, and we started slowly circling each other.

"So you are Alesul. The One. The others were not strong enough, but somehow you survived."

We were still circling each other, my mind racing. *Crap. How am I supposed to get away from him?*

"Do you think you can beat him?" he continued. "You will never beat him." He stopped. "You look pretty smart—join us. You can rule by his side and have more than you could ever imagine."

I shook my head. "What the *hell* are you even talking about, Strigoi?"

He squinted his eyes at me. "Don't play coy with me, little girl. I know what power lies within you."

But I was still stumped. "Who are you? What do you want from me?"

"I am Andrei. One of the most faithful servants of the Order. Join us," he repeated. "It is your destiny. The oameni are weak—they don't stand a chance against us. Rule with him—it is what you were made to do. Otherwise, you will die."

The Order? Humans are weak? Rule with him? What the hell? The train slowed to a stop and the doors pinged open. My assailant was momentarily distracted by the people coming onboard. I ran to the taser and swiped it off the ground.

"I don't know who the fuck you're talking about, but I'm not 'joining' anybody." I fired it at him without hesitation.

Being a Vampyre didn't protect him from the electric currents flowing through his body. He glared at me as he sank to the ground, twitching. Screams filled the air as people jumped away. I was starting to get a headache from all the high-pitched sounds. Dropping the taser, I ran off the train, scaring a few passengers on the platform. I noticed I still had three more stops before I needed to get off, but it didn't matter. I had no clue what was going on, and would rather run home than take my chances on the train with the unknown Strigoi.

My adrenaline was pumping and I flew up the stairs and onto the street, startling people who were making their way to the train. I cast a quick glance at the street signs, then raced in the direction of my condo. *I have to get home. I need to speak to Mamă.* It was the first time I had truly used my new ability of speed, and it was an amazingly freeing sensation. I would have taken the time to marvel at this new talent if the situation were different, but instead continued running. People shrieked and jumped out of the way as I zoomed by. I was nothing more than a blur, but they didn't need to have powers to know that *something* was approaching fast.

Protection! I need protection! Think, think! I wracked my mind for a protection chant, but it was hard to focus on anything while I was running. Finally, I threw something together and mentally prayed. *I call upon the protective energies of the Universe. Let no harm come to me. Let me be free of pain and rise above all fears. Grant this upon me. So mote it be.* My arms were pumping by my sides, and the breath was flowing rapidly into my lungs. I tried to visualize a white light surrounding me, but all I could focus on was not bumping into people while I ran. *Almost there.*

I felt a chill and knew that someone was coming quickly towards me. *Shit. Guess I didn't pray soon enough.* I sped up, trying to outrun the person, but I wasn't able to pinpoint exactly where he or she was coming from. A second later, I tasted gravel as someone tackled me head first into the pavement. I felt my skull split open from the impact. The screams started up again, which made the pain shooting through my head ten times worse.

I was dizzy, but tried sitting up. Blood dripped down my face and I winced, lightly touching the fracture on my head. I looked up in time to see the punch aimed for my face and blocked it, but just barely. I stood up quickly and almost fell back down because of my head injury, barely stumbling out of the way as my attacker planted his foot in the ground where I'd been only moments before. His stomp was so powerful that his boot became stuck in the pavement. This allowed me a good look at him, and I glared at the familiar face: *Barry.*

There were people running in every direction, but a few stragglers remained to record the scene. I heard sirens in the background and I knew it was only a matter of time before the cops would arrive. The bones of my skull shifted as they started to knit back together, and it alleviated the pain enough for me to make a move. I spun and kicked Barry in the solar plexus with enough force to send him flying. He crashed into a parked car, setting the alarm off.

He quickly recovered and soared towards me. I met him head on. I heard the crunch of bone breaking as I delivered a hammer fist to his nose. At the same time he punched me in the jaw, dislocating it. I stumbled as my head snapped backwards. The sirens were getting closer—the cops would be on the scene any second. I straightened and saw blood gushing from Barry's face. He was spitting it out, trying not to choke. I ran towards him and jumped in the air, spinning slightly before hook kicking him in the head.

Barry was thrown into the air and landed in a heap several feet away. His neck was bent at an odd angle, and he didn't rise. I took off down the street just as the first cop car pulled up. I was only a block from my condo, and prayed nothing more would happen before I reached my building. There were cop cars lining my street and dread filled me at the sight. The doorman gasped as I ran past him, and called out to me but I didn't stop.

I ran through the door leading to the stairs taking the steps three at a time until I was on my floor. My anxiety heightened when I saw cops and my neighbors in the hallway. I quickly ran to my door.

"Miss, you can't go in there!" One of the cops held out his hands to stop me. He looked me up and down. "What happened to you?"

"Move," I said roughly. "I live here! Mamă!" I called out.

I pushed him out of the way, eyeing the yellow crime scene tape across the doorway. I ducked under the tape.

It was a wreck. There was shattered glass and paper strewn everywhere. A detective walked towards me.

"Nadia Gabor?" I walked past him, glass crunching underneath my feet. I called out to Mamă again, but still she didn't answer me. "Ms. Gabor," he tried again, rushing to get in front of me. "My name is Detective Stephens. We need to talk." I stopped.

"Where is Mamă?"

"Ms. Gabor, I'm afraid I have some difficult news..." I shook my head and pushed him aside.

"No," I said. "Mamă?" I called out more softly. I crept down the hallway, passing more cops, and nearly slipped on a dark puddle on the floor. The familiar iron scent of blood greeted my nose, and I hurried down the hallway. Pictures, candles, and wall sconces littered the floor. I threw open the bathroom door, but didn't see anything except a few more dark puddles. The guest bedroom was the same. My room was next and messier than the living room; even my bedspread had been torn to shreds.

I didn't stay to investigate, and instead continued down the hallway to Mamă's room. I shivered at a sudden drop in temperature and my heart pounded in my chest. Her door was ajar, and I whispered her name as I pushed it open. The smell of blood was overwhelming; instinctively, my fangs grew. There were dark streaks everywhere, making the room look like a war zone. I focused on her bed, on the blanket thrown over a figure. The bed was drenched in blood, and my chest tightened as I walked closer to it.

My hand trembled as I reached for the blanket. I took a deep breath, and slowly pulled the blanket down to reveal the figure lying beneath it. Mamă stared up at me with lifeless eyes. Blood still flowed from the deep gash across her throat. I felt like the wind had been knocked out of me.

"No!" I howled. Tears welled up in my eyes. "Mamă, Mamă!" I sat on the bed and picked her up, holding her close to me—she still felt warm. I started rocking back and forth. There were bite marks on her neck and arms, and it made me cry harder. "Why!" I yelled. "Mamă, I'm so sorry!" Incoherent words spilled from my lips as I rambled, completely overcome with grief. I don't know how long I sat there with her blood seeping through my clothes, but it was long enough the fluid started to coagulate.

Detective Stephens softly knocked on the door. "Ms. Gabor, the coroner's here..."

I stopped rocking and looked at Mamă, admiring the beautiful soul that had raised me. *I never got to apologize to her.* I felt a pang of guilt at realizing that the last time I spoke to her, I had been upset and yelling. *Te iubesc, Mamă.* I stood up and gently laid her back on the bed, smoothed out her hair, and closed her eyelids. As I kissed her forehead, a few of my tears dropped onto her face.

"I will kill whoever did this to you," I vowed, whispering so no one could hear.

I took a deep breath and pulled the covers back over her. After making sure my canines were their normal length, I walked past Detective Stephens back into the living room. I felt completely numb. Plopping down on my couch, I felt a furry body weave itself around my legs. I looked down at Nefi, relieved that she wasn't harmed. She stared back at me—I'd never really noticed just how blue her eyes were until now. *It's like the whole Universe is in them.*

It took me a few minutes to realize that Detective Stephens had asked me a question. Behind him, I could see the coroner leaving with the body bag of Mamă's remains.

"What?"

"I said, do you have any idea who may have wanted to harm your mother?" I shook my head and looked down, feeling more tears forming. "Ms. Gabor, I'm sorry to have to ask you this, but where were you this evening from five to eight?"

I glared at him. "Are you suggesting I had something to do with this?"

"I'm sorry," he repeated, "but I have to ask." I ground my teeth, then explained that I went straight from work to dinner with Gabby. He nodded. "I will need to corroborate your story."

"Of course," I said, looking at him icily. He cleared his

throat.

"Do you have someone you can stay with? Your father, perhaps."

"My father is dead," I responded, still glowering. He sucked in a breath. "I have someone I can call." I got up and walked out to the hallway before he could say another word. I had to call Vi a few times before she answered the phone.

"Girl," she greeted me, slightly out of breath, "this better be important. I'm with Adrian," she added.

Despite the situation, I found myself smiling slightly. I could only imagine what was going on with them. But that quickly changed as I remembered why I had called her in the first place. *This can't be happening.* I opened my mouth to respond, but no sound came out.

"Nadia? Are you there."

"Vi, Mamă..." I closed my eyes and felt more tears roll down my cheeks. "Mamă is dead."

"Oh my God, Nadia! How?"

"She was...she was murdered."

"What?! Where are you?"

"I'm, I'm at the house." My voice quivered. "The cops are here..." I trailed off.

"I'm coming to get you."

"Okay," I murmured.

I hung up the phone and took a deep breath. Slumping to the ground, I rested my head on my knees. I closed my eyes. *This happened because of me.* I shuddered as a fresh wave of grief and guilt overcame me. I could no longer keep up my mental blocks. Some neighbors were still dawdling in the hallway, all too shocked to approach me but speculating wildly in their heads. I could hear the cops in my condo discussing everyday things, even laughing as if they were sharing jokes over coffee. Like this was normal. Like this was okay. *My life will never be normal again.* I suddenly grew angry at those who did this; at myself for letting it happen; at the cops who could return home. *It's not fair!*

Before I knew what I was doing, I went back to the living room and yelled, "How dare you! Mamă was *murdered* and you're in here talking and laughing like this is an ordinary thing!" Several pairs of eyes focused on me. They were all too stunned to respond. "This was my Mamă –the sweetest woman I knew. She raised me all on her own. She didn't deserve this!" I swallowed a sob. "You're in here touching her things and making more of a mess. Mamă was always neat..." My voice cracked and I lowered my head. "Leave," I whispered, then lifted my head and raised my voice to address them. "Get out." No one moved; instead they all glanced at each other, unsure what to do. This made me even angrier. "I said get out! Get out now!"

Detective Stephens took charge and ushered the other officers out until he was the only one left. He turned to face me and held out a business card. "Ms. Gabor, if you think of anything, please do not hesitate to call me."

I frowned and didn't take the card. "Go."

He nodded. "I'm sorry for your loss." He placed his card on the end table before making his exit.

As soon as he crossed the threshold, I slammed the door shut. Minutes later, there came a knock. I roughly opened the door with my face scrunched up, ready to start yelling again. Then I saw it was Vi, and I couldn't stop the tears from falling. She hesitated, eyeing my blood-stained clothing, but then embraced me in a tight hug and held me in her arms, rocking me from side to side.

"Shh," she said, "It's going to be alright. I'm here for you." She rubbed my head as I cried into her shoulder. Soon, my sobs quieted and I hiccupped. I let go of her and sniffled, wiping my nose on my sleeve. My eyes felt swollen and puffy and I had a splitting headache. Vi offered me a weak smile and took my hand. "Come."

I let her lead me to her car. I'd mentally checked out, and was unaware of the drive to her aunt's complex. She opened the door for me and held my hand as I silently followed her to the apartment. We received some concerned glances along the way—it hadn't registered to me that I was still covered in blood. I didn't care; let them think what they want. *What does it matter?*

Once inside the apartment, Vi went to the bathroom and I heard her start the bath. Several minutes later, she came out and took my hand again, leading me to the bathroom. She'd left a towel and fresh clothes on the toilet. There were candles around the tub, and I was greeted by a pleasant lavender scent. Immediately, I could feel myself start to calm, but still I said nothing. She pointed to my tattered and bloody clothes.

"Off," she commanded, and I obliged. Then she pointed to the tub. "In" And again, I did as I was told. Vi grabbed a washcloth and sat on the edge of the tub. I didn't react when she soaped it up and began washing the blood off my face. She started humming while she scrubbed my back and arms. Then she put the washcloth down and squirted shampoo into her hands. She rubbed them together, creating a nice lather before massaging it into my head. After rinsing out the shampoo, Vi did the same with conditioner. Once done, she kissed the top of my head and stood up.

"I'll be outside if you need me." She left the bathroom, closing the door behind her. I reached for the washcloth and slowly started cleaning off the rest of me. When I was done, I sat there and stared at the water.

This is my fault; I should have been there to protect her. Who would do such a thing? This can't be happening—she can't be dead. I have to plan a funeral...Oh Zeită, a funeral! My mind was racing, and I choked back a sob. *Mamă...*I inhaled deeply, letting the aroma of lavender flow through me. Then I submerged myself into the water. I could hold my breath longer than before, but I was scared to close my eyes for fear of seeing Mamă covered in blood again. Eventually my eyes closed, and soon I felt myself drifting into a Vision.

It was dark and I couldn't tell where I was. I had to rely on my other senses, but I felt at peace here. I could hear Enigma's "Return to Innocence" playing softly in the background. A gentle breeze blew past me followed by the scent of lily of the valley. Bit by bit an image of a maple tree appeared. It was in full leaf and surrounded by the delicate lilies. There was a blue jay perched on a branch, chirping excitedly. I expected to see Mamă, but there was no one.

"You must be strong," said many voices collectively, from everywhere yet nowhere. I twirled around, looking for the source of these voices, but it took a little more effort and concentration than usual—almost like I wasn't fully *there*. I didn't see anyone. My necklace seemed to thrum with energy, and I closed my fingers around it just as the voices repeated themselves. "You must be strong."

"Who are you? Where am I?"

"All the answers you seek are within. As is your power," the voices said. "Be strong—you are never alone."

The tree started fading from view, and the scent of lilies was being replaced by lavender.

"Wait!" But it was no use. I opened my eyes and gasped, almost choking on the water, which was much cooler now. There was a knock on the door.

"Are you ok in there?"

"Yes, I just fell asleep," I said. "I'll be out soon."

"Take your time."

More time was unnecessary—the water was now uncomfortably cold. I took my time drying off and getting dressed, spending longer than usual looking in the mirror. My eyes were shaped so much like Mamă's. My smile so much like hers. My chest tightened as more tears threatened to spill.

Be strong, I thought, repeating the message that I'd received in the Vision.

"Te iubesc, Mamă," I whispered, and then kissed my reflection. Hanging up the towel, I walked into the living room. Vi was in the kitchen. "What time is it?" I asked.

"A little after eleven. You hungry?" she asked, and I gave her a small smile and nodded. I was so thankful to have Vi around at a time like this. Truth was, I didn't really have an appetite, but it gave Vi something to do. "Is Chinese okay?"

"That's cool."

"Great. I'll order and go pick it up. It feels really nice outside; you should go sit on the balcony while you wait," she suggested.

I merely nodded and made my way outside. Vi was right—it was very comfortable on the balcony. I took a deep breath of fresh air, and my head cleared somewhat. I settled in a chair, thinking. *You have to be strong.* I had no idea who the voices belonged to, but they were right. I decided I'd spend tomorrow informing my family, friends, and Mr. Dalca of her death and planning Mamă's funeral—closed casket, of course. Shuddering, I shook my head. *Don't think about that now.* I needed to investigate; I was determined to find and kill whoever did this. *Nicolae knows something about this. Somehow, I'll track him down and confront him.* This was my last thought before sleep took me, and all I dreamt was darkness.

∞

I opened my eyes and reached over my head in a stretch. I smiled broadly—that was the best sleep I'd had in a long time. My smile faded as I looked around and the reality of what had happened hit me like a ton of bricks. *Mamă is dead. Mamă is dead.* I found myself repeating this over and over. My eyes started burning with unshed tears. *No. I must be strong.* I thought back to the message I'd received while bathing. Even hanging onto this recent memory, it was still a challenge not to give in to the urge to disappear under the covers forever. *Covers?* The last thing I remembered was falling asleep on the balcony.

I looked around the room, and spotted Vi sitting on a chair in the corner with her head slumped over her shoulder. *Did she carry me? Or did she wake me and walk me half-asleep?*

"Vi," I said, but it came out in a whisper. My throat was dry and scratchy, and I swallowed to try and moisten it. I pushed the covers aside and sat up. "Vi." I giggled when she snorted and blinked a few times before looking at me.

"Nadia!" She rushed to my side, squeezing me in a tight hug.

"Whoa! Good morning to you, too."

"I'm so glad you're awake! I was starting to get worried."

I scrunched up my face in confusion. "Why?"

She pulled back and looked at me intently. "Nadia, you've been sleeping for almost two days."

"What? Seriously?"

"Yes! I was going to call 911, but I've been checking on you and you seemed to be okay. I just figured with...um...what happened...that maybe you needed a lot of rest."

My chest ached as I thought about Mamă. I threw my arms around Vi, pulling her into an embrace. I shuddered as the tears I'd held back finally broke free and rolled down my cheeks. She held me and rubbed my hair as more tears flowed.

"I'm here for you," she whispered into my hair. She kissed my head and I pulled away to wipe my eyes, sniffling. "Nadia, you don't have to get up. Take as much time as you need."

I wiped my face with my hand and nodded. "I know—but I can't hide here forever. I have so much to do..." I trailed off.

Vi put her hand on my shoulder. "Whatever you need."

I stared at the ceiling, thinking about life without Mamă. Then my eyes met Vi's. "Can I get a ride home? I just need to be alone right now."

"Of course. Let me get my keys."

I followed her to the living room, looking for my shoes. I'd just opened my mouth to ask where they were when Vi offered that I take her flip flops. Vi handed me my phone before we headed out the door. Besides the occasional reassuring smile, Vi focused on driving, for which I was thankful. My mind was relatively blank—nothingness surrounded by a steel wall; I was just *there.* Cars, bikes, and people passed by in blurs. It felt like no time had passed when Vi slowed to a stop in front of my complex. As she turned to me, I felt a rumbling in my belly.

"Do you want me to get you something to eat?"

"No, thank you."

"Are you sure? Or I can make you something?"

"Yes, I'm sure. Regardless of what my stomach says, I don't feel too much like eating." *Lies. I honestly don't want to start eating you, Vi!* I became anxious at the thought of feeding. The sooner I could get away from her, the more comfortable I'd feel. Vi grinned and nodded.

"Alright, then. If you need anything at all, let me know."

"Thank you." I smiled and stepped out of the car, watching as Vi drove off. My phone went off as Gabby called, but I sent her to voicemail. I ignored the texts from both her and Rian asking me how I was; I didn't have any energy to speak to them right now. My hunger forgotten, I kept my head down as I walked through the lobby. I sped up; I was beginning to feel nauseous hearing people's ideas on how Mamă died. I was practically running by the time I reached my hallway. Feet from my door, I stopped. There was bright yellow CRIME SCENE: DO NOT CROSS tape going across it.

I stared at the tape with loathing. It solidified all that had happened there and made it real. *My mother is gone...forever.* I ran my hands through my hair and bit back a scream of anguish. Tears formed in my eyes as I angrily ripped the tape from the door.

"Nadia." I froze upon hearing my name.

I looked up to see Mrs. Agnes standing outside her door. She hobbled over to me and wrapped her arms around me. I closed my eyes and hugged her back, missing that maternal connection.

"Are you okay?" She placed her hand on my cheek, gazing at me sympathetically. I shook my head and my lips quivered as I started crying again. "Oh, my poor sweet child." Mrs. Agnes took my hand and led me to her condo. She turned on the stove, placing her kettle on top, and we sat at the coffee table. She nudged a box of Kleenex in my direction.

"The world can be a harsh place sometimes." She reached into her pocket and pulled out a pack of Newports. "Do you mind?" I shook my head, and she took out a cigarette and placed it between her lips. "I know what you must think, but I'm getting old and am going to die anyway. Might as well enjoy the ride how I want to." She winked at me, lighting her cigarette, and I smiled. "Anica was such a compassionate woman, always there to lend a helping hand."

The kettle whistled loudly and she got up to turn it off. She took out two mugs from a nearby cabinet, and pulled out a couple of tea bags from a container sitting on the counter. As she placed a steaming mug of tea in front of me, the aroma of lavender filled my nostrils.

"Grab that box over there," Mrs. Agnes instructed, pointing to the mantle of her decorative fireplace. My eyes followed her finger, and I saw a beautiful wooden box with a golden latch. I walked over to the fireplace and picked up the box. It thrummed slightly in my hand. "Your mother gave that to me many years ago, and asked me to hold onto it for her," she continued. I returned to my chair and placed the box on the table. "Drink your tea before it gets cold." She put out her cigarette and picked up her mug, taking a slow sip, and sighed. "Now, she asked me to give that box to you when the time was right—I believe that time has come."

"Thank you," I said softly.

Mrs. Agnes dismissed my thanks with a wave of her hand. "No thanks necessary." She settled back in her chair. "Your mother was a mysterious person. I think she knew a lot more than she let on." I glanced at her and bit the inside of my cheek. I slid my hand across the top of the box, admiring its carvings. As I went to unlatch it, Mrs. Agnes spoke again. "No, don't open it here." I dropped the latch and grabbed my mug instead. "That's between you two—take it home and see what's inside."

For the next several minutes I pretended to listen to her stories while I finished my tea, but all I could focus on was the box.

"Well, I think you've entertained this old lady long enough," she said finally, standing up. "Go home and rest. I will check on you later and bring you dinner."

"Thank you again, Mrs. Agnes."

"Hush, child." She hugged me tightly. "If you need anything before then, just come right over." I nodded and she kissed my forehead.

I left her condo, holding tightly to the box like a pirate who'd found lost treasure. I marched to my condo, and took a deep breath before opening the door. I felt a pang of sadness as I looked around the living room. It had been cleared of all blood and debris, but furniture, family photos, and other little items were missing—it made the room seem empty. I heard a door open down the hall and quickly stepped inside the condo, shutting the door behind me. The last thing I wanted was to hear more thoughts on how Mamă died.

I heard a meow and saw Nefi peek out from under the couch. She ran to me, and my heart swelled. *At least I still have you.* I bent down and stroked her fur, then picked her up and carried her with me towards Mamă's room. My chest tightened as I got closer to her door, but I pushed on anyway. I wrinkled my nose at the strong scent of bleach. An image of how it had looked when I was last here flitted across my mind, but I pushed it aside. Just like the rest of the condo, it was clean in her room, but several things were missing, including her bed.

I put Nefi and the box down and walked to Mamă's closet. I ran my fingers across her clothes before picking out a blouse and taking it off the hanger. It was her favorite one, dark blue with gold embroidery around the neckline. I rubbed the silky fabric between my fingers and put it on—it still smelled like her. I inhaled deeply, feeling her warmth and love. In that moment, I felt extremely close to her.

I shook my head. *How could I have let this happen to you?* A single tear rolled down my cheek. I wiped it away and picked up the box. Nefi settled down next to me as I sat on the floor, leaning against the wall. I blew out a breath and glanced at her.

"You ready?" She rubbed her head against my leg and purred. I shakily lifted the latch and opened the box. The first item to catch my eye was an antique iron key resting on the satin lining. It was next to a little bottle and an ancient scroll. I picked up the key, noting how heavy it was compared to modern ones. The bow of the key was shaped like a bird, though I couldn't tell what kind, and the whole key was about four inches in length. *I wonder what this goes to.* I shrugged, placing it back in the box, and went on to the next item.

I eyed the scroll curiously, but hesitated to pick it up. *This thing looks like it'll break apart if I even breathe on it.* I carefully lifted the aged paper from the box, frowning as bits of the corner fell off. I slowly unraveled the parchment. It was in Romanian, and the scratchy penmanship made it difficult to read, but still I tried. Almost at once, I realized it was a letter.

My dearest daughter,

If you are reading this, then my Visions have come to pass. Yes, the events of this day are not news to me. You are different, but your eyes tell the truth of who you really are.

I couldn't read the next couple of sentences, so I skimmed the letter, searching for a word I understood. Finally, a paragraph before the end, I noticed the word *need.*

...need to tell you about Mi...

That was all I got from the letter. *Go figure.* I looked at the letter again, willing for something new to stand out to me. What looked to be the initials *ED* were written on the bottom of the page. Other than that, the rest was unreadable. Sighing, I shifted my weight; my bottom was getting numb. I stood up, deciding to sit in my room. I slumped into my chair and placed the box on my desk.

I'd picked up the bottle and started examining it when I felt pinpricks of negative energy. My eyes darkened. In one swift motion I grabbed my knife from my desk and turned, chucking it at the person behind me. She slumped to the ground with the carved phoenix hilt sticking out of her head. I didn't recognize her. I rushed to her and removed my knife from its new fixture. As I stormed towards the living room, I felt a stirring within me.

It was the same sensation I'd gotten when Barry first attacked me, before I lost control of my body. Whatever this energy was, I acknowledged and welcomed it. When the second intruder appeared, my lingering sadness over Mamă's death was replaced with the deepest fury possible. This feeling was new to me, but I'd recognized it from my readings on Vampyre lore as Blood Rage. I threw my head back and let out an ear-piercing scream. It shattered the windows and the intruder dropped to his knees, covering his ears. I charged at him and with an outstretched hand, ripped out his throat with ease. He flopped over with his blood spattering on the floor—he was human. Lebada Neagra. Black Swan.

The knife flew from my hand as a new intruder attacked me, throwing me backwards. The strength of the tackle made me believe this person was Strigoi. I threw him off me and was back on my feet in an instant. I watched as more people came pouring in. The Vampyres narrowed their black eyes at me, while the Fledglings sneered at me with baby fangs. Being weaker than their counterparts, some of the Black Swans had silver knives. I was surrounded, and I felt my blood boil. How dare these people take Mamă away from me? How dare they have the audacity to come back here to face me? I gave an unearthly growl that caused the hairs on my own neck to stand up. Lunging at the nearest person, I punched him with enough force to send my hand through his chest. I jumped into the air and flipped over a Black Swan who was about to attack me, throwing my leg out in a kick that sent her crashing through my wall.

I spun around and delivered a low kick to a Fledgling. Her legs went out from under her and she landed on the floor with a loud thump. I rammed my elbow into her chest and she gagged on her own blood. There came a blow to the side of my head, and I fell to the floor. Immediately, people pinned me down, kicking and punching any part of me they could reach. The stirring within me grew and my body got warmer. The pain and guilt I felt at losing Mamă doubled.

She was taken from me...again. The voice in my head was not mine, and yet it was. Everything I felt was new and old.

My Mamă had been taken from me; life as I knew it had been taken from me. All because of this *Curse*, this Awakening. What else could they do to me? How much more would they take? I balled my hands into fists and shrieked, startling my attackers. They stopped punching and kicking, staring at me wide-eyed. *No more. Sa terminat. You will take no more from me!* My necklace thrummed against my chest, my body glowing from every pore. I let out a burst of energy that sent my attackers flying in every direction.

I lunged at the nearest Swan, latched onto her like a leech, and began to feed from her. My rage wouldn't let me stop until I drained her. She stumbled around, squealing, trying to pull me off. Her colleagues tried to detach me, striking at my head and face and carving gashes into my skin, but it was useless. Only after I was done did I release her, and she dropped to the floor like a sack of potatoes.

I caught my reflection in some broken glass and shivered. My expression was venomous; I had the Swan's blood all over my face and dripping down my chin. It was a perfect match to how I was feeling inside. Ripples of hate swam through me, and I knew in that moment that naïve Nadia was gone.

I gazed around the room in search of my next victim. I could easily tell the Lebada apart from the Tinerei and Strigoi. Not only by their heartbeats, but also by the look of fear in their eyes. They were all at fault and all needed to die. No matter what, I would see to it that everyone involved in Mamă's death met the same fate. I would do that for her or die trying.

I shot through the room like a bullet, blocking, kicking, and tearing at everyone around me, leaving several bodies in my wake. I had the image of Mamă lying in a pool of her blood to fuel me. The Swans took steps back, while most of the Fledglings and all the Vampyres approached me, up for the challenge—I went after them next, snatching the closest Vampyre by the throat. I lifted him over my head, squeezing slowly.

"I want you to suffer like Mamă did." I watched with pleasure as his eyes began bulging out of his head and he struggled for air. He clawed at my hands, peeling the skin as he tried to break free, while the other Strigoi stood back in amazement at my strength. I turned to face the others with him still dangling from my grasp. "You will *all* suffer like Mamă did."

I took pleasure in watching them cower away from me, smiling when I caught some glancing at their fallen comrades. Their level of fear increased and I drank it in like fine wine. I returned my attention to the Vampyre I was holding and tightened my grip around his throat. The lack of oxygen would only make him light-headed and that wasn't enough. No; I had to make this torturous. I wanted his head to pop off. His trachea started to collapse in my hand, and I gave an evil smile.

He went slack, and that was all it took to break the trance of those who still remained. All at once, they came after me and crushed me under a rain of blows. I'd managed to get a few hits in when I felt a prick in my shoulder blade, followed by an excruciating pain. I tried to turn my head to see who stuck me and caught a glimpse of a syringe filled with residue up to the 1mL marking.

Silver.

I screamed and sank to my knees, scratching at the floor. My insides felt like they were boiling, and in my mind I saw my organs blistering and popping. My necklace was on fire, and I called to its power. The silver might affect my Strigoi side, but it could do nothing to the Vrajitoare running through my veins.

I felt a breath on my ear. "Not so powerful now, are you?" I had a surge of strength and caught Andrei's gaze.

Travelling deep into his mind, I saw a massive amount of pressure. I sent the little waves of energy I had into him, building up the pressure in his head. He shrieked in pain at the sudden inflammation. He threw his hands to his head and started shaking violently, his face turning cherry red.

"What is she doing?"

"Andrei!"

"Stop her!"

In the next instant, the screaming stopped as his head burst open, covering those closest to him in blood and bits. I slouched over, energy depleted...and let out a maniacal laugh.

"Put her out FOR GOOD!" a woman yelled shrilly, and I felt another prick—this time in my neck. Immediately, my vision went blurry and my face met the floor. Then all was black.

∞

My eyelids felt heavy but I managed to open them slightly. All I could see were blots of color. My head was pounding and I heard someone speak before I slipped out again: "You've done well."

Then all was dark once more. I thought I saw a pin-prick of light. The light grew and with it, a burning sensation shooting up my left leg. It grew hotter as the light grew brighter; my leg was on fire, and I could feel the skin melting off my bones.

My eyes flew open, an earsplitting scream erupting from my throat. I didn't stop screaming until I had no voice left; only then was the room silent.

"Ahh—so, you're finally awake." A dark-haired woman strode towards me, her heels clicking against the tiles. I recognized her immediately as the woman who had been looking at me through the window at the restaurant. I was handcuffed to a gurney in nothing more than a bra and my underwear, and surrounded by white walls. "I knew the injection would work—it *always* works," she added, snapping gloves on her hands. From where I lay, she was attractive, but as she closed the gap between us, I could see the signs of aging. Her skin looked weathered and her eyes told centuries' worth of stories—she was *very* old.

When she reached me, she frowned. "Unfortunately for my taste, the pain wears out too fast."

At her mention of pain, I finally registered the burning along my wrists and ankles. I grunted, struggling against the silver cuffs that bound me, and shrieked as nails pierced my skin. She walked around to the other side of the gurney, grinning broadly. "Silver nails were added to the insides of the cuffs—my own personal touch. Do you like them?"

"Who...are...you?" I struggled to get the question out, then started yelling as she flicked out a silver knife and trailed it up my leg, leaving behind a thin line of welts.

"Ah, ah, ah. That's not how this goes—*I* will talk and you will listen. If questions are to be asked, *I* will be the one asking them." She walked closer to my head. "If I don't like your answer, you get this." She waved her knife. "But if I do like your answer, you'll only get a tiny prick."

I couldn't turn my neck to see her, but I heard her tap a tray as something jingled on it. I looked at the ceiling and noticed it was a mirror; I could see her behind me, moving things on the tray. The clicking sounded on the tiles again.

"However, since it relates to this conversation, I will answer your question." She came into my field of view again and peered down at me. "They call me the Blood Countess."

My eyes widened as it dawned on me who I was in the presence of: Elisabeta "Erzsebet" Báthory—the most prolific female serial killer. She'd been compared to Vlad the Impaler, known for many atrocities like covering naked victims in honey and leaving them outside for bugs to feed on. She smirked at my realization and stood there proudly. "I see you recognize the name."

"But," I shook my head slightly. "You died...in the castle."

She scowled. "No," she said harshly, getting in my face. "Those fools tried to kill me, but my master saved me." She reached over my head and I heard a rattling sound on the tray. She gingerly took my hand, and a sharp pain shot up my arm as she jammed a pin underneath my fingernail. "And you do not listen." I gritted my teeth and let out a slow yell as the pin burned through my skin. Using the same hand, I attempted to remove the pin with my fingers, but Báthory firmly held my hand. This made me wriggle my hand even more which amused her; she watched my struggle with an evil gleam in her eyes.

"No, no—we will have none of that." She stuck another pin underneath a different nail. I bit back a scream and she came close to my face. "But you can keep screaming—it's like music to my ears."

The pins underneath my nails felt like they were melting my skin and bones away. I tried so *very* hard to remove them, but she placed them in just the right spots, making it impossible for me to snatch them with my free fingers.

She released my hand. "Now, tell me—where is the key?" I furrowed my brows at her, unsure what she was talking about. "Oh, don't play dumb. I know you know where it is, *Princess*." She spat the last word.

Princess? What the hell is she talking about? The only key I knew of was in the box Mamă had left for me. Perhaps the Vampyres took it when they attacked me? *Then why was she asking for it?* She walked away from me towards the hearth on the other side of the room. When she turned around, she held a red-hot poker. My eyes widened as she came back to me. She was inches away and I could feel the heat of the poker, not only because it had just been pulled from the fire, but also because it was made of silver. *That's why she's wear-*

ing gloves!

"I will ask you one more time, where is the key?"

"I don't know what you're talking about!"

Báthory curled her lip and tisked at me. "You're making this more difficult than it has to be."

She took the poker and slowly pushed it into my foot. I let out an ear-piercing scream as the silver coupled with the intense heat ate at the sole of my foot. I thrashed about, the nails on my cuffs burning my wrists and ankles, but I was beyond caring. As soon as it started, the pain stopped as she pulled the poker out. My breathing quickened and tears formed in my eyes.

"Please," I begged, "I really don't know what you're talking about."

"If that's true, then you're in for one hell of a night." She tapped a gloved finger on her lips. "Well, you're in for a hell of a night, anyway." She smiled and pressed the poker into my shin. The skin instantly melted away from the silver, and soon she was branding my bone. My throat was raw from screaming, and my eyelids fluttered as I started to give in to the pain.

"Not so fast," she said, removing the poker and slicing the side of my leg. Blood ran from the gash. She dipped a finger in the blood before rubbing some on her arm. Instantly, her wrinkles smoothed out, making her skin look younger. She looked at her arm, impressed. "Wow, better than virgin's blood," she muttered. She gave me her full attention again. "You know, my orders were to hand you in, but I may have to keep you as my pet. Your blood seems to work wonders for my skin."

She traced her finger through a puddle of my blood from the gurney, and wiped it on her face. Again, the skin where the blood touched became youthful once more. She faced me. "Change of plans." Báthory replaced the poker and picked up her knife again. I yelled as she jammed the silver into my side. "I can't have you trying to escape, now can I?"

I couldn't focus on her words through the excruciating pain of silver. She unlocked the cuffs from around the gurney, but still left them tight around my limbs. She tugged on the ones that held my wrists, and I fell to the floor. The impact forced the knife further into me and I yelped. I looked up and saw shackles dangling from the back wall. Báthory roughly yanked my cuffs and began dragging me across the white floor, leaving a trail of red in my wake. She lifted me up, careful not to let the cuffs touch her exposed skin, and snapped the wall-mounted silver shackles around my wrists. She did the same to my feet, and only then did she remove the cuffs completely.

"That's better," she said, observing my limp body hanging a couple of feet from the floor. "Oh! I almost forgot!" She ran to a sink on the far side of the room and came back with a bucket. She looked as excited as a kid in a candy shop as she placed the bucket underneath me. "There!" She gazed into my eyes. "Can't let a single drop go to waste, can we?"

"Please, let me go..." I whimpered. Blood dripped down my arms from the silver searing into my wrists, and I closed my eyes.

Báthory slapped me and my head snapped back. "Tell me what I need to know."

I tried to swallow, but my throat was too dry. "I don't know of...a key," I repeated.

She shook her head and walked to the tray, this time coming back with a pair of pliers. Bending down, she took my foot in her hand. "You know," she began, "your mother said the same thing when I asked her about the key." She grabbed my big toe nail with the pliers and separated it from my skin. I yelled as she continued to remove my nails with the pliers. I felt a surge of anger at the mention of Mamă, but it was short lived as Báthory dropped the pliers and took a handful of pins, digging them into my bloody toe.

My side started to go numb where the blade punctured me, and my skin was taking on a blue tinge. Báthory cupped her hands together underneath my wound, capturing some of the blood leaking from it. She smeared it all over her face, and I watched in awe as her skin tightened and blemishes disappeared. She picked up a mirror from the tray and admired her beauty. The change didn't last, however; minutes later her skin shriveled back to itself.

She growled and rushed towards me, roughly yanking the blade from my side. "I guess I'll just have to get more, then." She thrust the blade into my intestines and tugged down my abdomen. I howled at the fiery sensation as my skin blistered before splitting open. As the crimson liquid flowed freely, I realized I was going to die. *No one even knows I'm here.*

My hands were turning blue from lack of circulation. I focused on Báthory again. She was transferring my blood to a larger container. *I need to get out of here...*And yet I could barely formulate a sentence, let alone a plan. Báthory walked back in my direction, and frowned when she noticed my skin had started healing where the slice had been only moments before.

"Well, that won't do," she commented. Again she went to her tray of tricks, coming back with a syringe. She injected the mixture into my abdomen, and the scorching pain I'd felt earlier came back with a vengeance. My skin stopped healing and she smiled. "That's better."

Fire swam through my veins, and it felt like my insides were melting. I could picture the muscles dissolving from my bones, and I just wanted it all to end. I begged my Higher Power to take me right then, but instead Báthory spoke.

"Your mother, Anica, was it? Anyway, she was quite a fighter. I didn't expect such strength from a mere human."

It was then that I found my voice. "Don't talk about my

mother," I spat through my clenched jaw, but she ignored me. I struggled against the shackles and winced at the pain.

"Of course, that was until I let my children feed on her. Then she was howling like a child. Such a beautiful sound."

Fury bubbled inside of me, and I stared into those dark eyes set in a face covered with my blood. "I will kill you for what you did to her."

She raised an eyebrow. "Is that so? Well, I've got news for you—you won't be alive long enough to lay a finger on me."

And with that she grabbed yet another device. This time, she held up a whip made of silver chains with sharp hooks at the ends of them. She swiped at me and the hooks lodged themselves into my stomach, some of them into my un-healed wounds. I threw my head back and screamed loud enough to make the mirrors shudder. My vision started to blur and I welcomed the darkness that was coming for me.

I failed you Mamă, I'm sorry...

Just then, a door that had blended in with the walls came flying off its hinges into the room. Nicolae rushed in covered in blood, followed by Jeni. I squinted, utterly confused. *What hallucinations are these?*

"Get the Păzitor," he instructed her, his eyes never leaving Báthory. She turned on her heels and rushed out of the room.

"So, you're the boyfriend. Such a shame to kill one as good-looking as you," Báthory growled at him. She jerked the whip from my body and began swinging it back and forth, chunks of my skin still dangling from the hooks. I wailed and closed my eyes as I was engulfed in darkness.

CHAPTER THIRTEEN

WALLACHIA/NEW YORK

*T*rees whizz by me as I sail through the air. I crash into the side of a cliff, and leave a small imprint of my body before slumping to the ground. The loud crack and sharp pain in my chest tells me that my ribs are fractured and my lung is punctured. Still on the ground, I begin to wheeze. I wince, and blood spatters on my lips as I go into a coughing fit.

I rest for only a moment. Ignoring the pain of my now-healing ribs and lung, I am up and running before my attackers can locate me, my arms pumping by my sides. Trees blur as I run past, careful to avoid branches and animals alike. My breaths are hurried and visible in the early morning air, but my adrenaline keeps me warm. A sense of dread washes over me, and I cry out as the silver arrow pierces my back just under my shoulder blade.

I stumble slightly but keep running. I can feel the silver slowly eating away at muscle and sinew, inching closer to my heart. I reach over my shoulder to try and remove it. Pulling at the arrow, I scream out as I accidentally push it deeper into my skin. The wood snaps and I begin to panic—I need to remove the arrow as soon as possible.

Seconds later, another arrow lodges itself into my calf, followed by one in my lower back. My feet grow heavy and I trip over a branch. I fall face first into the ground and start to crawl away, pulling at the grass in front of me. I wince at a sharp pain in my back, and my legs go numb as the silver starts feeding on the nerves. I crawl faster, every inch made challenging by the *sudden dead weight of my own legs.*

A twig snaps behind me and I look over my shoulder. A boot slams into my face before someone roughly turns me over. The arrows in my back wedge deeper. I can feel the silver enter my heart. I grunt and look up at the archer. My eyes widen as recognition dawns on me.

"You?"

"Aye."

"But why?" I struggle to get the question out.

"It was my next mission."

"How could you do this to him? To us?"

"He should have followed suit when I left—we would be on the same side." She lifts her bow, and with sad eyes, shoots an arrow into my head. "Mayhap I can have my son back now."

Oana quickly turns and hurries back into the woods.

"She came this way!" I hear Nic's voice moments later. He emerges from the trees and takes one look at me before sinking to the ground. His shoulders rise and fall as he starts to sob. The Keeper comes out behind him and lowers his hand onto Nic's shoulder.

"We must act fast," he says, and I notice that I'm rising, slowly floating towards the trees and away from my body. Nic nods, and both he and Fabian rush to my side. Fabian pulls out a small corked potion bottle, popping it open and holds it over my mouth. "Your soul emerged, but not yet purged. In this bottle you must coast, 'til reunited with your host."

I begin to descend back towards my body. A light appears in the bottle, and the closer I get to my body, the brighter it becomes. Both Fabian and Nic's eyes widen at the sight.

"The Seer gave this to me long ago, apprising me of the events of today," the Keeper whispers. "I tried, but I could not dissuade the Princess from her mission..."

Nic glances at his father. "We have both failed her. She was my betrothed and I could not save her." The last wisp of white light leaves my mouth, and I am again one with my body. "Until we meet again," he whispers to me.

The last thing I see is Nic lowering his lips to mine. Then all is black. The darkness is everywhere, cold and complete. I begin to suffocate on it, on the nothingness it brings me. Just as the darkness promises to fill me, it gets lighter, and I start spinning weightlessly. I find myself surrounded by a watery fluid, and I merge into another being. My ears perk up at a rhythmic thumping; I realize that for the first time, I have a heartbeat.

I opened my eyes, glancing around me with a newfound clarity. I hadn't realized how incomplete I felt until just then. Finally, I was whole. I was no longer shackled to a wall, but was instead in what looked to be a living room, lying on a couch. I winced when I tried to sit up and felt hands on me, gently pushing me down.

"You must rest," Jeni said, smiling at me.

I looked at her very closely, two words appearing in my head. "Young Phoenix?" I whispered, and her eyes widened as she nodded. As I lifted my hand and stroked her cheek, her eyes watered. "No longer a youngling." She laughed through her tears, then looked up, and I turned my head to follow her gaze. Nicolae stood in the doorway, with bruises on his face. He stared at us with a wide grin.

"Welcome back, Antanasia."

∞

Elisabeta was kneeling and trembling underneath her master's gaze. They were in the chamber, surrounded by only those most trusted in the Order—the Black Circle. Located in a secret room in the basement of an abandoned building, there was no chance of them being seen.

"Please," she begged.

Her master turned around, glaring. "You disobeyed me." Mihnea picked up a sword and took a step closer to Elisabeta. "I told you that my plans had changed and she mustn't be harmed. She is more powerful than what I or the

Sorceress had predicted. And you tried to drain her for your own selfish gains!"

"No, master!" Elisabeta said, crawling towards Mihnea's feet. "I wasn't going to kill her, just torture her a little. I wanted her to know who she was up against," she added, grabbing her master's hand and kissing it. "I would never deliberately disobey you. Don't you remember when we used to torture together?" She shimmied up to Mihnea. "It was us swimming in the blood of our enemies. Why can't it be that way again?"

Elisabeta fell back as Mihnea shoved her. "Enough! I don't do well with treason. You are no longer needed." Mihnea raised the sword.

"No! Wait!"

The sword swiftly cut through Elisabeta's neck. Blood sprayed everywhere as her head rolled away and her body slumped to the ground. Mihnea tossed the sword away and turned to the three remaining Strigoi, glaring at them with steely grey eyes.

"Burn the body! Tell your Fledglings and Swans that no one is to harm my sister, is that understood?" They bowed their heads in understanding. Mihnea focused on one Strigoi in particular, staring into his green eyes. "As for you, Rian—keep up the good work."

GLOSSARY

Alesul
The One

Am crezut că ar dori să aibă această înapoi
I thought you would like to have this back

Aștepta
Wait

Atentie
Be careful

Bună dimineata
Good morning

Ce s-a întâmplat?
What's wrong?

Conexiune de Spirit
Connection of Spirit

Crească din nou pentru noaptea este a mea. Eu merg pe străzi a cordere a de timp. Luna este închis dar mintea mea. Este luminous câştige puterea mea di noaptea
I rise again for the night is mine. I walk the streets claiming time. The moon is dark but my mind is bright. I gain my strength from the night.

Crezi prea tare
You think too loudly

Da
Yes

Desăvârşit
Perfect

Dragă
Dear

Esti patetic
You are pathetic

Fiică
Daughter

Fiintă
Essence

Frumoasa
Beautiful/Handsome

Iţi promit
I promise

Lebada Neagra
Black Swan

Mamă
Mother

Multumesc

Thank you

Ne vom întalni din nou
We will meet again

Nimic
Nothing

Nu
No

Oameni
Humans

Ochii tăi
Your eyes

Papanaşi cu brânză de vacişi affine
Romanian cheese donut with blueberries

Păzitor
Keeper

Permiteţi acest comportament în unitate dumneavoastră
You allow this behavior in your establishment

Sa terminat
No more

Stai aici
Stay there

Strigoi
Vampyres

Tată
Father

Te iubesc
I love you

Te simti durere
You feel pain

Thalers
Currency

Tinerei
Fledgling

Undete duci?
Where are you going?

Vârsta de Maturitate
Age of Maturity/Adulthood

Vrajitoare
Witch

Zeită
Goddess

A NOTE TO MY READERS

Thank you for taking the time to read my debut novel, *Awakening*! I really appreciate the support that I've received while creating this piece, and what I continue to receive now that it's completed. I couldn't have done this without you there rooting me on!! I hope you continue this journey with me to the next installment in the Bloodline series!

If you have comments, questions, or just want to say "hello", I would love to hear from you! Feel free to email me at tieratlrice@yahoo.com.

ABOUT THE AUTHOR

Tiera Rice was raised in Rockland County, New York and is a realtor in Rockland, Westchester, and Orange Counties. She earned her degree in criminal justice from Temple University, is the founder of Laughter and Lemonade: a project that focuses on motivational posters for those experiencing a chronic illness, and co-founder of #26forTiera: a foundation that provides financial resources to single parents battling life-threatening illnesses.

∞

Having recently survived a battle with cancer, Tiera decided to use her writing to entertain and motivate her readers. When not writing or selling houses, Tiera can be found spending time with her friends and family, especially her young daughter, fish, and kitty cat. Her other interests include singing, drawing, and dancing.

To: Blauvelt Library

Thank you for supporting me & helping me share my story!

Enjoy!

♡ Tiera

Made in the USA
Charleston, SC
26 October 2016

63169780R00154